# DEATHLY DELINQUENCY

## EVA CHASE

GANG OF GHOULS

BOOK
4

Deathly Delinquency

Book 4 in the Gang of Ghouls series

First Digital Edition, 2022

Cover design: Yocla Book Cover Design

Ebook ISBN: 978-1-990338-42-7

Paperback ISBN: 978-1-990338-43-4

# one

*Lily*

It took all three of us to haul Nox back to my car, and then only with the help of the emergency blanket I kept in Fred 2.0's trunk. After it'd become clear that no amount of hefting and hauling between Jett, Kai, and me could budge the Skullbreakers boss's massive frame more than a few inches across the matted grass by the marsh, I'd gone running back for it.

We'd shifted him onto the blanket with a lot of heaving and tugging. Now Kai and Jett were dragging him along by the upper corners, kicking rocks out of their way so he didn't have to jostle over them, while I held up the back end in an effort to stop him from sliding off.

A procession of frogs hopped along on either side of us, croaking like it was a funeral march. My stomach twisted tighter with every step. I wanted to tell the little creatures to scram, but they were here because of me. I was lucky the tension roiling through my body hadn't summoned half the lake to pour down on our heads.

Actually, it wasn't luck. It was the fact that I'd run the supernatural energies in me nearly dry in the past several hours. That was why we were moving Nox rather than seeing if there was anything we could do to help him where he'd fallen.

The Gauntts had fled, but that didn't mean they wouldn't send their lackeys to try to finish the job they'd started.

They *hadn't* finished. I had to take a little comfort in that fact. Nox looked dead to the world: his eyes shut, his jaw slack, and his face waxy pale other than the small blotch in the middle of his forehead where Nolan Gauntt had smacked him. But every now and then, his chest lifted with a breath. We'd been able to feel a sluggish but steady pulse when we'd checked his neck.

He was alive, on the most fundamental level. He just wasn't exactly *with* us. And we had no idea what precisely Nolan had done to him. The effects of this mark were clearly different from the ones that had blocked off memories in the heads of the young victims he and his wife—and possibly the younger generation of Gauntts as well—had used for their sick purposes.

It was a good thing we hadn't come on the guys' bikes. I wouldn't have had the blanket, and there'd have been no way to stick Nox on one of the motorcycles to drive him home. I pictured us struggling to get him balanced on the seat while he teetered this way and that, like a scene in a slapstick comedy, but couldn't summon any amusement at the idea.

It might have been easier if Ruin had been here. He knew how to put a positive spin on almost any situation. But he was back at the apartment healing from the brutal gunshot he'd taken earlier this evening. I didn't know when he'd even be able to walk around with full exuberance again.

That was two of my men down in different ways in the course of one night. How much longer would we have before the Gauntts came for the rest of us, especially now that we knew their darkest secret?

At least, I sure as hell hoped they didn't have any secrets darker than what we'd just discovered. Adopting kids so you could murder them and take over their bodies when you got old or ill was pitch-black already.

Once we made it to Fred 2.0, it took a lot of maneuvering to get Nox actually inside. We basically snake-slithered him onto the back seat, first sitting him against the car, then easing him up over the side of the seat. The whole time, his brawny body stayed slack. His breath didn't so much as stutter. His eyelids didn't give the slightest twitch.

Once he was inside, we stopped for a moment, staring at him and catching our breaths from the exertion of moving him there.

"We'll figure it out," Kai said, but his voice didn't hold half its usual know-it-all confidence.

"Let's get him home," Jett said gruffly.

Kai opted to drive, fishing the keys out of Nox's pocket, where the boss had stuck them after racing us out here. Since Nox had taken over the entire back, I sat on Jett's lap in the front passenger seat.

Another time, cozying up to him might have made for an enjoyable trip. After what we'd just experienced, I was simply glad that he'd gotten over his awkwardness around being physically close with me. That meant I could tuck my head against his neck and lean into the warmth of his embrace, and he hugged me to him without hesitation. Breathing in his familiar scent with its lingering tang of paint soothed my nerves just a little alongside the thrum of the engine.

When I closed my eyes, images from the bizarre watery ritual we'd witnessed rose up from the depths of my mind, like a body floating to the surface. Which seemed appropriate, given that those memories involved more than one body being shoved into the marsh's water. Only one had emerged.

Both Nolan Senior and his ten-year-old grandson, Nolan Junior, had gone into the water. In theory, it'd been Junior who'd come out. But his comments afterward had made it clear that the elder had possessed the younger.

The way Nolan talked about the ritual, his frustration that they'd had to conduct the transfer "early," held other implications. We'd forced his hand when I'd damaged his heart by using my watery magic to manipulate his blood, but they'd already been prepared. They'd already *had* a ritual.

"This wasn't the first time they've transferred a soul over like that," I said abruptly, opening my eyes to peer at the darkness beyond the windshield.

Kai nodded. "Definitely not. They gave every appearance of being fully comfortable with the proceedings and sure of the outcome."

The nausea that'd briefly eased off flooded my gut again. "How many times do you think they've done it?" How many bodies had the Gauntts taken over before?

He shrugged. "There's no way of knowing. At least a few times, I'd guess. I'll see what I can find out about the history of the family when I'm back at work on Monday."

Right. He'd have to return to the lion's den. The job he'd charmed his way into at Thrivewell Enterprises, the Gauntts' immense corporation, seemed like more of a liability than a benefit now.

"How can you go back?" I asked. "They saw you tonight."

"This is the first time they've ever seen me. It's not like they come down from the tip of their tower very often. The most they could know about their new employee is my name, which we didn't give them out at the marsh. Even if one of them happens to cross paths with me at the office, I doubt they'd connect me to a face they saw only in the darkness while emotions were running high."

I frowned at him. "You can't be sure of that."

"I'm sure enough to think it'd be silly not to take advantage of my position there while I still can," Kai said matter-of-factly.

Jett rubbed his hand up and down my arm before giving me a gentle squeeze. "We've got to get at them somehow. They'll be gunning for us even more now. And the girl…"

I tipped my head to glance up at him. "The girl? *Oh.*"

Nolan and Marie Senior had two grandchildren—the son Nolan had taken over, and the slightly younger daughter…

"She's meant for Marie," Jett filled in as the same conclusion hit me.

Kai clicked his tongue. "I think that goes without saying. They must have adopted the two kids for the primary purpose of having younger vehicles for the older generation as their bodies failed. It's a sound strategy… if you're looking at it from the perspective of a total sociopath who doesn't care about any life other than their own."

He and my other guys had come back to life in a similar way. But they'd stolen the bodies of four vindictive assholes at my college rather than kids, and they'd done it not for themselves but to protect me. Which I guessed made them partial sociopaths rather than total ones?

In any case, it seemed pretty obvious that Team Not Murdering Children had the moral high ground.

"We already knew that the Gauntts are deranged psychos," I muttered. They certainly didn't give a shit about *our* lives, or my sister's, or any of the kids they'd molested over the years.

We still didn't know for sure why they messed around with any of those kids in the first place. From the descriptions we'd gotten, it sounded like it was about more than perverted gratification. Their victims had mentioned times when they'd felt strange energy passing through them—or out of them. Was that how the Gauntts fueled their awful magic?

I pressed my hand to my forehead, but the contact didn't push my thoughts into any better order.

"There were a few things that went right tonight," Jett pointed out, the glass-half-full approach so unnatural on him that his voice came out stiff. He was trying his best to fill in for Ruin, I suspected mostly for my benefit. "We slaughtered a shitload of Skeleton Corps pricks, including the assholes who slaughtered *us*. Which also means fewer foot soldiers on the Gauntts' payroll. And we put the Gauntts themselves at a bit of a disadvantage."

Kai hummed to himself. "Yes, Nolan won't be able to command the same kind of authority while he has to pretend he's as young as his current body looks. The family will have trouble even bringing him into the office, since he's much too young to plausibly intern— or be taken out of school for that matter."

"That's why he was pissed off about the timing," I said. It was hard to feel like I'd scored much of a victory, though, when that victory had resulted in the death of a kid. I'd wanted to *save* any more kids from being tormented by the Gauntts, and instead my actions had led to one losing his life completely.

A particularly determined frog had hitched a ride with us. It chose that moment to hop up onto my knee. I gave its sleek back a careful pet, wondering if it wouldn't have been safer staying back at the marsh too.

When we reached my apartment building in Mayfield, I was relieved to see that the Skullbreakers recruits were still standing guard in the shadows off to the sides of the entrance. There hadn't been any attack on this place. Which made sense, considering that we had struck a major blow against the Skeleton Corps gang this evening.

They were probably still licking their wounds. It'd become clear tonight that for decades, the Gauntts had been paying off the gang with favors to do some of their dirty work. Maybe the Corps would reconsider their association with the family now.

A girl could dream.

After Kai parked Fred 2.0, we realized we now had the problem of getting Nox's substantial frame up two flights of stairs to the third floor. Since thumping him across the steps one at a time on the blanket didn't seem like a great strategy for his continuing health, whatever was left of it, we ended up calling over a couple of the recruits who'd been staked out inside the building.

Between the five of us, we managed to cart the boss up the stairs holding the blanket like a makeshift stretcher, with a lot of huffing and puffing.

As we carried Nox into the apartment, Ruin sat up a little straighter where he'd been recovering on the couch. "Lie back down!" I hissed. The last thing I needed was to see him at death's door again too.

He sank down like I'd asked but craned his neck to continue peering at us. "What happened to Nox?" he asked, his brow furrowing. I guessed even he couldn't come up with a cheerful way of looking at this situation.

He kept his voice low like I had, and my sister's bedroom door was closed. I hoped Marisol had finally managed to get some sleep.

"The Gauntts happened," Jett said darkly.

"I'll fill you in on everything," Kai added. "It's been a wild night."

We lay Nox down on the floor between the dining table and the couch. His chest rose and fell at that moment, confirming that his body was still performing the basic tasks of life. Small wins.

As the recruits tramped back out again, I knelt by Nox's head. "I'll see if I can figure out what magic Nolan put on him—and if I can break it like the other marks."

Kai inclined his head, nudged his glasses up his nose, and went to give Ruin the full low-down. Jett grabbed a cola from the fridge and started chugging it.

I brushed aside Nox's red-tipped black hair where

9

it'd drooped across his forehead and focused on the mark, tuning out Ruin's startled noises of excitement and consternation in response to Kai's story. The hum of my powers reverberated through my chest and out into my limbs. I rested my fingers over the mark and closed my eyes.

I *could* sense a barrier inside Nox's head, one that didn't feel terribly different from the kind that had locked away my and the other victims' memories of the ways the Gauntts had manipulated them. This one was larger, though, and… heavier somehow, as if a globe of thick glass had encased Nox's entire brain. My sense of it sent a shiver down my spine.

What would happen if I broke *this* spell? Shattering the others hadn't caused any ill effects other than the trauma that came from the recovered memories, so after a moment's debate, I decided I should at least try. It wasn't as if Nox could end up in a state much worse than the one he was currently in.

Drumming the fingers of my other hand on the wooden floorboards, I roused more of the energy inside me, as much as I'd recovered during the relative rest of our drive home. Picturing it condensing into a shape like an ice pick, I rammed the supernatural power at the wall around Nox's mind.

It ricocheted off, making the hum of energy inside me quiver erratically. My nerves jangled. I inhaled deeply and tried again.

I flung my magic at Nolan's spell over and over until sweat was trickling down my back and a headache expanding through my skill. Then I sat back on my heels. I had no impression of the barrier being affected, not the slightest crack. Was I just too weakened still, or was this spell that much more powerful?

I rubbed my forehead and realized Kai and Jett had come over to stand near me. I looked up at them, a lump clogging my throat.

"The spell's wrapped right around his whole mind," I said. "I can't make a dent in it. Maybe tomorrow after I've gotten more rest, I'll be able to shatter it."

Jett swiped his hand through his rumpled purple hair and grumbled a curse. Kai bent down next to Nox and studied his prone body. His mouth slanted into a deeper frown.

"Nolan knew what he was doing," he said. "If he'd killed this body, there'd be a decent chance Nox's spirit could have leapt free and we could have gotten him into another one. This is worse than death. He's trapped inside."

"Could *we* do the killing?" Ruin suggested in a tone that was weirdly hopeful considering he was suggesting murdering his best friend.

I hugged myself. "We don't know for sure that he *would* be able to possess anyone else the way he did before."

"And we don't know that even death would free his spirit now," Kai added. "This spell might seal his spirit inside no matter what happens to the body."

Just when I thought the outlook couldn't get worse. I swallowed hard. "All right. Then we've got two things to get to work on. One, figure out a way to break the spell. And two, destroy the Gauntts for good so they can never do anything like this again."

Too bad accomplishing either of those goals wasn't going to be anywhere near as easy as saying them.

# two

*Kai*

Behind my placidly friendly expression as I walked into the Thrivewell building, I stayed sharply alert to the reactions of every employee I passed. Even people talented at holding their cards close couldn't hide their emotions completely, and I highly doubted that the Gauntts had managed to staff their entire corporate headquarters with Oscar-caliber actors.

Nothing I saw gave me so much as a prickle of concern. Some people ambled by without more than a passing glance at me, not a hint of recognition crossing their faces. Others offered a casual tip of the head or a brief smile. The only employees who looked tense were those who were already hustling around when I walked by. They didn't seem to even notice my existence, they were so wrapped up in their own business.

By all available evidence, our stand-off with the Gauntts last night hadn't resulted in a bounty on my head. The family of psychotic pricks was probably too busy figuring out how to handle the fact that one half of their company's leadership now appeared to be elementary-school age to start speculating about mutinous sharks in their work pool.

By the time I'd reached my desk, I'd downgraded from high alert to understated wariness. I was going to continue keeping a close eye out for any signs of suspicion or concern, of course, but I had other goals to fulfill here that meant I needed to stick out my neck a little.

One of the guys who sat near me, Mike Philmore, had taken something of a liking to me ever since I'd shown mild support of his crush on Ms. Townsend, the secretary to the higher admin assistants. It made sense to start with him. After clattering away on my keyboard for a little while to give the impression of dutiful dedication to my work, I ambled over to the break room just as he happened to be grabbing a coffee.

"Mike," I said in a friendly tone, raising the empty cup I picked up toward him as if in a toast.

"Zach," he replied with a nod and a grin. I'd given the company the name of my host, since that was conveniently on my existing ID. It hadn't been hard to fudge the birthdate a little so I appeared to be the right age for my made-up employment experience.

As I filled my own cup, I kept my tone warmly conversational, as if I were just shooting the breeze but with a little more trust than I might have shown the average colleague. People liked feeling trusted. It made them want to prove how much they deserved it. "You've been at Thrivewell for a while, haven't you?"

Philmore cocked his head. "I'd say so. Coming up on five years now. Started out six floors down. We'll see if I ever make it any higher than this." He let out a self-deprecating chuckle that I could tell was designed to hide the fact that he really did hope to be making his way into the uppermost ranks eventually.

I chuckled back in solidarity. "Lots more years to accomplish that in. And when the company has been around so long, you know this place isn't going anywhere. More than a century since founding! Pretty impressive. Did you ever hear any interesting stories about the history? Hard to imagine what it takes to keep a business going this strong for all that time."

Philmore hummed to himself. "I know they had a big bash for the hundredth anniversary, but that was a little before my time. I get the impression a lot of their success comes from keeping it in the family. It's been Gauntts since the beginning as far as I know."

"Lucky for anyone born into the family, then," I said. "I wonder what the next generation has in store."

"Yeah." Philmore's brow creased momentarily. "I'm not even sure if there is a next generation yet. Guess that makes sense. The big bosses wouldn't have *that* much of their family time at the office."

Then one of our colleagues motioned him away to help with a file, but that was all right. It hadn't sounded like the guy knew much of anything about the Gauntts' personal history anyway.

Of course they wouldn't parade the kids around the office. If the plan was for Marie Senior to take over her granddaughter's body eventually, they'd probably want as few people as possible thinking about the fact that the power couple she and her supposed adoptive brother would make down the road had once been siblings. There was no blood relation, but it was still creepy as hell.

Could they even get legally married in their new personas? Maybe Thomas and Olivia would un-adopt one of them somehow to make that possible? Or it could be they'd never fully legally adopted one or both in the first place. You could get away with a lot of fudging of proper procedure when you had as much money and reach as the Gauntts did. One of them could be listed as a foster sibling or similar without the same permanent implications.

After puzzling over that conundrum for a few minutes, I decided I was spending too much time worrying about our enemies' marital prospects and went back to my desk. If we got our way, they'd be dead long before they had to worry about getting re-hitched.

Throughout the morning, I found opportunities to chat up a few other coworkers, but none of them were much more helpful than Philmore had been. No gossip about our head honchos' pasts or ancestry appeared to have circulated through the office in recent years, and no one could point me to anyone who might have some dirt, not even Molly from accounting, whose eyes lit up with a manic gleam at any mention of drama.

At the start of my lunch break, I meandered over to Ms. Townsend's desk to approach my quest from a different angle. She was the most professionally in-the-know person out of all the colleagues I had access to, and I'd already established a good rapport with her. All it took was a couple of subtle compliments and expressing enthusiasm about growing my understanding of the company so I could serve it better, and she coughed up the location of an archives room in the basement where I could do a little digging into Thrivewell's history.

"Thanks," I said, flashing her a smile, and headed straight to the elevator.

My body still hadn't totally adjusted to the whole possession-by-ghostly-energies thing, so it was a good thing I'd stuffed a good assortment of snacks in my satchel. I chowed through them to stave off the grumbling of my stomach as I peered at faded labels and sorted through dusty boxes.

The dustiest ones, naturally, were from the longest ago. After a half hour's excavation, I unearthed a trove of newspaper clippings and press releases from the 1960s. Sitting down on the floor cross-legged, I pawed through them for any mention of the Gauntts.

There, in an article about a big donation the CEOs had made to a food bank organization. Partway down the page, I found a reference to "Nolan and Marie Gauntt, their son Thomas, and his wife Olivia." Just like that, as if it'd been written today.

But the Nolan and Marie Senior *we'd* tangled with couldn't have been more than young kids back in 1964. The Thomas and Olivia who were currently in their thirties would have barely been a figment of anyone's imagination. A sense of dread crept up through my chest. Just how far back did this go?

I dug farther, faster, knowing I was running down the clock. I could get away with failing to be seen at my desk for a little while after my break was technically over, but I didn't want to draw unnecessary attention. The archives room would still be here tomorrow... but now that the mystery was unraveling in my hands, I was chomping at the bit to chase it to its end.

There were a few more references to the Nolan and Marie of the 1960s in earlier files going back a couple of decades before then. Interestingly, the articles from longer ago didn't mention their supposed son and his wife at all, or any earlier generations either. It appeared that the Gauntts were very good at keeping the news focused on only one generation at a time, two at the most.

Which was presumably for strategic reasons, because when I got to the increasingly fragile papers left over from the 1930s, there were a few references to Nolan and Marie taking charge of the company... after the company's founders—Nolan's parents, Thomas and Olivia—had passed on, one within months of the other.

There wasn't much at all from farther back than that. I hauled out the last few boxes, sneezing at the copious clouds of dust, and found only sparse, scattered references to the company around its founding in 1912 by Thomas and Olivia Gauntt. So they'd been the first. It was all Thomases and Olivias, Nolans and Maries, back to the very first generation.

If I was adding things up correctly going by ages, that made for three of each. The current Thomas and Olivia and the current Nolan and Marie Junior were the third of their names in the family.

Were the current Thomas and Olivia the spirits of the very first of their namesakes, born well over a hundred years ago? Or had they initially only been passing on the names as part of a more typical family legacy, and the spooky supernatural aspect had only come into it later?

There'd definitely been something hinky going on by the 1960s, when the second Thomas Gauntt had ended up married to a woman who just happened to have the same name as his theoretical grandmother.

It would have been a little much to expect anything in the business archives to shed light on the paranormal aspects of the Gauntts' life. At least I'd come away with more information than I'd started with.

I snapped photos of all the key articles, making sure the sources were clear in case we wanted to track down other copies later, and put the boxes back in as close to the right order as I could remember. I couldn't replace the dust, so I took a rag I found in the corner and swiped it over a bunch of the lids so it wasn't obvious which ones I'd focused on if anyone came poking around not long after me. Then I headed back to my cubicle upstairs, my mind already spinning through the possibilities of how we could pry even deeper into the Gauntts' personal affairs.

We needed to know how they'd developed their spiritual powers and what those powers involved—the full extent, both so we could narrow down what might be afflicting Nox and be prepared for whatever they might throw at us next. Would the older generations have kept any sort of written record in case the transfers didn't leave all their memories intact? We hadn't found anything like that in their house, but with the amount of wealth the Gauntts had accumulated, they had to own multiple properties.

I was just stepping off the elevator on the fifteenth floor when a short, plump woman bustled over to me looking very stern.

"Mr. Oberly," she said. "Marie Gauntt would like a word with you. You're to proceed to her office on the top floor. Ms. Townsend is waiting to allow you elevator access."

As prepared as I liked to be for every eventuality, I hadn't been anticipating this request at all. My pulse hiccuped, but I had enough self-control to compose my expression into a mild smile. "Of course. Let me just collect the reports for that meeting from my desk and I'll be right up. Thank you."

My unfazed reaction seemed to reassure the

messenger, as I'd intended. She swept off to see to some other business, and I wove through the cubicles toward mine—and then doubled back as soon as I was out of both her and Ms. Townsend's line of sight. I ducked into the stairwell and headed downstairs at a brisk but not panicked pace.

When you panicked, you made stupid mistakes.

Marie Gauntt wanted to see me—now, after I'd been working at Thrivewell for weeks without any interest from the top brass, only twelve hours after I'd witnessed some of her most questionable supernatural practices. The chances of the summons being a coincidence were nil. My best guess was that someone had made an offhand remark about my interest in company history that'd gotten back to her, she'd looked up my file, and somehow she'd put together the pieces.

Maybe she'd simply noticed that Lily and I had interviewed for our jobs there at the exact same time. She might not *know* anything, only want to verify her instincts. I'd rather not give her the opportunity to do it.

I'd milked my time at Thrivewell for everything it was worth anyway. If Marie wanted to stop me from uncovering the dirt buried here, she was too late.

In the front lobby, I sauntered toward the front of the building at a leisurely pace, peering through the broad windows. It only took a few seconds to pick out a couple of figures outside that I recognized from our recent dealings with the Skeleton Corps, loitering on the sidewalk. No doubt there were more gang members I couldn't see positioned farther from the entrance.

Yes, Marie had definitely caught on that *something* was rotten in the state of Thrivewell, and she was pulling out all the stops to contain the problem.

Too bad for her that this once I'd stayed one step ahead of her. I looped around through the main floor, slipped out through the rear delivery entrance, and hopped into the back of a mail truck while the delivery guy was carting a large package over to the building. I let the truck carry me several minutes away from Thrivewell, and then scrambled back out during another delivery stop, well away from any prying Corps eyes.

If they were after me at work, they'd come at us on our home turf soon enough. I flagged down a cab and sent the driver speeding toward Lily's apartment as fast as I could convince him to go.

# three

*Lily*

"Is he going to be okay?" Marisol asked, peering down at Nox with her forehead furrowing.

It was a fair question, considering I'd been asking the same thing since the Skullbreakers boss had fallen into his coma. And considering he looked half-dead already. And also considering that his condition had left him so continually immobile that we'd set him up on a bed made up of a couple of blankets and a pillow on top of a shipping trolley one of the recruits had brought around for us.

It looked odd, but it did make it easier to move Nox's brawny body around the apartment as need be without worrying about hurting him more with our efforts at dragging.

Fitting him onto the wheeled platform had required lying him on his side with his legs folded in and his head ducked down. His sneakered feet still dangled over the end of the trolley. Lying unconscious people on their side was a good thing, though, right? Or was that only in cases of inebriation?

Well, there was no way of knowing how Nolan's spell would affect Nox in the long run. I'd count his pose as a better safe than sorry approach too.

"We don't know," I admitted to my sister, the knot in my stomach tightening with the words. "We're doing everything we can to snap him out of the spell, but we don't really understand what the Gauntts did to him."

Marisol rubbed her temples. "I wish I could remember more from when they called me away from you. It's all so blurry. I remember eating pancakes with you and then running with you to the car at that farm, but everything in between is just bits and pieces... It's like trying to sort out the details of a dream I had a month ago."

I gave her arm my best reassuring squeeze. "It's okay. It sounds like you weren't around the Gauntts much if at all anyway, only the gang they're paying off, so there probably isn't anything to remember that would make a difference."

"I just wish I could help him. I know you care about him. And he obviously cares about you. He helped *me* when I needed it." Her hand dropped to the small pistol she'd been carrying with her everywhere in the pocket of her hoodie. Nox had given it to her and taught her the basics of how to shoot it so that she could defend herself if trouble came when the rest of us weren't around.

Crazy as it might sound, that'd been the first time I'd really felt like we could all be a family together. A bizarre and chaotic family, but one I'd take over what Marisol and I'd had with Mom and Wade any day.

I didn't know if we could get back to that without Nox ruling over the Skullbreakers and offering his fiercely cocky version of protectiveness.

"I'm sure he'd appreciate that sentiment," I said. "But really, I don't want you going out of your way to get even more mixed up in all this—the Gauntts' powers and gang wars and everything else." I bit my lip. "I wish there was somewhere I knew was safe where you could hole up until we figure things out."

My sister shook her head vehemently before I could go on. "No. I don't want to hide. I just spent days forced into hiding away from you. There's got to be some way I can help in this whole situation. I want to be part of it. I want to hit back at those assholes."

A little shudder traveled through her body, but her eyes flared with determination as fierce as anything I'd seen from Nox. We hadn't talked in detail about the things she'd remembered about the more distant past, the ways the Gauntts had used her, but from talking to their other victims, I knew it couldn't be pleasant. I wasn't going to force her to dredge up those awful memories before she was ready.

I understood her vehemence—it resonated with my own resolve to take down the psychotic dickwads who'd gotten me consigned to the looney bin for seven years, molested and manipulated my little sister, nearly killed two of my guys, and wreaked who knew how much other havoc. But part of my own resolve was wanting to protect her.

I had to grapple with the words before I said, "I get that. And however you can be a part of it, I'll let you. Just… let me and the guys take the lead, okay?"

Marisol's mouth twisted, but she nodded. I was about to ask her if she wanted me to make her a late lunch from the limited supplies in the kitchen when Kai burst into the apartment with an unusual air of urgency whirling around him.

He flicked his dark brown hair away from his glasses and peered around the room with more typical analytical precision. I paused, my hand coming to rest on my sister's shoulder. "What's going on? Did something happen at work?" It must have, mustn't it, for him to be home this early?

Kai inclined his head with a jerk and motioned to Jett, who'd come out of the guys' bedroom at his arrival. "Pack up. I think we should get out of here, at least for now. The Gauntts know something is up with me, and they had Skeleton Corps guys staked out around the Thrivewell building. I'll be surprised if they don't come at us again here soon, especially when they know at least one of us is down for the count."

His gaze dropped to Nox, and his mouth tightened. Then he marched over to the dining table to grab the laptop he'd left there.

My heart started thumping faster. I hustled Marisol over to her bedroom, where she'd only just started unpacking the suitcase she'd brought from our childhood home. I hurried into my own bedroom to grab everything I couldn't bear to leave behind, leaving the door open so I could still talk to the others.

"Where are we going to go?" I asked.

Ruin's voice wavered up sleepily from where he'd been dozing on the sofa. "Go? Are we taking a trip?"

"Something like that," Kai said grimly. "You keep resting for now. I'll pack your stuff too—lots of snacks —and we'll help you down to the car. I don't think you should be trying to balance on a bike just yet."

Ruin let out a little huff. "It's my insides that fell apart. The rest of me is fine."

"Your outsides do affect the insides, you know," Jett muttered, emerging with a duffel bag slung over his shoulder. "We can't go to the clubhouse. They know about that place too."

"They do." Kai let out an exasperated sigh. "And Lily's car isn't really big enough for all six of us, especially with Nox in his current state. I suppose we could squeeze him into the trunk…"

I grimaced. "We're not making anyone ride in the trunk, regardless of level of consciousness. Don't you guys have your cars from your hosts?"

"I think they're all back in Lovell Rise since we switched to two-wheeled travel." Kai paused and hummed to himself as he grabbed Ruin's medicine and several packs of beef jerky from the kitchen. "Lily,

Marisol, and our invalids can squeeze into the car. Jett and I will flank you on our bikes. That might be a better defensive position than all of us in enclosed vehicles anyway."

"We still haven't decided where we're going," I pointed out.

And we didn't get to decide even then, because a gunshot rang out from just beneath the window. My nerves jumped.

Jett rushed to the window. "Fuck," he snapped, which was all I needed to know about the situation.

I stuffed the sweater I'd been holding into my backpack and flung it over my shoulder. Marisol dashed out of her room with suitcase in tow as I rushed to get her. She yanked her pistol out of her pocket with her free hand, her face pale and her jaw clenched.

Footsteps thundered in the hall outside. More shots boomed through the air. Kai loped to the front door, his own gun in his hand, the fingers of his other hand flexing. "I'll help clear the way."

Jett grabbed the handle of Nox's trolley, and I helped Ruin up off the sofa. He slung his arm over my shoulder, setting his feet carefully but steadily on the floor. His eyes darted from the window to the door nervously, but he still managed to smile as he tipped his head a little closer to mine. "At least I get a bonus hug out of this."

As fast as my pulse was racing now, I couldn't help snorting at that comment—and hugging him to me as tight as I dared in consideration of his still-healing injuries. As we all barreled toward the door as quickly as we could move without causing loss of life or limb, Kai stormed out. His supernatural energy was already so keyed up that a faint sizzle sang through the air with his movements.

We still had the few new recruits who'd survived the shoot-out at the clubhouse standing guard here. I caught sight of a couple of them in the hall, wrestling with the guys in skeleton masks who'd come for us. The Gauntts hadn't wasted any time siccing their gangster lackeys on us.

Kai charged right into the fray, smacking his free hand against the first masked head he could reach. "Take down as many of the Skeleton Corps people as you can," he ordered with a crackle of paranormal voodoo. Then he shot the next-nearest masked man, who'd just lunged at him.

The guy he'd worked his spell on whirled around and stabbed his knife straight into the belly of one of his colleagues. The opening gave the Skullbreakers recruits enough room to fire off more shots of their own. The rest of us pushed into the hallway.

More Skeleton Corps men were hurtling up the stairs. The tension inside me expanded into a frantic thrum. We had to get out of here before the hall turned into a death trap.

The bloody aspect to my magic couldn't hurt more than one person at a time, so instead of reaching toward our attackers, I threw the supernatural hum inside me back toward my apartment. At the tug of my attention, every faucet and fixture in the kitchen and bathroom groaned to life. With a swing of my arm, I propelled all that gushing water toward the stairwell.

It rushed past us in separate airborne currents like thick, watery snakes, only dappling my face with a faint sheen of droplets as they soared by. The torrents smashed together right as they crashed into the onslaught of masked men.

From the looks of it, I might have stolen all the water from the entire building. The tidal wave knocked all the men I could see off their feet and swept them down the stairs, limbs flailing. Jett let out a low whistle of approval.

Kai wheeled his arm. "Come on!"

We ran on across the now sopping carpet to the stairwell, the recruits and Kai's dupe charging ahead. As Ruin wobbled down the steps next to me, Jett eased the trolley along with a series of muted bumps. Nox's body jerked and swayed, but he was heavy enough that his center of gravity held him in place. Even that jostling didn't do a thing to wake him up.

We came around the second-floor landing and found a mass of dripping, pissed off dipshits waiting for us with guns raised. Jett looked down at his boss, mumbled an apology under his breath, and gave the trolley a shove.

At the sight of the cart with its massive cargo racing toward them, the Skeleton Corps guys took just a second to gape. A few of them scattered; others raised their guns. But the trolley, with Nox's weight adding to its heft, was already ramming right into their midst.

And so the Skullbreakers boss helped pummel our way out to safety without even being conscious.

The recruits and Jett fired off more shots. Kai's dupe lunged and thrust with his knife. And somehow we found ourselves barreling out the building's entrance amid scattered bodies.

The gang war had already made a mess of the building a couple of times before. This time we couldn't stick around to clean up. I was going to guess that today's evacuation might be permanent.

My heart sank, but I didn't have time to mourn the loss. When we hurried to the parking lot around the back of the building, Jett pushing Nox's trolley again, we found several more Skeleton Corps guys converging on us.

The recruits and Kai's dupe leapt forward. The masked guy managed to take down a couple of his fellow Corps members before one of them realized he really wasn't a friend anymore and kicked him aside with a bullet in his chest. He slammed right into Nox's bike, sending it toppling.

Ruin let out a sound of consternation. "Look what they're doing to your ride!" he called to his prone boss. "You can't sleep through *this*."

If there'd been any external circumstances that could have shaken Lennox Savage out of his coma, a threat to his bike did seem like the best bet. But Nox's expression stayed as slack as ever.

Ruin fired off a couple of shots, hitting one Skeleton Corps guy. Then I hauled him and Marisol over to Fred 2.0, thankfully undamaged. By the time I'd gotten my sister into the front seat with her suitcase and Ruin into the back, the guys had dealt with the remaining Skeleton Corps members—although for all we knew, there were more on the way.

We'd lost one of our recruits too. As far as I could tell, there were only three left from the motley crew of a couple dozen Nox had assembled a few weeks ago. Despite the fate all their comrades had met, these few stuck with us to the end, helping Kai, Jett, and I heave Nox off the trolley into the back seat. As the guys threw the trolley into the trunk and I rushed around the car to dive into the driver's seat, Ruin patted his boss's head when it came to rest on his lap.

"We'll fix it up," he promised, glancing at the fallen bike again. "Or get you an even better one." He glanced through the window at his own bike with its gleaming neon trim, momentarily puppy-eyed about abandoning his ride too. Then I was hitting the gas and spinning the steering wheel.

*So long, dreams of a happy family home*, I thought as we sped away from the apartment building. At least we were alive to make new dreams somewhere down the line.

# four

*Lily*

I let Kai take the lead, roaring ahead of the car on his motorcycle and weaving through the city streets. He was the one most likely to have some idea where we should go from here. I sure as shit didn't have a clue.

Marisol peered out the passenger-side window with wide eyes and tensed shoulders, but a lot less shock than I might have expected from a sixteen-year-old who'd just witnessed a gunfight. Although I guessed it wasn't her *first* gunfight. There'd been a lot of guns blazing a couple of nights ago when we'd rescued her from the Gauntts.

It wrenched at me that she'd had to witness any

EVA CHASE

gunfights at all. Why couldn't we have had normal lives that didn't include bullets and blood splatter?

Because of the Gauntts.

But the bullets and blood had come with a few things I appreciated. When I stopped at a red light, I glanced over my shoulder toward the back seat. "Are you doing okay back there?"

"Everything's good," Ruin replied, unfazed even by the loss of the sofa that'd been his main home for the last two days. "I don't think any stitches came open."

"Thank God for small mercies," I muttered.

Ruin chuckled. "I don't think God had very much to do with it. If he exists, he probably wouldn't approve of my career choice."

Fair.

I kept my mouth shut after that and focused on following Kai. He drove around downtown and into an industrial area with factories, warehouses, and way less traffic. Following some sense of direction I didn't share, he pulled off the road onto a lane that led around behind one of the factories. There, he parked in a lot that was empty other than an assortment of trash drifting in the breeze.

As Jett zoomed in after us, I parked and opened my door. "I'm guessing this isn't our new accommodations," I said to Kai.

"I'd prefer somewhere with more walls, as much as I enjoy the fresh air," Ruin piped up from behind me. The breeze washing over us past the open door was pretty cool.

34

Kai glowered at us. "Obviously not. I haven't exactly had time to reach out to my connections and figure out where we'd be safest laying low. It just seemed like a reasonable place to talk undisturbed." He drew in a breath. "And we do need to talk before we decide exactly how low we're laying."

Something about his tone made my gut clench. "What do you mean?"

He cocked his head in the direction we'd come from. "The situation has escalated. The Gauntts are on the warpath, and they're throwing all their resources at us now. If we're going to stay and fight, we have to be prepared for an even worse onslaught. Or we could take off for someplace out of their reach at least for long enough to regroup and recover on our own schedule."

"If we're beyond *their* reach, then they'll also be beyond ours," I said. "We can't—we still need to figure out how to help Nox. We don't know how long he can survive in this state. And the kids—their granddaughter —everything else they've done… We can't let them get away with it."

"I'm not saying we should," Kai said. "I just wanted to lay out the options. If we're sticking around, then in my opinion, we can't stay on the defensive. We need to strike back at them, hard, as soon as we can. Otherwise they'll keep battering us until we're beaten down."

I inhaled sharply and glanced at my sister. I'd just been regretting her exposure to gang warfare, and now we were talking about instigating even more of that war ourselves.

But what were our other options, really? If we fled completely, we might buy ourselves a little time to heal, but Nox could slip away from us in the meantime. And we'd be giving the Gauntts and the Skeleton Corps time to regather their forces as well.

Marisol met my gaze and folded her arms over her chest. "I say we destroy the motherfuckers."

Well, when she put it that way…

I turned back to Kai. "What she said. The sooner we crush them, the better. But how are we going to do the crushing?" The thought of the tall tower of Thrivewell Enterprises intimidated me more than I liked.

Kai gave us a crooked smile. "I'm not sure yet. We still don't know exactly what we're dealing with. But while I'm finding us new digs, I can think of at least one way you can work at uncovering their weaknesses."

\* \* \*

Peering at ancient newspaper articles through a filmy screen wasn't quite what I'd have pictured as an act of war. Although it did seem to come with some possibility of physical injury. I'd been squinting at the display for so long that my eyes were starting to feel like they might melt into the backs of my eye sockets.

Ruin didn't look particularly impressed either. He spun on his stool next to me—not too fast, because I'd already given him a death glare when he'd risked toppling off it earlier—and chewed on a spicy gumball he'd brought along to keep him alert. At least, that was his official explanation.

He'd been assigned to keep me company mainly so we didn't end up leaving him undefended. Marisol had opted to cruise around with Kai and Nox to pick out a place to crash for the night, and Jett was off on some errand he and Kai had murmured about in low voices before he'd taken off. That left me and my sunshine-y invalid at the county archives office.

"So where did the girls come from then?" Ruin said abruptly, apparently just finishing mulling over some of the information we'd uncovered about an hour ago. We'd been able to find adoption or, in the case of the first three generations, birth certificates for the men in the Gauntt family, but there was no sign of any of the women having officially existed other than the very first Olivia and Marie. Not as kids, anyway. The marriage records confirmed that women who currently went by Olivia and Marie had married each generation of Thomases and Nolans.

"Siblings can't legally get married, even if they're not blood relations," I reminded him. "I guess they couldn't officially adopt both kids when they wanted to resurrect their marriage after passing the buck down the line. Maybe they figured it was easier having the boys be the legit heirs since that kept the family name the same."

"But where did the girls come from? They didn't fall out of the sky."

"No, but I'm sure there are a lot of ways you can set

up adoptions off the books if you have the money to back it up."

Maybe the Gauntts had gone overseas to poorer European countries. Maybe they'd preyed on struggling single parents here in the States. Kai had suggested it might have been a more temporary-sounding foster situation. Whatever the case had been, I had no doubt the Gauntts had orchestrated it with as much awfulness as they'd brought to everything else we knew they'd done.

A frog hopped by under my feet with a faint croak. "Keep a low profile, okay?" I murmured at it, shooting a glance toward the woman who oversaw this part of the office. Every now and then she glanced up from her metal desk on the other side of the room and narrowed her eyes at us like she was sure we had some nefarious purpose. I'd like to know exactly what sort of trouble a person could get up to with this kind of equipment.

I turned my attention back to the microfiche just in time to spot a mention of Marie Gauntt in a piece from the 1920s. Ah ha. I expanded the text on the screen, which made it a bit blurry but not unreadable. As my gaze skimmed over the article, my spirits leapt.

"Look at this," I hissed to Ruin, and immediately regretted my enthusiasm when he leaned over in his chair, probably stretching all kinds of patched up organs he shouldn't have been straining. I tugged at his chair so he'd scoot closer where he didn't need to bend over and motioned to the screen. "The first Marie was into spiritualism."

Ruin swallowed his gum, which probably wasn't any good for his internal situation either, and started gnawing on a piece of fiery jerky next. "She worshipped ghosts?"

"Not exactly." I skimmed over the piece, which didn't offer a whole lot of explanation because it assumed the reader knew the context, but I remembered reading a book that talked about the movement during my copious free time while under psychiatric observation at St. Elspeth's. "People got really into trying to communicate with the dead and wandering spirits. Receiving 'messages' from them, tapping into higher planes of existence and crap like that. It seems like Marie was gung-ho about that stuff. She hosted some big group séance at her house."

Ruin's eyebrows leapt up. "Then that's where they got the idea for shuffling spirits around, right? They figured out how to stop their souls from just wandering away."

"Something like that, I guess." I frowned at the screen. "Kai suspected they started with the possessions way back then. It seems like this confirms that they were in the right mindset. They must have found some practices and techniques that actually worked for manipulating the afterlife."

A shiver ran down my back. If the Gauntts had been studying the supernatural world for that long—if the four souls we were up against had more than a century of life experience under their belts—how much of a chance did we have of really challenging them?

They had the advantage when it came to money, political power, and now paranormal clout too.

I knew life wasn't fair, but it did seem like the scales should have been tipped a *little* less in the asshats' favor.

As I started scrolling again, the woman at the desk stood up abruptly. I glanced down, prepared to defend my amphibious interlopers if need be, but it was Ruin she was staring daggers at.

"Are you *eating* while viewing the archives?" she demanded, in a tone that suggested that offense would be on the same level as ethnic genocide.

Ruin's head jerked up, his face forming an expression of apologetic guilt. The apology part was probably not helped by the fact that he was still chewing.

Before the office manager could turn any redder with indignation, I decided we were better off distracting her than attempting to suppress Ruin's appetite. He had internal organs to reconstruct, after all. So with a small twinge of guilt of my own, I tapped a soft rhythm on the table in front of me and focused my supernatural energy on the water cooler in the far corner near the woman's desk.

The jug started gurgling. A small spurt of water ejaculated from the faucet, followed by a more emphatic sploosh. The woman spun around with a yelp and ran over, groping around for something she could use to mop up the sudden puddle.

Ruin shot me a grin and popped the last of his current pack of jerky into his mouth. Then he composed his face into a model of perfect innocence for when the office manager happened to look our way again. I snatched the empty jerky packet from him and stuffed it into my bag where she wouldn't see it.

The rest of that microfiche didn't turn up anything else interesting about the Gauntts, and neither did the two I checked after that. I found a brief mention from some local paper so small it'd faded from existence over the past century, referencing Marie's "avid spiritual interests" as a passing remark, so at least that was independent confirmation of her supernatural dabbling. It didn't tell us anything about where that dabbling had led her, but maybe that was too much to expect.

Swallowing a sigh, I moved to one of the more modern computers. Ruin wheeled his stool after me, bobbing with the squeaking of the wheels. "What are we hunting for now?" he asked.

"I don't know," I said. "This is my last-ditch effort to get something more useful out of this place. Probably Kai and Jett will come up with more than we do, but Kai said I might as well look through *all* the different types of records they store here just in case."

Along with the birth and adoption records, I'd already checked death certificates and written down their sparse information about when each of the previous Gauntts had passed on. So far, there was nothing recorded for the Nolan Senior I'd met. I wondered how the family would handle his death. As far as I knew, they'd left his body in the marsh for the fish. Had they gone back and dredged it up later? Or maybe they simply had a doctor on their payroll who'd write up a certificate with no questions asked.

Now I entered the name Gauntt into every database the archives office contained. I got either nothing or boring business-y looking documents until I reached a list of property deeds.

The first few held no surprises. There was the mansion in the suburbs that we'd broken into a little while back, the immense tower of the Thrivewell head office, and a couple of satellite offices in the neighboring towns. But at the end of the list, after those, was a transfer agreement for a small plot of land not far outside Lovell Rise.

As I read through the details, understanding tingled through my mind. Ruin noticed my sharpened focus and tipped his head at the screen. "Is there something special about that one?"

"I think so," I said. "The Gauntts own about an acre of land along the lake—the description and the coordinates make it sound like it's right where we found them on the spit the other night. And they bought it back in 1937, just a month before the first Thomas died."

I looked over at Ruin, my chest constricting. "It's been all about the marsh all along."

# five

*Lily*

I parked at the end of the road that took us closest to the Gauntts' spit and got out with a full brigade of protectors around me. All of my guys who were currently conscious had insisted on accompanying me out to the marsh in case our enemies were hanging around. Nox had come along for the ride too, currently slumped in the back seat of Mr. Grimes's old car, which the other guys had picked up after we'd been ousted from my apartment. He hadn't had much choice in the matter.

I motioned for Marisol to stay in the car while I scanned the landscape ahead. I couldn't see the spit itself because of the cluster of scrawny trees between us and it, but I couldn't make out any other vehicles in the area or any signs of human presence. After several seconds, weighing the risks of leaving my sister here versus bringing her with us, I waved for her to come out.

"Things might… get a little weird," I warned her. My sister knew about my watery talents, but she hadn't witnessed them up close all that much. The last time I'd come out to the marsh for my own purposes, I'd practically drowned myself to tap into enough power to break the Gauntts' memory-blocking spell on me.

Marisol shrugged with typical teenage nonchalance. "I can handle it. I *want* to see your superpowers." She gave me a sly smile. "And if you can figure out a way to give me some, I'd be happy to put on a cape and tights."

Jett snorted with a rare outward show of amusement. I couldn't resist reaching over to ruffle my sister's hair. "I'm not sure how it works, and considering I had to almost die to get mine, I'd rather we didn't experiment. But if I come across some kind of magic potion, I'll be sure to grab a portion for you."

She gave a playful huff. "I guess I can live with that."

Speaking of conditions for life… I glanced at Nox's prone form. "Should someone stay behind with him?"

The other guys held each other's gazes, appearing to have a silent debate. Kai, who'd taken over as the highest authority figure in Nox's technical absence, nudged Ruin. "You shouldn't be walking around much anyway. Hang out in the car with him, and shoot anyone who looks like a problem."

Ruin waggled his gun. "I can do that. Just make

sure you fill me in on the whole story when you get back."

Jett and Kai kept their guns out as we headed down to the water. We didn't encounter any people on the other side of the trees, though, only a small squad of frogs who'd hopped out of the marsh to meet us. They bobbed their heads to me as if kowtowing to their ruler.

"That's really not necessary," I told them. "You can go back to whatever you were doing." I hadn't meant to interrupt their froggy lives.

My assurances didn't persuade them. They bounded after me along the spit. I stopped by the spot where the Gauntts had conducted their ritual and peered down into the water, braced to see Nolan Senior's corpse staring up at me.

I couldn't make out anything through the murk and the tangled vegetation. Was he still there, just out of sight beneath the swirling silt and the reflections that played off the water? The cool breeze raised goosebumps on my arms even through my sweater.

The Gauntts had taken over this spot nearly a century ago, claiming it as their own in both a legal sense and, it seemed, by supernatural means as well. Had the marsh already contained paranormal energies, or had the Gauntts used it as a conduit for powers they'd developed elsewhere?

The frogs couldn't tell me, but maybe the water could, one way or another.

I knelt down at the end of the spit. Kai, Jett, and Marisol stayed at the foot, the guys surveying the area around us for trouble, Marisol focused on me. I tuned them all out, matching the rhythm of my breath to the whisper of the wind through the reeds.

These currents had seen so much. And there might be more than water out there. The Gauntts' spirits had passed on from body to body, but the kids those bodies had belonged to must have died for the transfer to happen. Had any of them lingered on like the Skullbreakers' souls had?

They'd certainly have plenty of unfinished business to hold them in this world.

I dipped my hands right into the water and reached my awareness out through it, searching for any sign that there was a presence that I could communicate with. Weeds tickled against my fingers. A few of the frogs croaked. The current twined around my hands, and I thought I felt the faintest tug.

"Who's there?" I murmured. "Talk to me. Let me see you. Reach out to me however you can."

A shiver of sensation traveled up my arms and through my skull. I propelled more of my magic into the water that'd granted it to me, letting the vague impression forming in the back of my mind take shape in front of me.

The surface of the water directly ahead of me bulged upward. It quivered and stretched toward the sky, smaller protrusions jutting out of it like it was some kind of aquatic gremlin, but gradually arranging into a more clearly humanoid form. A translucent face mottled with imprecise dips and peaks of eye sockets, nose, mouth, and ears gaped at me. Arms dangled at its sides. From the size of the figure, it was a kid—if I could expect this watery apparition to be to scale.

Even as I stared back at the liquid spirit, another tug came. I fed more of my energy into that sensation, and a second figure rose up from the water next to the first. Then a third and a fourth. They all stood around the same height. It was impossible to identify them with the vagueness of their features, though it wasn't hard to guess who they might be. More impressions nipped at my fingers, but I was already stretching myself thin just holding these four up. An ache was spreading down my spine.

Behind me, Marisol let out a little gasp. Jett muttered something inaudible to himself. I didn't dare glance back at them in case losing my attention would destroy the beings I'd conjured out of the water.

"You're here because of the Gauntts," I said. "They left you in the marsh." Whether they were the victims of past adoptees who'd been co-opted as hosts or victims of other sorts, I figured those two statements were almost definitely true.

The figures all nodded emphatically, though not in unison, with an erratic bobbing of their watery heads. One of them lifted an arm with a blob of a hand at the end and made some gesture I couldn't decipher.

"What?" I asked. "I don't understand. Is there something you can tell me that'll help us stop the Gauntts?"

That question spurred the figures to greater life.

More energy rushed out of me with a greater strain on my nerves, as if the aquatic ghosts were dragging it out of me in their enthusiasm. They launched into a grand, watery pantomime, limbs whipping this way and that, the wells of their mouths opening and closing.

Unfortunately, I couldn't make much sense of any of it. They looked like they were performing a drunken interpretive dance that could only have been explained in the production's program, which no one had bothered to give me. Could beings made out of water get drunk?

Okay, that was probably the wrong question.

"Er…" I said, not sure how they'd respond to constructive criticism of their methods.

Finally, they acted out one scene I could easily recognize. One of them pushed another into the water just as we'd seen the Gauntts do to Nolan and his younger counterpart.

My stomach twisted. "Yes, we know about that. Is that what happened to all of you? They drowned you and then used your bodies?"

Another chorus of nods, this one so eager a thin spray whipped off their heads and misted my face. It kind of felt like being spit on, even if I didn't think they'd meant it that way. I wanted to swipe the moisture off my skin, but I wasn't sure what would happen if I removed my hands from the marsh.

"Have you seen any of their other powers?" I asked, and immediately regretted it when I was treated to another extended drunken pantomime. Maybe they were saying that the Gauntts worked figure skating voodoo? Or that they regularly wrestled tigers? Somehow I didn't think I was interpreting this dance correctly.

When they slowed down, I broke in with the most important question I hadn't asked yet, even though my hopes had sunk as my energy dwindled. I didn't know how much longer I could keep giving them form.

"My boyfriend," I said. "Well, one of them. I don't know if you saw—when we were out here a few nights ago, Nolan smacked him on the forehead and left one of their marks, and now my boyfriend is unconscious and won't wake up. Do you have any idea how to snap him out of that spell?"

I braced myself for another bizarre dance show, but what I got was somehow worse. One by one, the watery figures shook their heads or splayed their hands in gestures of helplessness. My throat constricted.

What else could I ask them? I'd come out here, I'd managed to summon them out of the marsh, and I hadn't gotten a single useful thing from them. How could I give up now? A few of the frogs had plopped into the water next to my submerged fingers, but they didn't offer any insights.

Then Marisol's voice rang out from behind me, firm and full of teenage sass. "You've got to tell my sister something! Come on. Don't you *want* her to help you kick those pricks' asses?"

My mouth twitched into something somewhere between a smile and a grimace, but it was pride that swelled in my chest. Maybe she wasn't expressing her opinions in the politest way ever, but I loved that Marisol was confident enough to speak up at all after everything she'd been through.

The translucent forms swayed back and forth for several seconds. I couldn't tell whether they were wavering indecisively or if they were reacting to my fraying control. The ache in my spine was stretching right through my back and along my ribs now.

They looked so mournful that I opened my mouth to tell them it was all right—it wasn't their fault we couldn't figure out how to communicate. Maybe we could teach them sign language like researchers did with gorillas in the jungle?

Before I could say anything, the nearest figure sped between the reeds toward me. My mouth snapped shut just in time, because the next thing I knew, the body of water was leaping out of the marsh and crashing down over me with a splash.

In the first instant, I thought it was some kind of attack, that the spirits were pissed off that *I* hadn't been more useful to them. But as the chilly water drenched me, soaking through my hair and trickling over my scalp, images washed through my mind.

I saw Nolan and Marie Senior barking orders at the kid whose memories I was receiving. A pinch of Marie's fingers around "my" arm, and a sense of panicked obedience rushing through me. Choking down gulps of food while the four adult Gauntts chattered around me as if I wasn't there, their voices warbled like I was hearing them through water. Staring up at the ceiling from "my" bed, unable to fall asleep. Then sinking down into the cold darkness of the marsh in the middle of the night while voices chanted over me.

The moment those images faded, the second figure threw itself over me. More water soaked me; more ghostly memories floated through my mind. Nolan and Marie looked decades younger, though still recognizable. An older man I didn't recognize—the previous Thomas?—chortled to himself as he prodded my sides. I was left alone in a kitchen for hours, unable to move, my fingers starting to itch to grab one of the knives and stab it into my own chest. Then another dunking into the frigid slurry of the marsh water.

The third and fourth figures cast themselves over me next, sending images full of the same desperation and anguish coursing through my mind. A sob congealed in my chest. I wanted to reach out through the filmy impressions and hug the children they belonged to close.

But they were already gone—at least all physical presence they'd had was. What remained was slipping away from me as water dribbling into the muddy ground beneath my feet.

Just as I thought it was over, a deeper, broader sensation swept up from my fingers where they were still submerged in the marsh. A cold, turgid wave of horror and revulsion rushed through my nerves and rippled through my chest.

I gasped, my hands clenching. The feeling fell away,

leaving only my chilled, sodden body and an ache that now seemed to fill every part of me.

I stood up, and my legs wobbled under me as if I'd lived for over a century myself. I swiped my dripping hair away from my face and looked toward my sister and my guys.

"The spirits aren't happy," I said, "and I don't think the marsh is either. I don't think it likes what the Gauntts have put into it at all."

"Who would?" Jett muttered.

Kai studied me through his glasses. "What does that mean for us?"

"I'm not sure," I admitted. "But I think it means we've got all that water on our side... if we can figure out what we'd want it to do for us."

## six

*Ruin*

The windows of the medieval restaurant that'd become our new clubhouse glinted with broken glass. I cocked my head at the sight, summoning the cheerful spin I knew I could bring to the situation if I just reached far enough. The painkillers I'd been taking helped, giving every sensation softly fuzzy edges.

"The police haven't messed with our stuff," I said. "No caution tape or chalk outlines. They must be scared of getting on our bad side."

"Or of getting on the Gauntts'," Kai said flatly, easing open the door on its battered hinges. "The Corps guy we talked to did say that they pay off the cops not to bother the gang."

Kai was not so great at looking on the bright side. But that didn't matter when I was so good at it, and he was brilliant at so many other things. I guessed that was why Nox had brought both of us onto the team.

Thinking of Nox brought up frustrations I couldn't put in any kind of positive light. I grimaced inwardly and stepped through the doorway into the mess of the restaurant, walking carefully so I didn't stir up any new pangs in my stitched-up insides.

The interior of the restaurant held the same autumn chill as outside, since the broken windows obviously weren't holding any heat in. In one particular way, the space was less messy than it'd been when we'd last occupied it. Blood stains marked the floor amid the toppled chairs and shards of glass, but someone had carried off all the bodies. And there'd been a *lot* of bodies.

"The Skeleton Corps—or maybe the Gauntts themselves—must have decided it was better for them not to leave a bunch of corpses around for anyone to see," Kai said, answering the question that'd only just begun to form in my mind in that eerie way of his. His ability to predict what you were thinking had been nearly supernatural even before the whole resurrection thing.

"Whoever came through, they were very enthusiastic," I said, taking in the newer parts of the mess. Someone had wrenched a bunch of the decorative weapons off the walls and tossed them around the place. The banquet table by the throne was cracked down the middle, and the throne itself had its seat caved in and the back snapped off halfway down. Spray paint streaked across the floors and walls with the Skeleton Corps's crossed bones symbol and a whole lot of obscenities aimed at us.

I was glad Lily didn't have to see them. Hopefully she and the others were staying safe in the foreclosed house we'd broken into as a place to crash for the night.

I wandered over to the area along the walls where the tables that'd held the platters of party food were now lying on their sides. Finger foods and dip scattered the floor, giving off an odor that was just crossing the line between greasy deliciousness and sour rot. I wrinkled my nose and dipped my head in a moment of silence. What a waste of tasty snacks.

Kai kicked aside an axe here and a platter there, the faint clangs echoing through the large room. We were supposed to be checking to see if the Skeleton Corps had left anything here that might be useful to an attack on them—and to make sure *we* weren't leaving anything they could use against us—but nothing jumped out at me in the mess. I supposed we could take some of those swords and run the assholes through, but guns worked faster.

Anyway, it seemed like we needed a more permanent solution than regular death when it came to the Gauntts. They kept resurrecting themselves like something out of a horror movie.

"Do you see anything?" I asked Kai, walking slowly around the throne. Remembering the fun I'd had with

Lily on that seat—my first time with her—made me want to fix it, but I was afraid I'd bust something open inside me if I tried to wrangle the heavy pieces. She wouldn't be happy about that. It could wait until my organs had fused back into place a little better.

Kai blew out a breath and shook his head. "Not so far." He ducked into the room at the back, which had once been the kitchen area, and came back out frowning. "The guns and ammo we stashed here are all gone. No surprise there. I can always get more."

I glanced at the walls with their mottling of bullet holes and couldn't help chuckling. "It looks like we could load a lot of pistols with what's in the plaster."

Kai rolled his eyes at me and headed toward the front door. "Come on. We don't want to stick around any of our known haunts for longer than necessary."

I hummed to myself as I followed him. "I'd kind of like to run into a prick or two. Put some fear into them." I smacked my fist into my palm, and just then a guy appeared outside the shattered front windows.

He stopped when he saw us, and so did we. Kai's hand snapped to his gun, but before he'd even lifted it, the guy raised his hands in a gesture of surrender.

"I just wanted to talk to you," he said. "I promise, I'm not here to fight."

Kai narrowed his eyes at the guy. "I've seen you before. You're with the Skeleton Corps."

The dude didn't look particularly familiar to me, but I wasn't as keenly observant as Kai at the best of times, and the fuzziness of the medication was definitely making my memory more sluggish too. My friend was obviously right, because the guy nodded.

"I am, but I'm not here for them. They— I'm here for me." He moved one arm—slowly, as if he was worried we'd shoot him for any sudden movements— and touched his other bicep. "You asked before about the Gauntts and marks we might have on us. That girl did something to one of the bosses, made him remember something that got him angry at them… I've got one too."

"A reason to be angry?" Kai asked.

"A *mark*," the guy said. "I can show you—I want her to do whatever it is she does for me. I want to know what happened."

Kai and I exchanged a glance. The guy looked pretty harmless by our standards. I didn't see any weapons on him, and he was shorter and scrawnier than either of us alone, let alone both of us combined. I probably could have taken him even with my internal injuries and without my supernatural powers, if I didn't mind another trip to the doctor afterward.

And one of the enemy coming to us for help had to be more useful than anything else we'd found around here, right?

"Come inside," Kai said carefully. As the Skeleton Corps guy stepped through the empty window frame, Kai eased closer to the opposite window to peer down the street.

"I came alone," the Corps guy said. "Believe me, I

don't *want* them knowing I'm here. What they did to the boss…"

Curiosity gripped me. "What did they do to him? He didn't come to the party!" Not that he'd missed anything other than a massacre. But it'd been a very impressive massacre.

The guy made a face. "I don't actually know. But after that meeting with the bunch of you, he was ranting about the Gauntts, and then the bosses all went off together… and I haven't seen him again since. The bosses get paid off by those rich pricks. They don't want to piss them off. So I've got to think they cleaned house."

Kai folded his arms over his chest. "Then you might not be able to go back after you've talked to us. What's so important about this that you're risking your life over it?"

"What do you think?" the guy said. "Obviously something fucked up is going on with these Gauntt people. I never liked that we let them jerk our chains in the first place. And there was…" His forehead furrowed. "I'm missing something. How the fuck am I supposed to know what to do about them if I don't know what *they* did?"

His words tugged at something deep inside me—not anything currently held together with staples and stitches, thankfully. I found myself thinking of the aimless days in my childhood home when it'd felt like I was just drifting on, barely even existing to anyone other than myself. Like nothing I said or did meant

58

anything. Until I'd decided that I'd make it mean something. I'd find my own joys wherever I could, whether the people around me bothered to notice or not.

And then in a weird way I'd been free.

This guy wasn't free at all, in the opposite way. He had all kinds of assholes telling him his life was theirs, and he didn't even know all the shit they'd done to him. But he was trying to do something about that problem however he could. He was trying to make his life his, like I had. I could respect that.

Kai didn't look particularly impressed. I might not be a master at reading people, but his expression was all skepticism. "And you're coming to us about this *now*? Why?"

The guy spread his hands. "I was thinking about it. Like you said, it's a big risk. And then there was the epic fight and everything... People are saying crazy things... But I don't care about any of that. I decided I want to know, and you're the people who can make that happen. Simple as that. So are you going to do it or not?"

"Out of the goodness of our hearts?"

"No." The guy scowled at Kai. "If the Gauntts messed with me half as much as it sounds like they did the boss, then I'm on your side. I'll help you go after them—and the Skeleton Corps fuckers who let them get away with that shit—whatever way I can. There might even be more guys with the marks that I can bring on. But I can't promise anything until I know what's up."

Kai glowered back at him. "When you're asking for access to our woman after everything you pricks have done to us, that isn't going to cut it."

"Hey!" I said, holding up my hand. "We can make sure he's telling the truth. I'll just make him want to."

Kai's face brightened a little with approval. The Skeleton Corps guy looked significantly less enthusiastic. He backed up a step. "I'm not sticking around to let you beat me down."

I snorted. "That's not what I meant. All I've got to do is give you a little tap. Then you can be part of one of those crazy stories for a little while, and we can get our confirmation. Win-win!"

His eyes darted between the two of us. Kai was nodding. "I think that's fair. If you're not willing to trust Ruin that much, there's no reason we should trust you."

The guy's jaw clenched. For a second, I thought he was going to storm off on us. Then he propelled himself toward me. "Fine. Do it. Just get it over with."

That seemed like pretty good proof in itself, but when it came to Lily's safety, I didn't want to go just by my admittedly off-kilter instincts. I paused for a moment to think about the emotion I'd want to send into the guy and then gave him a light smack across the shoulder.

Energy crackled over my skin with the sense of awed respect I'd aimed at him, drawn from my own feelings for my friends and my love. The guy blinked at us, and something in his face relaxed. He sank down to his knees, staring up at us like we were a fountain he'd reached after a long trek across a brutal desert.

"I can't believe you're considering helping me," he said in a breathless rush. "You really are great. Amazing. Fantastic."

"And all the other adjectives," Kai said dryly, shooting an amused glance toward me. "Why do you really want our help? We expect full honesty if we're going to believe you're really committed."

"Of course! I'm putting myself in your hands. I'm sick of living under the Gauntts' thumb, and if they did something even worse to me that I can't remember…" He shuddered. "You're the only ones who can stop them. Who can get their mark off me, if they're the ones who put it there. There's no one else I can turn to. Please."

"And you aren't going to go running back to your buddies telling them what we're up to?" I asked.

He shook his head so emphatically it nearly popped off his neck. "No, I'd never do that to you. You deserve so much more loyalty than that. If you take me on, I'm with you until the end. Those fuckers who think they can cover up what the rich pricks are doing to the rest of us can suck my dick."

That sounded pretty similar to what he'd already been saying. I was ready to believe him, but Kai with his smarts made extra sure.

"Before my colleague here gave you a smack, did you have other plans?" he asked, taking on a smoothly reassuring tone. "Were you planning to betray us before you realized how fantastic we are? We won't punish you for it, of course. We just need to totally understand where you're coming from. Full honesty is key."

"I understand," the guy said, clasping his hands together. "But I'd already made up my mind before I came here. I mean, I was kind of concerned about how you'd all react, but I'm done with working for the Skeleton Corps. The assholes at the top showed that *they* don't care about loyalty."

A smile stretched across Kai's face, and I knew we were good. He motioned the guy onto his feet. "Come on then. It seems like we've got a lot of talking to do."

# SEVEN

*Lily*

The guys had propped Nox up against the wall where we'd wedged his trolley into a corner of the empty dining room, under the theory that there was more chance he'd come back to life if he looked at least a little alive. I wasn't sure how much validity there was to that idea, but I had to admit it was a bit of a relief not to see him constantly sprawled on his side like he was already fully dead.

I sat next to his motionless form, watching the other Skullbreakers, who'd gathered around the Skeleton Corps guy they'd brought back with them. I'd broken the Gauntts' mark on his arm at his request, and he'd gone off into one of the house's other rooms for a while to stew with the memories I'd released. Now he was back, talking with the other men in low tones with a look on his face that was equal parts anguish and rage.

The Gauntts had hurt so many people in their ghastly quest for… for what? I wasn't even sure what their endgame was. Did they simply want to live forever? To use their accumulated wisdom and experience to make their corporation even more powerful? Or did they have even bigger, more disturbing plans?

I wasn't sure I could wrap my head around anything more horrendous.

"So now we've got a Skeleton Corps guy becoming an honorary Skullbreaker," I said to Nox quietly. "What do you think about that?"

He didn't answer, of course.

I cocked my head. "I guess you'd probably have gone by Kai's judgment anyway. He was convinced enough that the guy has the right intentions to bring him here. Ruin's always happy to make friends, so that wasn't a hard one. I don't think Jett's totally on board yet, though." The artist was hanging half a step back, his shoulders slightly hunched in a typical wary pose.

Nox continued to sit silently. Could he hear me from wherever his spirit was locked away inside his body? I reached over and squeezed his hand, which was at least still warm. Every time I moved to touch him, my pulse stuttered with the fear that I'd find his skin deathly cold.

The Skeleton Corps guy's gaze darted over to us and jerked away again, and I had to smile. "He's scared of you even while you're doing your best mannequin impersonation. You've definitely made an impact."

There were so many other things I wanted to say. *I'm sorry that I couldn't get any useful cure ideas out of those water-logged ghosts. I wish I'd realized what Nolan was doing and jumped in the way before he touched you.*

*I miss you.*

A couple of months ago, I hadn't had any of the guys in my life. I'd been overjoyed just to be leaving behind St. Elspeth's to begin the rest of my real life. But they'd wormed their way into every part of my existence both together and in their own separate ways.

No one had ever made me feel like Nox did, with the words so sweet and demanding at the same time rolling off his tongue. With the unshakeable confidence he brought to every problem the world threw at us.

We needed him. The longer he stayed under the Gauntts' spell, the farther away he seemed.

Kai ambled over, and I pushed myself to my feet to meet him. He glanced down at Nox with a discomforted twist of his mouth and then studied me, his eyes brightly alert behind the panes of his glasses.

"I think this development is going to be a real blessing in our favor," he said. "It's going to keep you busy. Our new friend Parker is planning to figure out who else in the Skeleton Corps has been marked and bring them back here so you can open their minds. We'll end up with our own little contingent of double-agents."

I studied the slim, scruffy-looking newcomer, who

was ducking his head with a shy smile at Ruin's playful cuff of his shoulder. "Are you sure we won't end up double-double-crossed again?"

"He sounded genuinely pissed off at the way the Gauntts have been bossing around his gang before we even cracked open his head," Kai said. "And he definitely doesn't have any friendly feelings toward them now. Revenge is an excellent motivator, as we should know."

"True." I dragged in a breath. "That'll help us defend against any future attacks from the Corps. But what about getting at the Gauntts? It doesn't sound like the gang has any access to them beyond taking their orders or any idea about their supernatural abilities. They jump when they're called to and that's it."

Kai grimaced. "I'd agree with that assessment. It's one piece of the puzzle. The more we can take away from the bastards, the harder it'll be for them to hold us off."

One piece of the puzzle. His words made me think of our earlier gambit to figure out who else in the area had been abused and marked by the Gauntts. The viral video had failed because of their meddling, but there were others out there who might want the same revenge and were in a different position from Mayfield's gangsters.

I even knew who at least a few of them were.

My chest constricted around the suggestion for a few seconds before I forced it out. "Maybe we need to reach out to other unlikely allies. Other victims who'd want to tear the Gauntts down if they had the chance to."

Kai raised his eyebrows. "I take it you have someone specific in mind—ah. Of course." He paused. "Are you sure you want to go there? Dealing with that contingent would stir up plenty of uncomfortable memories for *you*."

I shouldn't be surprised that he'd followed my line of thinking before I'd said half of it out loud. I shrugged, bolstering my resolve on the inside. "If you guys can manage to forge an alliance with people from the gang that murdered you, then I think I can handle making nice with a few college bullies. We don't even know how much they actually wanted to harass me and how much it was Gauntt voodoo winding them up."

"True. Who do you want to start with?"

I knew the answer to that question, even if I didn't really want to say *that* either.

We only knew three of my former bullies at Lovell Rise who'd been marked by the Gauntts, and it made the most sense to start with one of them and work from there to figure out who else had been affected. One of them had been Ansel Hunter, whose body Ruin had taken over and therefore had nothing to say for himself anymore. Another had been a guy named Fergus who'd gone practically catatonic when I'd released his memories. I wasn't sure he'd be of much use for anything.

And then there was Peyton, the worst of the girls. I'd already appealed to her once a couple of weeks ago, and she'd told me off. But the conflict between us had still been fresh then, and she hadn't had much time to think about what I'd said or the crazy things she'd seen.

I didn't like her, but she was a heck of a lot stronger-willed than Fergus seemed to be. And I knew how fierce she could be when someone had threatened something important to her. If we *could* get her on our side, even as an enemy-of-our-enemies rather than anything resembling a friend, that should definitely work in our favor.

Especially when she'd mentioned that her mom worked for Thrivewell.

"I think I need to go pay another call on Ansel's groupie," I said. "Which means Ruin had better come along too."

* * *

It was actually the perfect day for approaching Peyton, because I'd shared a class with her on Tuesdays before I'd left the school. So I knew exactly what building she'd be walking out of at two o'clock this afternoon.

In total stalker style, Ruin and I lurked in the shadow of the neighboring building until I spotted Peyton's thick chestnut hair swishing as she exited the lecture hall. We hustled over, a little less hastily than I might have preferred since I was still worried about Ruin's insides becoming his outsides all over again.

We managed to catch up with Peyton before she reached her destination, which appeared to be the campus bar. I wasn't sure if she was looking to grab a snack or aiming to get started on some day drinking, but either way, she was temporarily out of luck.

"Peyton!" Ruin called in his bright voice when I motioned to him.

Peyton swung around, her eyes widening over her arched nose. When she saw the two of us, she stopped, but she folded her arms tightly over her willowy frame. "What do you want now?" she asked, not even trying to act friendly for the guy-formerly-known-as-Ansel's benefit.

I willed my hackles to stay down even though her mere presence made the hum wake up in my chest. Through force of will, I kept my voice even. "Just to talk. It's important. And it involves Ansel too."

Peyton's eyes flicked to Ruin again. It was even harder now for me to see his host in his gradually shifting appearance, but I'd gotten to know the guy he was now pretty well. Peyton must still have made out a lot of her former crush in him. She bit her lip and then nodded. "Okay. Fine. I'll give you a few minutes."

We stepped around the side of the building, out of the way of other early bar-goers. A chilly breeze wound around us, and I tucked my hands into the pockets of my jacket. The hiss of the wind over the grass and the rhythmic pulsing of bass emanating from a dorm-room window steadied me.

"I know a lot of what we said when we came by before must have sounded strange," I started.

Peyton snorted. "That's putting it mildly. It sounded

fucking insane."

I resisted the urge to glower at her. "Well, it should be pretty obvious to you by now that a lot of strange things are actually going on. I mean, I'm assuming you've never been swarmed by frogs before. And then there's him." I jerked my thumb toward Ruin.

He nodded, holding Peyton's gaze with the kind of gentle smile only Ruin would be capable of. I doubted Ansel had ever produced an expression half that sweet.

"You know I'm not Ansel anymore, don't you?" he said, equally gently.

Peyton's face tightened. "I don't know how that's possible."

"It's… complicated," he said. "And I'm sorry that you lost someone you cared about. But I can tell from the way you reached out to him and tried to protect him when you thought he was in trouble that you *are* a caring person. Someone who wants to support other people. Right?"

That was probably the most generous spin any person could possibly put on Peyton's behavior, but hearing it put that way softened something in her too. She swallowed audibly, and her arms loosened over her chest. "I'd like to think so. When the people deserve it."

"Do you think *you* deserve it?" he asked.

Peyton blinked. "I—I don't know what you mean."

I held out my hand to Ruin, and he passed me Ansel's phone. We'd left the screen on the photo of Ansel in his bathing suit with the Gauntt mark clearly visible. I showed it to Peyton, pointing to the mark. "I tried to talk to you before about your mark. Ansel had one too. A lot of people do. Because someone with more strange powers has been messing with all of you. We want to stop them from doing more."

Peyton's eyes narrowed. "Is this that crazy talk about the Gauntts again?"

I gave the phone back to Ruin. "The point isn't who's doing it, not right now. The point is, do you really want to let someone else control you and manipulate what you do? Don't you want to know that your life is totally your own? Don't you want to hit back at the people who've hurt you before—who hurt Ansel?"

She shifted her weight on her feet, and it didn't surprise me at all that her hand rose to scratch at the spot on her upper arm where I knew her own mark was. A shiver ran through her. "I don't know anything about any of this."

"Exactly," Ruin said in his upbeat way. "But Lily can help you with that. Lily can break the memories open so you see everything they did."

Peyton backed up a step. "No. I don't trust her. She might do something even worse to me."

And she'd deserve it if I did lash out. But I kept that thought to myself. "If I just wanted to hurt you, I could have done that a dozen times. I never did anything to you at all until you came at me so much I had to make you back off. Don't make me out to be the villain here."

"It's your fault he's like this," she said, waving her hand toward Ruin. And the thing was, she wasn't wrong. Ruin had taken over Ansel's body to be with me.

71

I opened my mouth, still struggling to find the right words, and Peyton started to walk away. "Leave me alone. I'm done with all this crazy talk, and—"

Ruin leapt forward before I had to do anything at all. He clapped his hand to her arm, his expression almost apologetic.

Peyton halted and turned around. "I'm sorry," she said in a small voice. "I shouldn't have talked to you like that. Whatever you think you need to do, go ahead."

I shot Ruin a sharp look. "We were going to let her make the choice."

"She needs to know, doesn't she?" he said. "We *would* be villains if we let her go around without any clue what the Gauntts did to her. And we're not villains. So we're doing this for her own good. We *should* do it."

I didn't know how to argue with his optimistic logic. Maybe he did have a point. They were Peyton's memories. She couldn't know that she didn't want them when she had no idea what they even were. She didn't even believe me that she was missing anything.

"*I'm* sorry," I told her, and stepped up to grasp her arm. She stiffened just slightly and then relaxed. As the hum of my power rose up inside me, I sensed the barrier of magic inside her skin.

"This will only take a minute or two," I said. "Then whatever happens after is completely up to you."

I focused all my attention on the magic in the mark. My heart thumped in my chest, driving the supernatural energies inside me forward. Gathering them, I flung them at the wall of magic, again and again and—

The cracking sensation quivered through my nerves. I dropped Peyton's arm immediately and eased back to give her space.

Like it'd seemed to before when we'd gone through this process with Fergus, Ruin's influence faded as the unearthed memories rushed through Peyton's mind. She stared at us and then brought her hands to her face. Her arms trembled. "I— Oh my God."

"Yeah," I said quietly. "They did shit like that to Ansel too. And my little sister. And a ton of other people we've found. But we're going to make them pay. You don't have to like me or what's happened to Ansel to help us. Are you in?"

She took a few gulping breaths, seeming to be gathering herself. Then her hands balled into fists. "I can't believe… My *mom* knew, she let them…" She met my gaze, her eyes flashing. "What are you planning to do?"

I hadn't really thought that far. I hadn't known if we'd have anyone on our side to carry out a plan. Inhaling deeply, I found myself thinking of Nox in his silent vigil over the rest of us, locked away inside his body.

I knew what he would have said, and we were doing this for him too.

"I'm still working out the details," I said. "But one thing's for sure: we're going to go big. There's no way they're getting out of the mess they've made this time."

# eight

*Lily*

"Are you sure you're okay with this?" I asked Ruin when we parked at the far end of the block from Ansel's family home. "I could go in alone. Or have Jett or Kai come with me later. We only need the keys."

"And I have them," he said cheerfully, holding up Ansel's keyring with a metallic jangle. "It shouldn't be a strain. All I've got to do is sit and type. My fingers don't have any stitches."

"Well, no." But I had other reasons to worry about his internal state. The memory of how furious he'd been the last time we'd come here, the way he'd stormed into the house and laid into Ansel's mother, remained stark in my mind. It was the only time I'd *ever* seen him really

74

angry about anything other than someone trying to hurt me or his friends. "You just— Thinking about his parents seems to bring up a lot of unpleasant feelings for you."

Ruin cocked his head as if *he* had a little trouble remembering his last visit. Then he shrugged and beamed at me. "This will be more payback that they ought to make. Even if they won't be making it themselves. That's a good thing. And we're sure no one's home anyway, so we won't have to talk to them, right?"

"Yeah, Kai made a couple of calls to confirm they're at work." I dragged in a breath and smiled back at him. "Okay, let's do this."

I tucked my hand into his as we walked up the street and along the front walk to the porch. It took him a few tries to find the right key to open the door, but I didn't see anyone around who'd notice. When we stepped inside, he closed the door and immediately nudged me up against it, his head dipping close to mine. The warmth of his body and the familiar smell of him melted any desire I had to skip this mission.

"I like you looking after me, Waterlily," he murmured. "No one could be as sweet as you. If we didn't have some *very* important things to do, I'd show you just how happy you make me right now."

My voice came out a bit breathless. "I'm sure there'll be plenty of time later. Time that I'll be looking forward to a lot."

He grinned. "Good." Then, rather than totally leave me hanging, he pressed a kiss to my mouth that lit up my body from head to toe as if he'd channeled some of his supernatural electricity into my nerves.

We stalked through the house, quickly identifying a small room on the first floor as a home office. Ruin sat down in the chair in front of the computer, and I perched on the edge of the desk, watching the monitor blink on. Ansel's parents had enough faith in their home security that they hadn't bothered to put a password on it to wake it up.

"Check the email app," I said, swinging my legs where they dangled over the edge. "Hopefully they check their business accounts on this computer. But we can still use their personal contacts even if they don't."

It appeared that the computer belonged to Ansel's dad. There were two accounts, one a standard public one and another with the domain for the company he worked for, both in the name of Ronald Hunter. A wider smile stretched my mouth. "Jackpot."

Ruin tapped through to the contacts list for the business email, and his eyes brightened eagerly. "Look at all these people he talks to for work! Are we going to tell all of them?"

"Every one," I said with a rush of nervous adrenaline.

We weren't the only ones taking this step. Peyton and a few of the other local college students with marks we'd found and broken were taking similar action in their own homes. But it was the first attempt we'd made at bringing broader awareness to all the crap the

Gauntts had been pulling instead of simply going at them directly.

This whole war was about to get so much bigger. I didn't totally know that it wouldn't blow up in our faces.

We had to try, though. They hadn't left us with many options. We were going to hurt them in every way we could until we found something that'd actually break them.

Ruin opened up a new email and gleefully tapped each of the contacts to add them to the CC list. "Important information about Thrivewell Enterprises and the Gauntt family," he said under his breath as he typed those words into the subject line. Then he tapped away at the keyboard some more to create the body of the email, pretending to take on Ansel's father's voice. Here and there, he was pleased enough with a line that he spoke it out loud too, putting on a falsely deep voice.

"I'm so incredibly ashamed that I let this go on for so long… My son deserved much better than this from me."

"And so do all the other children in Mayfield, Lovell Rise, and everywhere else the Gauntts have preyed on them," I suggested as an addition.

"Perfect!" Ruin typed that in too, wiggling in his seat with eager anticipation. Then he continued with his part of the message. "I looked the other way while they carried out their psychotic perversions because I'm a selfish bastard who—"

I touched his shoulder. "As true as that might be, it's probably laying it on a *bit* thick for being believable."

Ruin tsked at himself and deleted the last few words. "Because I saw an opportunity to advance my own career." He glanced at me for approval, and I nodded.

It only took about ten minutes to compose the entire email between us. By the end, "Ronald Hunter" had laid out the abuse against his son and his awareness that the Gauntts had pursued various other kids as well, and called for all the companies that associated with Thrivewell to demand just punishment. I didn't know how much any of those corporate goons would believe it or how much they'd be willing to do even if they believed, but it was something.

And when more and more stories started popping up pointing out the same crime, eventually the tide would shift and it'd be harder for people to ignore it than to react.

"Good to go?" Ruin asked me, hovering the mouse over the Send button.

"Let's blow this thing up," I said.

He chuckled to himself as he clicked. With a whooshing sound, the beginning of the Gauntts' public exposure flew off into cyberspace.

As Ruin wrote a slightly adjusted version of the email for all of Ronald's personal contacts, because who knew whether any of them might be in a position of influence that'd help us against the Gauntts, I texted Peyton to let her know we'd done our part. I wouldn't have blamed her or the other victims we'd located if they wanted to wait to make sure we stuck out our necks before they extended theirs.

But Peyton wrote back in a tone similar to the warily brisk one she used with me in person now. *Already sent mine too. Those assholes are going to pay. And I don't just mean the Gauntts.*

She'd been pretty furious with *her* parents when she'd realized how much she'd paid so that her mother could get her promotion.

After another whoosh, Ruin leapt up from the computer—so fast I grabbed his arm and frowned at him. "Careful."

"I feel fine!" he announced. "I feel fantastic. Stitches aren't going to slow me down. Can we go see the float now? I don't want to miss it."

I couldn't help grinning at his enthusiasm. And I had to admit I wanted to see all of the larger spectacle we'd arranged too, rather than only arriving in time to act as the getaway driver.

Checking the time on my phone, I nodded. "Kai was going to get it started right around the end of the workday when lots of people are leaving the buildings downtown. We've got half an hour before they'll launch it."

The second phase of our current plan had involved using our new allies' funds rather than their contacts. Or rather, their parents' funds. Peyton wasn't the only one who'd been happy to stick it to the people who'd stepped aside and benefitted from the perverted treatment the Gauntts had put them through.

It was horrifying but somehow not all that shocking how much people were willing to look the other way when a powerful figure wanted something. And I guessed looking the other way meant they had the plausibility of not *really* knowing what the Gauntts had done with their kids. Maybe some of those parents had been marked themselves decades ago, and Nolan and Marie had made use of that influence, but there wouldn't have been any need to reward them if the Gauntts had full control.

The result of our fundraising efforts was currently traveling down the street toward the Thrivewell headquarters. I caught a few glimpses of it as I maneuvered Fred 2.0 through the city traffic. We parked on the opposite side of the street a few buildings down from Thrivewell and watched it approach.

One of our few remaining Skullbreakers recruits was driving Professor Grimes's former car down the middle of the street. It was dragging a platform holding an immense parade float that loomed as high as the third-floor windows on either side of the road. The inflated figure was a massive child, a little boy in a school uniform with a jaunty sailor's cap on his head.

Okay, so it wasn't a super accurate representation of the Gauntts' recent victims, but we'd had to work with what we could get our hands on with short notice.

The chorus of honks from the cars annoyed at the traffic slow-down provided an urgent soundtrack to the float's gradual process. They were going to be even more pissed off when it outright stopped... like it was right now, directly across from the Thrivewell building.

Ruin bounced in his seat, his eyes alight as if he were a little kid in the biggest toy store he'd ever seen. I squeezed his knee to remind him that we needed to stay in the car. We didn't want to be spotted by Thrivewell people, and we needed to be ready to take off at a moment's notice.

There was a thin wall at the back of the float, which I knew was hiding two figures much smaller than the inflatable boy who were ready to give it a voice. A moment after the float lurched to a halt, Kai's even tone rang out with the thrum of a loudspeaker. It carried down the street and must have penetrated the windows of offices all around.

"The leaders of Thrivewell Enterprises have a dark secret that's been hidden for too long. They're sickos who like to feel up kids and make them prance around naked for them to ogle. We're not letting them get away with this any longer."

People had started to emerge from the office buildings along the street—including a security guard from the Thrivewell building. Our float driver moved to intercept them. We weren't done here yet.

Several of the other spectators had pulled out their phones to record the spectacle. Excellent. I'd like to see the Gauntts try to suppress all *those* videos.

Kai must have passed the megaphone over, because it was Marisol's voice that pealed out next. "Nolan

Gauntt started coming to see me in my bedroom when I was just nine years old. He'd stare at me and touched me all over…" She faltered for a second, and my heart stuttered. But before the urge to race over there gripped me too strongly, she gathered her resolve again. "He'd kiss me sometimes, on my neck and shoulders and arms. And sometimes Marie Gauntt came too, just to watch."

My hands balled at my sides as I listened. She'd told us about what she'd say today, but it was different hearing her announcing it to the whole world now. I'd told her she didn't need to tell her story like this, that we didn't need her to, that it was okay if she sat this one out. But she'd been determined to give a first-hand account of her treatment, in case it'd make some small difference in taking down the Gauntts for good.

What she was talking about wasn't everything. She'd mentioned other things to me: that Nolan had often murmured words she didn't understand while he touched her, and she'd gotten a shivery electric shock feeling. Sometimes she thought he'd been taking energy or some other kind of power from her rather than predatory gratification. It'd have been hard to explain that part of the Gauntts' exploitation to anyone who hadn't experienced it, though, so we were sticking to the child molestation parts that everyone could understand.

Kai took the megaphone back. "If you need further proof, the evidence is all here. We're exposing decades of lies and corruption. Don't let innocent children suffer because you're afraid of the power the

Gauntt family holds. We have to stand up to them and show that we won't let this kind of deviancy go unpunished."

As his voice faded, a news van roared around the corner. Ruin let out a little whoop, and I smiled. That was exactly what we'd been waiting for.

A woman got out alongside a cameraman who looked like he was already filming. I spotted another crew hustling over at the other end of the street.

Kai must have noticed them too. He let out one more burst of accusations. "The Gauntts think they can get away with molesting kids all over the county because of their standing. I've heard more than a dozen stories from their victims. The family will try to explain it away, but we can't let them drown out the voices that need to be heard. It's time for justice!"

The news reporters were pushing closer to the float. I caught a flicker of motion as Kai and Marisol ducked out from behind the inflated boy. We'd set up the platform so they could stay out of view until they stepped onto the sidewalk between two of the cars, acting like they were just regular pedestrians who'd abruptly appeared to take in the show.

As they walked quickly toward us, one of the reporters clambered onto the platform. She prodded the float and picked up the object Kai had left behind—an unlocked phone with voice recordings from several of the other victims of the Gauntts.

That was all we'd wanted. Kai jerked open the back door of the car so he and Marisol could dive inside, I whipped Fred 2.0 around in a hasty U-turn, and we sped away from the scene of our anti-crime.

A giggle spilled out of Marisol's mouth. She looked pale, her eyes overly bright as if slightly panicked, but the smirk she shot me in the rearview mirror was all triumph. "We really did it. They came to listen to us. Do you think they'll believe it?"

"What's important is getting people talking," Kai said. "They'll definitely be doing that now. Even if we couldn't pull off anything else after today, those accusations are going to stick in people's minds no matter how the Gauntts try to brush them off. I doubt their magic can erase a story on this scale."

"But we're going to do even more," Marisol said. "This is only the beginning."

"That's right!" Ruin said. "Humiliation and then death to the Gauntts!"

"It's been a long time coming," I said darkly.

Marisol started to sway in her seat, humming a victorious tune. The melody wound its way into my bones and up my throat. I hesitated for a second, so out of practice that I automatically balked against putting words to the song.

But if there was ever a time to let my own voice out, wasn't it now? I'd always been able to sing for Marisol —*with* Marisol. I could reach for that dream alongside her. She'd already been so much braver than I needed to be.

I opened my mouth, and the lyrics that sprang into my mind tumbled out alongside her little dance. "We'll bring them down, one by one. They couldn't fall any farther. We'll tear them up, and when we're done, nothing will ever be harder."

A giddy laugh spilled out of my sister, nothing but joy and approval, and the same emotions swelled inside my chest. We were really going to do this, our strange little family, together. Right then, I believed we could conquer anything.

## nine

*Jett*

I froze at the base of the billboard as a lone car rumbled by on the street below. I was crouched in a thicker shadow amid the night's darkness, but I still waited until the headlights had swept by me before moving again.

Giving my spray can a quick shake, I finished the message I'd been adding to the Thrivewell advertisement: *CHILD GROPERS*. Normally I preferred to paint with my fingers, but the can got the job done much faster.

I was doing some work with my hands. After I'd sprayed the last letter onto the billboard, I pressed my palm to the part of the image that showed Nolan Gauntt's smiling face. With a jolt of my supernatural energy, I added demonic horns to his forehead and shaped his mouth into a leering grin.

Easing back, I considered my work in the dim light that glowed from the nearby streetlamps and nodded with a rush of satisfaction. People would notice that. And I'd given a makeover to billboards and other public advertisements for Thrivewell and its various subsidiaries all over town.

Talk about our stunt with the float was all over the news now, and tomorrow morning Mayfield's inhabitants would drive through the city with all kinds of visual reminders of what kind of people they'd let dominate so much of their city.

I rolled my shoulders, working out some of the strain that'd built up there over my hours of slinking through the night to do my guerilla artwork. Then I scrambled down the narrow ladder to where my bike was waiting.

Exhaustion was starting to creep up over me. I grabbed the bottle of Coke I'd been nursing and chugged the last of the cola, but the tart soda only gave me a faint boost with its lacing of caffeine. Definitely time to call it a night.

I revved the engine and took off toward the house where we were holed up for the night. There were enough foreclosed buildings in the shadier parts of Mayfield that we'd been able to hop from one house to another over the past few days, always parking at a distance and having a couple of recruits prowling the streets keeping watch in case the Gauntts or their Skeleton Corps minions tracked us down.

So far we'd gone unassaulted since the battle at Lily's apartment. Maybe the remainders of the Skeleton Corps were taking more time to regroup now that they'd seen we could still fight back just fine even without Nox's powerful fists in the mix. But I doubted we'd get a reprieve for long now that we'd gone so much more brutally on the attack ourselves.

Eventually, our efforts had to be enough. We'd beat the Gauntts down until they couldn't get back up. Maybe their defeat would break the spell on Nox. Maybe we'd be able to demand the cure in some kind of deal, exchanging it for a tiny particle of mercy, even if that was more than the pricks deserved.

I wasn't going to think about any scenario where we didn't get Nox back. He *was* the Skullbreakers, smack-dab in the middle of the picture. We didn't exist without him. So one way or other, we'd drag him out of the black hole he appeared to have fallen into.

I parked my bike out of sight down a secluded laneway and hurried the rest of the way to the house on foot. The recruit leaning against the house next door melded into the shadows enough that I only noticed him because I was looking for him. He gave me a small nod of acknowledgment.

This house had an enclosed front porch, no chillier than the rest of the house since the heat was off, so the whole place was pretty cold. The porch was our second line of defense, and both Kai and Ruin had hunkered down there in sleeping bags.

Kai let out a soft rasp with each perfectly even breath, like he was being strategic even in his slumber. Ruin hugged one end of the folded blanket he was using as a pillow, his mouth set in a dreamy grin. Of course that guy would be cheerful even when he was dead to the world.

Neither of my friends stirred as I slipped past them into the house. In the living room just beyond the front door, another bundle of blankets lay on top of an unfolded sleeping bag serving as a mattress. Lily was providing one final layer of defense for her sister and Nox, who we'd set up in the two bedrooms deeper into the bungalow.

My woman wasn't sleeping as soundly as the guys. Maybe she hadn't been sleeping at all. At the faint creak of the floorboards, she sat up, squinting through the darkness.

"It's just me," I said quietly, walking over to her. The sight of her, her hair and skin luminous in the pale haze that seeped through windows from the street, woke me up the way the caffeine boost hadn't.

She was my muse and my lover and everything else I could have wanted. It'd been more than worth dying the first time to come back to this.

"You didn't run into any trouble?" she whispered as I reached her.

I shook my head. "Got a couple dozen billboards and posters doctored, and no one seemed to notice me working. The real buzz will start in the morning when people can really see them."

"Thank you."

"Hey, they're our enemies too. I want them gone just as badly as you do." I hesitated, still a little awkward about my welcome after how long I'd shut down the lover side of our relationship. "Can I join you?"

"Of course," Lily said without any hesitation of her own, and scooted to the side under the blankets. I kicked off my shoes, shrugged off my jacket, and crawled in after her.

The unfolded sleeping bag made pretty poor padding against the scuffed-up floorboards. I set my hands against it with a surge of determination to make Lily's night a little more comfortable. Electricity crackled through my nerves, and the stuffing in the sleeping bag inflated to twice its previous thickness.

Lily let out a soft laugh. "So many uses for this talent of yours that we didn't realize at first."

"There's a reason I'm the creative one in the bunch," I said, and tucked my arm around her waist, tugging her close.

I'd only meant to cuddle with her. I might not have been huggy like Ruin, but with this woman... every inch of her body that deigned to rest against mine was a gift. But as her watery wildflower scent filled my nose and her hip brushed my groin, certain parts of me woke up *way* more than before. Suddenly I was thinking of the art we'd made with our bodies just days ago. The type of act I hadn't gotten to repeat in all the chaos afterward.

Since we'd first hooked up, I'd tried to show her in every way I knew how that I had no regrets. That I was totally here with her now. But maybe I should make a complete demonstration of it, just so there was no room left for doubt. Who knew when I'd get another chance?

When I trailed my hand up Lily's torso to her cheek, she automatically turned her face toward me. There was barely any distance to cross to bring my mouth to hers.

She let out a small sigh into the kiss, rolling her body to lean into me. I savored the heat of her mouth and the softness of her lips, intent on etching every sliver of sensation into my memory.

That first time, I hadn't really known what I was doing. I'd still been too stuck in my head to fully let go until we'd already been wrapped up in each other. Tonight, I wanted to do this properly from the start.

Lily kissed me back with increasing fervor. Her fingers traced over my face and into my hair, winding around the strands with a little tug that turned me on like she'd flicked a switch.

I teased my tongue across the seam of her lips, and she opened her mouth to me. Our tongues tangled together in a dance that felt as much like art as the shifting rhythm of her breaths.

One day, maybe I'd be a muse to her too. Spark a song inside her the same way she fueled my paintings. For now, giving her pleasure was a craft I could gladly immerse myself in.

And a craft I could bring my creative side to just as avidly as any other activity. Nox had talked about how we all offered Lily something different—that even if all four of us were hooking up with her, we still had something special. I intended to make my time with her as unforgettable as she was to me.

All kinds of ideas whirled through my mind, but I wanted her to be good and ready first. As I continued kissing her, I slid one hand up under her shirt. My fingers traced over the bare curves of her breasts. She'd taken off her bra to sleep—lucky me.

I swiveled my thumb over her nipple, gently and then with more force. Lily's hips canted toward me, a strained whimper seeping from her throat into our kiss. She bit her lip, her breath turning shakier. "We need to stay quiet. I don't want to wake Mare up."

True, having her little sister interrupt would definitely put an end to my plans. A sly smile curved my mouth. "Feel free to bite me as an alternative."

Heat flared in Lily's eyes. She kissed me again with even more passion, but when I pinched the peak of her breast, her head jerked down so she could take me up on my offer, clamping her teeth against the skin of my neck with a strangled growl. The little pricks of pain that came with the gesture turned my dick even harder.

"That's right, Lil," I murmured, easing my hand farther down. "Mark me up any way you like." I'd wear any nicks and bruises she gave me like badges of honor.

She exhaled with a stutter and buried her face in the crook of my neck. As I tucked my hand under the waist of her jeans and stroked her beneath her panties, she alternated between kissing and nipping my shoulder. Her slickness spread over my fingers, and the jerk of her hips became more urgent.

My own need was searing through me, my dick aching for release. But I wasn't ready to bring this interlude to its finale yet. I intended to give my muse a masterpiece.

Beneath the blankets, I flicked open the fly of her jeans and tugged them down her legs. Lily squirmed the rest of the way out of them and reached for my pants. When her eager fingers curled around my rigid cock, I muffled a groan of my own against her hair. But before she could strip the pants right off me, I grabbed the large tube of paint I'd left in my back pocket in case I needed it for more subtle work.

It was acrylic, so basically plastic on the inside. With a flare of lust driving my supernatural energies, I willed the contents to meld with the casing into a solid mass. Then I extended and sculpted that mass into an arched shape with two prongs.

So many possible uses for my new tool. "I've got something even better for you," I said, and eased the toy between her legs. As one prong slipped easily into her slick channel, the other rubbed against her clit.

Lily let out a gasp she couldn't manage to suppress and gripped me tighter. She planted her mouth on the side of my neck with a pulsing pressure and a chorus of strangled sounds that vocalized her pleasure well enough. I worked the toy deeper into her, rocking it so it stimulated her clit the whole time, and she dug her fingernails into me alongside the edges of her teeth.

"Jett," she mumbled, so full of longing that her voice sent a bolt of bliss straight to my cock. I wanted to give her even more than this.

I eased my other hand over her smooth ass and stroked a finger over her puckered opening. Lily shivered and yanked my mouth back to hers. As our lips crashed together, I massaged her back entrance in time with the thrusts of my toy. Then I withdrew the pronged tool and adjusted its position, the closer end gliding against her slit, the slick end that'd been inside her prodding her other opening.

"Want them both?" I asked under my breath, my mouth brushing hers with the question.

"Fuck, yes," she muttered.

As I pressed both prongs into her, Lily's head tipped back. I took the opportunity to nibble *her* neck at the same time. She yanked forward, slamming her mouth against mine so hard her teeth nicked my lip, not that I minded. The kiss only partly muffled her moan.

Her legs trembled as I pulsed the toy in and out of her, both ends at once. The steady stream of noises she tried to swallow told me how much pleasure I was creating in her body.

I'd finally found the one art I could get totally right. Even if none of my paintings ever captured every impression I'd been trying to convey, there wasn't a single thing lacking in the opus of ecstasy I could bring to life in my woman.

Lily's tremors spread through her whole body. Her hips bucked to meet my thrusts. She muffled another moan with a bite of my shoulder and then reached back between us to grasp my straining erection.

"That feels so good," she whispered, "but now I want you. Just you. There's nothing better than that."

Something cracked in my chest, but in a good way, like I was splitting open to welcome a light that'd never touched me before. For a second, I couldn't find my words. All I could do was kiss her deeply as I withdrew my makeshift plaything.

I fumbled for my pockets to find the packet I'd made sure to have on me, and Lily ripped it open for me. As she rolled it over my throbbing shaft, I tipped my face as close to hers as I could get without continuing the kiss and let out the deeper ache inside me.

"I love you."

Lily's breath caught. I didn't give her a chance to answer, just reclaimed her mouth as I claimed her body by plunging into her. She gasped against my lips, rocking into my thrusts. I rolled us over so I was on top of her and tucked my hand under her ass to give me a better angle for delivering every possible pleasure I could on my own.

Even her face in the dim light, taut and glowing with bliss, was a work of art. I gazed down at her as I thrust deeper, shifting my position just slightly to follow the flutter of her eyelids, the parting of her lips. I'd never said those three words to anyone before, had never thought I would, but they couldn't have been truer. They were my signature on this masterpiece we made together.

Lily clamped her hand against her mouth, and I took that as my prompt to speed up my pace. As I slammed home, she whimpered against her palm, her eyes rolling back. Her pussy clenched around me, and the force of her coming propelled me over the edge with her. I hissed through my teeth, cutting off a groan as my cock erupted.

I sagged down next to her, the two of us a sweaty tangle of limbs and shaky breaths. Lily wrapped her arms around me and hugged me close, nuzzling my cheek. And possibly the most perfect piece of art was the way she drifted off to sleep within just a few minutes, nestled in my embrace.

I'd given her peace as well as passion. Here was hoping we could extend that peace into tomorrow.

## ten

*Lily*

It shouldn't have been remotely comfortable waking up in an unheated, abandoned house where I'd slept on the floor, but I wasn't going to complain about the sense of contentment that washed over me when my eyes eased open next to Jett's sleeping form. I tipped my head closer to his shoulder and got to enjoy the soothing warmth of his body for about five more minutes before Kai burst into the living room.

A couple of frogs hopped after him as if they were ready to join whatever urgent action he felt needed to be taken. I sat up, scrambling to pull my pants back on under the blankets.

Kai jarred to a stop. "I got a text from our inside

agent. The Skeleton Corps are on their way here. Somehow they got wind of our location."

That didn't particularly surprise me. The Gauntts had been able to track us before, when I'd been looking for Marisol. And I'd bet the family had also gotten wind of our various additional attacks on them now that they didn't have a giant parade float in front of them capturing their attention.

"Is our guy on the inside going to help us against them?" I asked, pushing myself to my feet. At the movement, Jett grumbled and swiped at his eyes. He took in the scene and hastily started pulling together his clothes too.

Kai shook his head. "There isn't much he can do, and it's better if he doesn't break his cover so he can keep feeding us tips like this. He was going to bring around a couple of guys he figured out are marked today—I guess that'll have to be delayed. I need to work out a good place for us to move to." He whipped out his phone and frowned at his list of contacts.

Ruin's voice carried in from the enclosed porch. "They'll come and end up with nothing. Too bad for them! I say we go out to a restaurant to get some breakfast and chow down while they run around here looking like idiots."

Of course a trip for food would be his suggestion. A smile tugged at my lips despite myself, but as much as I liked the idea of walking away from the battle, my thoughts pulled me into a different direction.

"How long do we have?" I asked. "How close are they?"

"It sounds like they were just heading out when I got the text," Kai said. "We've got ten, maybe fifteen minutes. We'll need to get Nox to the car, and then we can just take off."

I inhaled deeply. "Yes to getting Nox in the car. We want to be ready to make a quick getaway if it comes to that. But I don't think we should leave."

All three of the guys paused to stare at me, even Ruin peeking in through the doorway. Kai's eyebrows drew together and then rose just as swiftly with a flash of understanding in his expression.

"You want to turn the ambush around on them."

He didn't sound like he thought the idea was totally insane. Of course, all of my guys were pretty insane in general, so maybe he wasn't the best judge of how crazy my plan was. But insane situations called for insane solutions anyway, didn't they?

"We have an advantage over the Skeleton Corps guys," I said. "We know they're coming, and they expect us to be unprepared. They're not going to stop attacking us until we convince them they're better off leaving us alone than getting whatever the Gauntts are offering them. We might as well emphasize that point now while we have the chance, don't you think?"

Jett nodded. "Next time our guy might not warn us soon enough."

Ruin bobbed eagerly on his feet. "I'm ready to pummel a few pricks."

Kai inclined his head with a jerk. "Let's get everything prepared, then. Like you said, we need to be ready to make a getaway as need be."

At that moment, my little sister ambled out of the bedroom where she'd slept. She peered blearily at all of us, blinking hard. "What's going on?"

My pulse lurched. I was all for going into battle on our terms—but one of my terms was that I kept Marisol out of it if at all possible.

"The gang that's working for the Gauntts—the Skeleton Corps—is heading over here," I said quickly. "We're going to get you out of the way, and then we're going to take down as many of them as we can so that hopefully they'll rethink the whole 'blowing away the Skullbreakers' plan."

Marisol's shoulders stiffened. She reached to the pocket of her hoodie, where I could see the bulge of the small pistol Nox had given her. "I can fight too."

A lump rose in my throat. "I know you can, Mare. But you've never even fired that thing before. And—" A stroke of genius hit me with a rush of relief alongside it. "And we need someone watching over Nox in the car in case the Corps end up noticing him there despite our best efforts. You can shoot anyone who tries to get at him or you."

The prospect of having a useful role in the scenario seemed to bring down her hackles. "Okay," she said.

Kai snapped his fingers. "Come on, let's get moving. We don't have much time to get ready."

He and Jett hustled into the other bedroom and hauled out the trolley we'd thankfully left Nox lying on in his permanent doze. Kai barked an order at one of the recruits, who jogged with them away from the house down the sidewalk to where we'd stashed my car. Unfortunately we'd had to abandon Professor Grimes's car with the float, so we were down to just one multi-person vehicle again.

I nudged Marisol after the guys. My sister gave my arm a quick squeeze before hurrying along behind.

Standing in the enclosed porch, I focused on the hum of energy ringing through me and let it reach out into my surroundings. The two frogs who'd thrown in their lot with Kai hopped around my feet with determined croaks.

I could call more. They should have been too far away to make it to Mayfield from their marshy home, but I could sense my amphibious friends all over the city, lurking in sewers and backyard ponds and swimming pools. They'd already assembled to be close at hand for whatever I might need them for.

The light tugged at my heart, but I wasn't going to tell them they couldn't be of service. The Skeleton Corps hadn't needed to face my froggy army yet. That was one more way we could throw them off their game.

*Come*, I thought at all the sleek green forms I could feel around me. *Come and show these bastards they don't own the marsh. We do.*

As those impressions streamed toward me with an

eager tickling of my magic, I extended my awareness in other directions. All the utilities in the foreclosed house were shut off, but that simply meant that turning on the taps or flushing the toilet the regular way wouldn't accomplish anything. The water was still running through the mains in the street. I could drag it out of the sewer grates or from the hoses of the neighboring houses.

And of course, if I needed to, I could make use of our attackers' own blood. I'd battered a few hearts from the inside out now.

The thought still made me a bit queasy, but I hardened myself against my instinctive hesitance. I was doing this to protect myself, my sister, my men, and possibly hundreds of children who might suffer if we didn't shut the Gauntts down. We'd reached out to the Skeleton Corps members who were marked. Most of them weren't under any supernatural influence, and they'd made their choice. They were still making that choice in light of the information that'd been spreading about the Gauntts' unsavory practices.

If they thought that family deserved loyalty, then they didn't deserve any sympathy.

A soft thumping reached my ears as a trickle of frogs leapt down the street toward the house. As I urged the new arrivals to nestle in the lawn's scruffy grass or around the sides of the house out of sight, the trickle expanded into a stream and then a torrent. By the time the guys came racing back to the house, I had a few hundred amphibious soldiers gathered around the place.

"I'm as prepared as I can be," I said to the guys. "How do you want to handle the rest?"

Kai glanced around the porch. "Open the windows just enough so you can shoot through the gaps," he ordered Jett and Ruin. "We'll pick as many of them off from here as we can, as soon as they arrive."

He frowned at the screen door we'd broken to gain entrance and slipped out of the house again. Seconds later, he returned lugging a huge garden gnome that he plunked down by the doorframe. "If they get close enough to try to get inside, that'll slow them down. When we need to take off, we'll run through the back. The fence there is low enough that we can hop it."

"*If* we need to run off," Ruin said with a fierce light in his bright eyes. He spun his pistol between his fingers and grinned with matching ferocity.

"Yes, if," Kai muttered. "Now get down or we'll lose all the surprise we're banking on."

We all crouched down below the level of the windows, which started at waist height. My pulse thudded in my chest. I rested a hand on the back of one of the frogs that'd come inside with me, feeling the bizarre urge to hold on to something, even though fighting with guns or other weapons had never been my style.

It was only a minute or two of tense silence before the growl of car engines reached our ears from down the street. Presumably not wanting to alert us, the noises cut out before they reached the front of the house. Brisk footsteps rasped along the sidewalk.

Kai eased up just enough to catch a glimpse through the windows. "Now!" he said in an emphatic whisper.

He sprang farther up as the other two guys did, opening fire on the figures converging on the house. I sent out a pulse of defensive energy toward the horde of frogs and then flung a surge of water from the nearest sewer drain.

There'd been maybe fifteen men hustling toward us outside. Several fell in the first hail of bullets, and the others leapt behind cars or hedges to take shelter. They were met by a torrent of frogs hurling themselves forward in a furor, and then a wave of sewer water that crashed down over them in a gray-brown deluge.

If I'd hoped that'd be enough to send the rest of the Skeleton Corps guys running, I was out of luck. Several more men rushed in from down the street, staying lower out of caution. The original shitheels who'd gone uninjured swatted away the frogs with expressions of horrified disgust, but they held their ground.

Then an SUV came roaring down the street and careened right up the front walk to crash into the steps.

We all fell back on our asses. The gnome shattered. Someone flung the porch door open—

And Jett whipped out his hands to snatch up the frogs that were sitting next to me. He hurled them at the men who were about to storm into the building.

At first, I thought he'd just been trying to distract our attackers. Then I noticed that the frogs looked about twice as big as I remembered them being.

And then they chomped fanged jaws they *definitely*

hadn't had before into the flesh of the Skeleton Corps guy they'd landed on. He yelped, flailing to try to shake them off.

Kai and Ruin leapt forward together. "We can make a monster too," Kai said to Ruin in a rasp, who must have understood what he'd meant. They both tackled the second guy who'd been charging in at us.

"Fight off the rest of the Skeleton Corps people," Kai ordered him. At the same time, the emotion Ruin had propelled into the guy contorted his face into a mask of fury. The Corps guy turned with a bellow of rage and barreled back down the front walk, spewing bullets from his gun in one hand, swinging punches with the other. It was really something to see.

One of the fanged frogs had sunk its teeth into the first man's throat. He toppled over, still pawing at it with increasingly desperate whimpers. I whipped another tsunami of sewage at the asswipes still standing outside, knocked a heap more off their feet—and sent a whole bunch of them running.

We watched as the crazed man barged after his colleagues down the street. The swarm of frogs hopped after them, and the men closest by shoved themselves away with widened eyes. They'd obviously seen the treatment one of their companions had gotten and weren't taking any chances.

A quiet fell over the street, nothing disturbing it but the sight of the corpses sprawled on the road, the gurgle of the fanged frogs' victim, and now-distant booms of gunfire. Oh, and a faint peal of a siren that was no doubt coming our way.

Kai shot us all a sharp grin. "Excellent collaboration. Now let's get the fuck out of here before we end up in handcuffs."

# eleven

*Lily*

There was something to be said for central heating. And running water. And doors with working locks. Lucky us, the motel rooms we'd booked in a shabby joint an hour down the highway from Mayfield came with all three.

That was about as much as we got as far as amenities went, nothing fancier, but no one was complaining. Kai had decided we needed a break after all the running around we'd been doing. Just for tonight, we were leaving the city behind and hunkering down in *very* relative luxury.

We'd taken a couple of two-bed rooms with an adjoining door, one for me and Marisol and the other for the guys. I'd gotten to take a proper shower. Life was about as good as it could possibly be given our other circumstances.

I wasn't totally sure how Kai had paid for the rooms, but he'd assured me that the means couldn't be traced back to us, and he rarely said anything he wasn't sure about. I'd decided to take that one worry off my mind.

I let the shower water flow over me for the five minutes it took before it started to cool, reminding me just how low on the luxury scale this indulgence actually was, and then hastily dried off. When I came out into the main room, Marisol was perched on her bed, TV remote in hand, gazing wide-eyed at a news broadcast.

The image of our float graced the screen. For a second, I caught my sister's voice floating up from the speakers. Her mouth dropped open.

"It's all over the TV," she said. "This and the vandalized ads and something about certain business associates and key employees stepping back from Thrivewell. It's really working!"

I couldn't help smiling even as an ache came into my chest at the hint of disbelief in her voice. "Partly because of you. You gave them your story, and they had to listen."

"They didn't have to," Marisol replied. "But they did." She swiped her hand across her mouth, looking at least as anxious as she did awed.

"They never have to know it was you," I reminded her. "All they needed was a voice. You never have to talk about it with strangers ever again." Although I might encourage her toward therapy when all this was over.

There had to be a way for her to talk through the gross-but-not-supernatural aspects, so some shrink wouldn't figure she was crazy over stuff that had actually happened, right?

I didn't think I was equipped to help her sort through all the trauma she must be carrying, and my guys… There was a lot to recommend about them, but more subtle shades of protectiveness weren't really their forte.

"I was going to go check on the guys," I said. "Do you want to come with, or are you good in here on your own?"

Mare cocked her head, considering, and flopped back on the bed. "I think I just want to chill. We're safe here, aren't we?"

"At least for tonight," I told her. And we did still have one of the recruits keeping an eye on things outside just in case.

I walked through the adjoining door into the guys' room and stopped in my tracks with a huff of amusement.

Jett had been redecorating. The pea-soup green walls were now a warm umber, the bedspreads a deep red to coordinate. He'd placed the room's single chair on top of the wobbly table for reasons I suspected I'd never totally comprehend, and arranged a few tissues and the complimentary bible beneath it. The only thing that looked the same as our room was the TV, where Kai was flipping through the channels.

He stopped and switched the TV off at my

entrance. All the guys turned toward me—well, all of them except Nox, who was lounging on his trolley like usual near the foot of one of the beds. Kai was perched at the foot of the other, with Ruin tucked into a sort of nest of pillows near the head of the same one, chewing on some snack from a plastic wrapper. Jett had been standing near the desk, but he swiveled and leaned against it, not seeming concerned about the way the chair swayed with its wobble behind him.

"You look like you've gotten cozy," I said.

"It's nice," Ruin said, waggling his feet amid the blankets. "I'm not that picky, but I do enjoy sleeping on an actual mattress."

"And lucky you, you get it all to yourself, since neither of us wants to put up with your squirming," Jett said dryly.

A mischievous gleam came into Ruin's eyes. "Maybe I'll convince Lily to share it, then."

I cocked an eyebrow at him. "Not overnight. I don't want to leave Marisol on her own for too long."

He lifted both of his eyebrows right back at me. "I'm sure we could find something to do that wouldn't take all night. Even if we let these spoilsports join in too."

The temperature in the room seemed to rise a few degrees just with that remark, as if I hadn't already had those sorts of needs satisfied very thoroughly by Jett just last night. A flush tickled up the back of my neck. But as I opened my mouth to respond, something in his words jarred loose a thought in a totally different direction.

"We did some other joining together today," I said. "You and Kai worked your powers together on the one guy, and Jett got creative with a couple of the frogs I summoned."

Ruin hummed to himself. "We did. It was good. There were only a couple of those guys close enough to touch, so we gave that one an extra whammy."

Kai nodded. "It generally seems like a waste to combine our powers on the same target, but in certain cases, I can see it being quite useful."

Jett's lips curved into the faintest hint of a smirk. "I just believe in making use of whatever materials are close at hand."

"Yeah." But that approach was niggling at me in a way I didn't totally understand. I cast my gaze around the room, and my attention settled on Nox. A weird twinge, as wobbly as the hotel table, passed through my stomach.

The words tumbled out before I'd thought them through. "What if there are other things we could do by combining all our powers together. I tried breaking the spell on Nox on my own, and it wasn't enough. But if we all contributed somehow, maybe… Maybe that would do it."

The somehow was the sticking point. But Kai sat up straighter with a thoughtful expression, and an eager grin stretched across Ruin's face.

"Yes!" he said. "He's got to listen to all of us if we're trying to wake him up together."

Kai rubbed his mouth. "I don't know. I don't think it could be that simple."

"No," I said. "But if we were strategic about it—if we figured out the best way to bring each of our talents to the problem and worked on it together…"

He looked up and met my eyes again. "It's worth a try. I think… You're still going to be the key. You're the one who's cracked open all of the Gauntts' marks before. We should check if you can pass a little of your energies on to us, so we're all connected toward that common goal on the most fundamental level. Then let's see what comes to us."

My spirits lifted. We had a chance—a real chance.

Without really discussing it, we ended up kneeling on the floor around Nox's trolley. It was just small enough that we could manage to form a complete circle if we stretched out our arms and leaned forward to reduce the distance. You'd have thought we were going to carry out a séance, which I guessed wasn't that far from the truth. Although we wanted to wake up his body with the spirit we had to assume was still in it, not just commune with his ghostly self.

I gripped Kai's hand on one side and Ruin's on the other. "I'm not sure what to do," I admitted.

Kai gave my fingers a gentle squeeze. "Whatever power it is that you normally throw at the Gauntts' magic inside people, maybe do your best to send a little of that through the rest of us where we're touching? Not quite as forcefully as you'd generally go at the marks, of course."

"Of course," I said with a nervous laugh, and closed my eyes. The hum inside me felt more erratic than usual with the jangling in my nerves.

This was my idea. What if it didn't work?

Well, what *if?* Then we'd just be right back where we'd started. It wasn't as if this attempt should hurt anything.

I took a deep breath and pictured the wave of energy inside me that I normally hurled at the walls the Gauntts cast around their victims' memories. The wave I'd hurled at the wall around Nox's mind not that long ago.

Could I pass a little of that marshy power on to my men so that their talents might be even better at tackling the Gauntts' magic too?

Only one way to find out.

I urged just a thin stream of the energy down both my arms. It tingled as it passed into my hands where my fingers gripped the guys'. Kai twitched, and Ruin let out a soft chuckle. Then Jett grunted as the quiver of supernatural power must have reached him too.

Suddenly I could feel all of them like their bodies were mine too. The thump of their heartbeats, aligning with the rhythm of mine. The rise and fall of their breaths. The mild strain in their muscles holding this interlocked pose. An unnerving giddiness swept up through me.

When Kai spoke again, his voice was quiet. "I think

this will make a difference. But not just to how we try to bring Nox back."

I opened my eyes and found him gazing at me through the panes of his glasses. "What do you mean?" I asked.

He wet his lips. "The way your energy tangles with mine... I'm getting a strong impression that if we work our powers in unison, our supernatural resonance will merge together in a way we might never be able to *un*tangle. Some part of you might end up tied to us in a way we won't know how to sever."

He didn't sound at all concerned about that fact. Ruin only looked curious, and Jett showed no reaction at all.

They were all watching to see *my* reaction, I realized. They'd already been bound together as friends, colleagues, practically family, before I'd come into the picture. I was the new element.

I was the only one who might feel I was losing something if a piece of my soul melded with theirs.

I didn't, though. The second that thought passed through my mind, the giddiness expanded through my ribcage, getting warmer and more mellow by the moment. I *liked* the idea of having a permanent connection to the men who'd done so much to prove they were mine.

If that connection made it harder for me to ever lose them, then I was all for it.

Another, starker revelation chased on the heels of that fact, but it was one I probably should have recognized earlier. The whole situation had just been so, well, crazy, and chaotic, and—

But I knew it now. I knew it with all the certainty that'd rippled through Jett's voice last night.

"It's okay," I said, and grimaced at myself. "No, it's *good*. I want to be tied to you. I want to be *with* you, now and wherever life takes us after this." I paused, swallowing thickly, and let my gaze travel around the trio. "I love you. All of you. And Nox too." My eyes dropped to his prone form with a twang of continuing grief.

When I glanced up again, Ruin was beaming so bright he outshone the light fixture overhead. "I've loved you since before we could even properly meet," he said. "If you want always, you'll get always."

Jett offered a smaller smile that provoked no less heat. "You know how I feel about you."

Kai's hand tightened around mine again, a little more forcefully this time. He blinked, looking momentarily, startlingly unprepared. Then a thin smile crossed his own face.

"I'm so used to focusing on reading what other people are feeling so I can use it to our advantage that I've gotten out of the habit of paying attention to my own emotions. But I don't have a sliver of a doubt that I love you with every bit of devotion I've got in me."

My throat constricted again, but I managed to smile back at them. "All right. Then let's bring Nox back to us, whatever it takes. I guess I'll just hit the barrier they put around his soul with everything I've got and hope whatever you all do gets us the rest of the way there."

Ruin shifted his position with eager vigor. "I'll send emotions into him to motivate him, get his spirit all riled up so he can fight hard from the inside."

A spark lit in Kai's eyes. "And I'll command him to do just that with everything he has in him."

Jett let go of Kai's hand to rest his fingers on Nox's forehead. "I'll feel for the structures inside him that aren't really him but the Gauntts' magic. If they've made a wall, then I'll reshape that wall until it can't hold up anymore, whether it's a thing we can actually see or not."

"All right." I squeezed Ruin's and Kai's hands and sent another pulse of my energy through them, knowing it would pass to Jett as well through Ruin's grasp. "Ready when you are."

And if it didn't work, then at least we'd know we'd given it our all.

# twelve

*Nox*

The worst thing about the overall shit sandwich I was currently stuck in was that the last image my eyes had taken in before I'd ended up here kept hanging at the edge of my awareness. It was like a fucking painting I could never quite turn far enough away from to escape. A painting of the twerp Nolan Gauntt had become when he'd made the leap into his adoptive grandson's body.

Just like any creepy painting, the impression of his gaze followed me no matter what I did too.

Not that I was doing a whole lot. Other than that image of kid-Nolan lingering in my mind, I wasn't aware of much other than a hazy grayness all around. Every now and then, I got a vague sensation of pressure or movement somewhere in my body, but not enough that I could have said which part or what might be going on. Faint murmurs of sound wisped by me, also too filmy to identify. And I couldn't see anything at all. I had no idea if that was because my eyes were closed or my brain wasn't connecting to them anymore.

I was pretty sure I *was* still in my head. When my spirit had been floating free after my first death, I'd been able to see and hear everything around me just fine, to move around through the world with more freedom than I'd ever had before, although significantly less ability to affect anything in that world. Unless I'd been trapped in a very boring version of hell, I didn't think I'd kicked the bucket again.

Kid-Nolan had done something to me. When he'd smacked his hand against my forehead, there'd been a sensation like a bear trap snapping shut around my skull. At least, what I imagined a bear trap might feel like, since I was lucky enough never to have actually experienced one. That was when everything else had fallen away into this grayness.

I turned in the amorphous space as well as I could, trying to grasp hold of something, anything, that I might be able to use to break out of this prison. Lily was out there somewhere. My friends were out there. Had the asshole given them the same treatment? Were *they* even still alive?

The uncertainty and my complete inability to do anything to combat it gnawed at me constantly.

How long had I been stuck in this state already? Time was moving in even more of a muddled blur than during my twenty-one-year limbo. It might have only been a few minutes. It might have been days. It *felt* like way longer than I'd have wanted to be out of commission, but I had no clue how accurate that impression was.

After a while, my thoughts started to drift more randomly. It was hard to stay focused on escape when every attempt slipped through my fingers. I found myself floating back, back, back to moments I hadn't thought about in ages.

There was the one time I'd seen my parents after Gram had taken me in. We'd been at the grocery store, and they'd slouched inside, looking hungover and crabby. Gram had been polite enough to nod. My heart had leapt, torn between the conflicting desires to run over and see if they'd offer any affection at all to my seven-year-old self and to hide behind Gram with the thought of all the not-so-affectionate responses I might get instead.

The latter had definitely been more common while I'd been living with them. But some little part of me couldn't help hoping. I'd been a kid, after all.

In the end I hadn't done either, just kept standing next to Gram while my dad averted his eyes and my mom grimaced before hustling into another aisle. Gram hadn't pushed the matter. She didn't want to risk them getting irritated and finding the energy to demand me back. But I'd heard her mutter under her breath as we'd gone to the checkout counter about how she didn't know where she'd lost her son.

Had she felt the same way about me once I'd started delving into my criminal activities? I'd never been like my dad—never thrown all ambition away to simply exist and take out my dissatisfaction with life on everything in my vicinity. I'd known from the start that I wanted to build something real with the Skullbreakers, even if it wasn't what most authority figures would have approved of as a goal.

I hadn't talked to Gram much about my activities, but she had to have figured. The money was coming from somewhere. She'd seen me come home worse for wear now and then in the early years when I'd been finding my footing. Her advice had always been more along the lines of *Don't bite off more than you can chew* than *Stick to the straight and narrow*, though.

I'd wanted to show her I was better than my dad. That I could look after her like she'd done for me. Damn it. The gloom of that thought made the fog in my head even grayer.

And now I might have lost the other people who'd stuck with me, the guys who'd made my ambitions seem possible. Ruin, who'd warmed up to me from the start for reasons I couldn't explain, other than maybe he recognized the batshit crazy that he kept under all that sunshine reflected in me. Full of boundless energy for any task I set him to, no matter how insane.

That could be it. He might have always sensed that I was going to give him an outlet for the relentless cheer that I had to think he might have eventually drowned in if he'd had nothing to aim it at.

And then I'd gone to Kai sometime during the last year I'd bothered to attend high school, hearing he was the guy to talk to if you needed something you weren't sure how to get. Despite the fact that his know-it-all attitude had gotten on my nerves even more then than it sometimes did now, I'd recognized him as a guy worth knowing. And the more I'd given him to figure out, the more people we'd needed to bring under our sway, the more he'd risen to the challenge.

I didn't know if anyone *had* really challenged him before. I'd seen him with his parents a few times, and they barely seemed to know what to make of him.

Jett had always been around on the fringes of high school life, keeping to himself. I hadn't even realized he was responsible for the little sketches and impromptu found-object sculptures that'd pop up around the building until later, after we were working together. But our paths had crossed when I'd come after some prick who'd owed me money while the douchebag was in the middle of hassling Jett, and I'd gotten to watch the artist let loose all the fury *he* kept inside.

But it'd been his smile that'd convinced me. That little satisfied smirk when he'd looked down at the dork he'd left crumpled and groaning on the ground. I wanted people backing me up who *liked* doing it. And Jett had always taken a certain pleasure in laying down the law for the Skullbreakers, whether he let it show all that often or not.

We'd really been going somewhere. And then the fucking Silver Scythes—and the Skeleton Corps—and now the Gauntts too… I had the urge to grit my teeth even though I had no sense of where my jaw even was.

How the fuck did I get out of this? I *had* to get out, because those fuckers needed to pay. We'd delivered our vengeance to our murderers, but so many people had so much more to answer for.

The sense of conviction held me through another muffled jostling. What the hell was going on out there? My thoughts scattered and wandered again, and I might have lost a few minutes or hours or days—I had no idea. The grayness wrapped around me tighter, until I was barely aware of even kid-Nolan's stupid face anymore. That realization didn't reassure me.

*I* was slipping through my fingers, and I had nothing to hold on to.

Then something pierced through the haze. A jolt of emotion from out of nowhere—a fiery bolt of lust and desire. My spirit stirred, aching even without a body for the woman I'd shared those sensations with to such amazing effect.

I needed her. I had to get to Lily and make every minute I'd been AWOL up to her. Nerves I hadn't even known were still working woke up with a fire to reach out to her, to worship her like she so often forgot she deserved.

A moment later, another sensation struck me. I needed to wake up in *every* way. Someone was calling on me—someone was commanding me to the surface of my consciousness. If I could just find the right approach…

I squirmed as well as I was able to within the dour gray space and got the faintest sense of a solid barrier around my consciousness. It was vibrating just slightly, enough to catch my attention. Ah ha.

Gathering all my mental energy and the fire of need searing through me, I hurled myself at that wall of magic. All I seemed to do was bounce off it, but the impulses urging me onward wouldn't let me stop, not that I wanted to.

I'd get through this. I'd get through to everyone who needed me. I had to give it everything in me.

I launched myself at the barrier again and again, more passion flaring through my awareness, more urgency yanking at my thoughts. The supernatural wall shifted a tad, and then a little more, as if it were made of overlapping plates that were sliding against each other into a new arrangement. Or was it simply cracking into pieces?

What did it matter? If there were seams, then there were gaps I should be able to break through.

Again. Again. My entire consciousness felt as if it were crackling with unfulfilled hunger. I caught a whiff of Lily's sweet scent, and it only spurred me onward. Faster. Harder. I would get *out*.

As I flung myself at the walls around me one last time, they splintered completely apart. The world spun. My eyes popped open, and I was abruptly aware of my mouth going slack, air rushing into my lungs, my limbs and back braced against some hard, flat surface.

And the faces. Not kid-Nolan, but all the people I'd actually wanted to see. Lily, Ruin, Kai, and Jett were leaning over me wearing matching expressions of strain, determination, and hesitant relief.

"Nox?" Lily said with a note of hope in her voice so fragile it nearly broke my heart. She must have been working even harder than the others, harder than I'd been. Strands of her hair clung to her sweat-damp forehead; the light in her eyes was almost feverish.

The lust that'd inflamed me while I'd been imprisoned had faded away like something out of a dream. But the woman in front of me was oh so real. A deeper need stirred inside me, rushing through every particle of my body.

I was back, and I was going to give her a fever that'd have her crying out with bliss instead of tensed up with anxiety.

I pushed myself off the thing I was sitting on and tugged her to me. "I'm never letting you go again."

# thirteen

*Lily*

The spark in Nox's eyes and the passionate growl in his voice shattered the last of my fears. It was as if the spell had put him into a magical stasis, all bodily needs on pause, and now he'd snapped out of it like he'd only been knocked out for a matter of minutes.

There was no mistaking the crackle of life that was now coursing through his body like electricity. It electrified *me*, sending a tingle through my skin as he wrapped his arms around my torso. The only hunger he appeared to be feeling was for me. Heat was already pooling between my legs when he yanked my mouth to his.

His kiss took the vibe around us from steamy to molten in an instant. It'd been too long since I'd felt his demandingly passionate mouth against mine. The next thing I knew, he was hefting both of us off the trolley where he'd been sprawled and tossing me onto the nearest bed.

Nox's eyes gleamed darkly as he braced himself over me, gazing down. "What a good girl you are today. You broke that fucker's spell on me. I think you deserve *all* the rewards, Siren."

A giddy shiver ran through my nerves, but I wasn't going to take all the credit. "I couldn't do it on my own. The guys all pitched in. We managed it together."

Nox glanced over his shoulder to where his friends had stood up. The three guys were watching us, Ruin beaming, Jett's face briefly relaxed with relief, Kai's eyes alight with interest as he took in our pose. Just as Kai had suspected, the magic I'd shared with them had left a new connection between us. Only a tremor of an impression, but I could still hear the quickening of their hearts like a rhythmic whisper, taste the anticipation tickling through their nerves.

I didn't regret my choice one bit. It was exhilarating, knowing how closely I was joined with them.

Not just them but Nox too, the man we'd poured all our power into. As he smirked back at them, the vibrant pounding of his pulse echoed into me, the ripple of his desire passing into me turning me on even more.

"Then they'll get the reward of a show," he said,

"and maybe the honor of taking care of you even more when I'm done. But for now"—his gaze snapped back to me—"you're all mine."

I had no interest in arguing, especially after he claimed my mouth again. Every heated press of his lips, every scorching touch as he trailed his hand down my body, proved just how much he'd truly returned to us.

If getting it on with me was the way he wanted to celebrate his comeback, I sure as hell wasn't going to deny either of us that pleasure.

Nox tugged my shirt off and opened the fly of my pants in a series of urgent movements, but for all his enthusiasm, he wasn't exactly rushing. He marked a path of searing kisses along my jaw and down the side of my neck. When I let out a little gasp, he lingered with a nip of his teeth at the crook. Holding up his substantial weight with one hand, he cupped the other around my breast. As he nibbled along my shoulder, he stroked and pinched the peak until my nipple was pebbled and aching and all sorts of other noises were working their way up my throat.

I yanked at his shirt, wanting to feel him against me skin-to-skin. Nox practically tore it off and tossed it aside. I was vaguely aware of the other guys still standing around us, taking in every beat of this dance with searing attention, and then I was drowning in the heat of Nox's touch again. But only in the best possible way.

He leaned down on his elbow, tucking his arm

EVA CHASE

under me and letting his brawny chest brush my
stomach as he brought his mouth to one breast and
then the other. His tongue and teeth made short work
of the rest of my breath. It was all I could do to keep my
whimpers quiet enough that I wasn't worried Marisol
would overhear from the adjoining room.

I curled my fingers into Nox's spiky hair, and he
grinned up at me. "I love it when you let out the claws.
You look so fucking beautiful when you're all flushed
and wanting."

His words jarred loose an impulse inside me—the
need to say to him what I'd said to the others now that
he could hear it too. Now that it was impossibly clear to
me how much I meant it.

"I love you," I said hoarsely, bringing my hand to
his cheek.

Something flickered in Nox's eyes. For a second, he
looked oddly solemn, and I wondered if I'd offended
him somehow. Then he was rising up over me, his
mouth crashing into mine all over again with enough
force to set me on fire.

"I love you too," he muttered between kisses. "My
Minnow. My Siren. My Lily. If I have my way, I'm
never leaving you again, not for one fucking second."

A giddy giggle spilled out of me. "Well, I mean, you
might need to take a shower now and then, or—"

"Not even then," he growled. "All showers come
with Lily included from now on."

I didn't think he actually meant that, but I couldn't
say I cared all that much in the moment anyway. He

wrenched down my pants and kicked off his, and the hard length of his erection brushed my mound. I swallowed a moan of encouragement.

"Anyone around here have a fucking rubber?" he barked out. Kai was there in an instant, tossing over a foil packet.

Nox kept making his promises as he ripped open the packet and prepared himself. "I'm going to take you so high you'll forget what the ground is. Give you everything I know you can take and keep giving as long as you're with me. Just keep on making those perfect little noises and showing me how much you like it."

Fuck, I just about came from hearing him talk like that. He rubbed the head of his cock over my clit, and I gripped his shoulders with a growl of my own, all eager impatience now.

Nox didn't leave me wanting. He plunged into me, filling me with the heady burn of stretched muscles like he always did. I groaned and bucked to meet him, already trembling for my release.

But the Skullbreakers boss clearly intended to make good on his promises. He thrust into me with powerful but even strokes, a little deeper each time, grasping my hip and adjusting me as he felt me clench with the burst of pleasure when he hit that particularly special spot deep inside. My head tipped back against the pillow. I rocked with him, tracing my fingers over the bulging muscles of his chest and shoulders, a whole litany of needy sounds tumbling over my lips.

"Just like that, baby. I think you can take even more

than this," Nox murmured, and called to the other men without breaking from my gaze. "Who's ready to help me send our woman right up to the stratosphere?"

He didn't need to ask twice. Kai was already close after bringing the condom. In no time at all, he was climbing onto the bed next to us, reaching to squeeze my breast as Nox continued plowing into me. As Kai flicked aside his glasses and leaned in to nip my earlobe, Ruin bounded onto the mattress on the other side. My fiery-haired sweetheart bowed his head to lap his tongue over my other nipple and then teased his hand between me and Nox to start fondling my clit.

I bit my lip against a louder moan, and then Jett was there by the head of the bed. He stroked his fingers over my hair and bent over me to claim my mouth upside down. The unfamiliar twist on the welcome sensation had me gasping, my lips parting to admit his tongue.

Nox kept his firm grasp on my hip, bucking into me even faster than before. His breath was getting ragged.

"Look at you," he said, with so much heated affection in his voice that it sent a tremor of delight through my chest. "Taking us all at once. You are a fucking wonder, Lily. Don't you ever forget that."

It was hard to remember anything at all amid the flood of pleasure I'd been caught up in. I arched and squirmed into all the hands summoning bliss from my body, surging higher and higher on that wave just like Nox had promised.

Ruin pressed hard on my clit just as Nox slammed

into me at just the right angle, and I careened over the edge. A little cry broke from my throat. My sex clamped around Nox with its ecstatic contraction, and he followed me with a stuttered groan.

But he wasn't done. He eased in and out of me a few more times, drawing out my release and his own satisfaction. As he withdrew, he studied me with eyes now heavy-lidded. "You took that so well. But I bet you could handle more still."

"Mmm," was all I managed to say in my hazy delirium.

A sly smile stretched across his lips. He motioned toward the other guys. "I want to see you try welcoming two at one time, Siren. Twice the joy? I know they'll make it good for you." He cut a glance toward his friends as if warning them of the consequences if they didn't.

I didn't fully understand what he meant, but the guys seemed to. Kai grinned and nudged Jett. "That was always one of your specialties, wasn't it?"

The artist licked his lips, the motion of his tongue inflaming me all over again whether I followed the conversation or not.

"Perfect," Nox said. "Then you can put yourself to good use too, Kai. Lie down—let her ride you."

Kai sprawled on the bed next to me without a moment's hesitation. As he undid his jeans, I sat up, my whole body feeling sensitized by the thorough fucking I'd already experienced.

"Strip him," Nox ordered, his voice like liquid fire.

I was happy to oblige. As I peeled off Kai's shirt, I ran my fingers over the footballer muscles he'd taken over with his host. He made a rough sound in his throat and tugged my mouth to his.

Through the kiss, I helped him disentangle his legs from his pants. "Get another one," I heard Nox command someone else, and then Ruin was pressing a packet into my hand. "Suit him up," the boss added.

He wasn't just aiming to get me off in as epic fashion as he could manage, I realized. He was also reinstating his authority after his relative absence—in the most enjoyable way possible. I didn't think any of us had complaints.

I slicked the condom over Kai's already rigid cock. His teeth nicked my lips, and then he pulled me into place, straddling him. I rocked against his erection and grinned at the groan he couldn't suppress. A whimper of need was building in my own throat despite the release I'd already gotten.

"You've got it," Nox said encouragingly. "Now ride him good."

I sank down, impaling myself on Kai's cock. We both exhaled in a rush. My sex throbbed around him, wanting to race with him to the next thrilling finale.

Before I could do more than bob up and down a few times, hands gripped my waist from behind. Jett tipped his head to kiss my shoulder and my neck, sweeping my hair to the side for better access. Then he teased his fingers down my spine all the way past my tailbone to my other opening.

My nerves jumped as he circled the rim, but with excitement as much as uncertainty. I glanced at Nox instinctively, and his warm grin steadied me.

"He knows what he's doing," the Skullbreakers boss said. "He'll fill you right up. Doesn't that sound good, Siren?"

A sound that wasn't much more than panting escaped me. Jett cursed under his breath and rubbed his fingers together, and a slickness spread over my skin. He'd created his own supernatural lubricant. Would wonders never cease.

A giggle fell from my lips, followed by a whimper as Jett worked his fingers over and then into my opening. He stretched the muscles there gently, sparking currents of bliss with each rotation. By the time he lined up his cock with my back entrance, I was almost dying to know how he'd feel there.

He took it slowly, easing me up and down over Kai and pressing a little deeper inside me himself with each motion. Kai squeezed my thigh with one hand and massaged my clit with the other, and I felt my own slickness gush over him as my arousal expanded beyond anything I'd ever felt before. The quivers of *their* bliss traveling through our magic-formed connection— ragged breaths I felt as well as heard, sparks racing through nerves—only further inflamed me.

I had just enough sense left to remember there was one other guy I didn't want to neglect. Ruin had stayed sitting on the bed near us, watching the proceedings with avid eyes. I beckoned him closer.

"I can take you too," I said in a husky voice that hardly sounded like my own.

Nox let out a low whistle. "That's our Siren," he said. "You are something else."

Ruin jerked down his pants, and I bent to the side as I started to rock more emphatically with the two guys who were penetrating me in unison. The first swipe of my tongue around Ruin's erection was shaky, but as the pleasure searing through me swelled, I managed to close my mouth right around him. He tangled his fingers in my hair, tickling the tips over my scalp, and arched toward me.

My awareness became a blur of heat and bliss and guttural sounds. I was filled in every way possible, joined both bodily and emotionally with these men, and it was the most incredible combination of sensations I'd ever experienced. I wanted it to last on and on and I also couldn't help chasing that peak that seemed to keep spiraling out of reach the faster I raced after it.

Jett and Kai surged into me. I sucked hard on Ruin's cock, and he exploded in my mouth with a gasped murmur that was both apology and praise. His flavor on my tongue and the force of his release tipped me over the edge.

I came and seemed to keep coming, over and over, wave rolling after wave, until I found myself sagged over Kai as if I'd washed up on a shoreline with him. Jett's sated sigh as he pulled back and a whisper of fulfillment tickling into me told me that he'd found his release just as the rest of us had.

"Now that," Nox said with a mix of pride and amusement, "is how we treat our woman right."

# fourteen

*Lily*

I woke up in my own bed next to Marisol's to the sound of crinkling cellophane.

"Rise and shine!" Ruin said. I rubbed my eyes and made out him standing by our room's table, laying out the most extravagant spread of vending machine food in the history of the universe. He set up the individual bags of chips and cheese puffs in rows bordered by chocolate bars, individually packaged brownies, and a few baggies of granola, the only breakfast-like food the motel's machine must have contained.

Jett, following behind him, tweaked a few of the items as if to arrange them into more artistic order.

Marisol sat up in her bed, blinking blearily. "Is that what we're having for breakfast?"

Ruin glanced at her uncertainly. "There weren't any restaurants nearby. But I could go looking if you want!"

"No, no, it's fine," my sister said, and shot a glance in my direction as if expecting me to protest the junk-food meal.

I laughed. "It's fine. I think we could all use a treat, huh?"

"I got the chocolate bars with nuts in them, so they're a little healthy!" Ruin announced, his smile coming back.

Nox came barging into the room through the adjoining door with an air of assurance like he'd never been laid low. Marisol's eyes nearly popped out of her head.

"You're okay!" she exclaimed.

In the middle of the chatter about breakfast, I'd forgotten that I hadn't been able to tell her about our success last night when I'd slipped back into this room —after Nox had, after all, let me step a few feet out of his sight. She'd still been fast asleep.

A grin sprang across my face. "Yep. We figured out how to beat the spell."

Nox flexed his arms, a fiercely pleased light gleaming in his eyes. "Good as new. They can't keep the boss down."

"But I'm going to kick you all out," I informed the guys, pushing off the covers. I didn't care about them seeing me in my sleep clothes, of course, but— "My sister needs a little privacy before we get down to breakfast."

Ruin's eyes widened, and Nox took on a look of consternation that he clearly aimed at himself. "Sorry, sorry," he said, holding up his hands in a more apologetic pose, and herded Ruin and Jett out.

I heard Kai's voice from their room just before the door swung shut. "Has anyone figured out how to get hot water out of this—" Then it was just me and my sister.

Marisol bounded off the bed as if she'd been infected with Ruin's typical energy and grabbed the one change of clothes she'd been able to pack out of her suitcase, which had thankfully survived all our hasty getaways. "I'm glad he's okay," she told me. "They're all — I'm glad you found guys who look out for you that much. And listen to you. They might be kind of crazy, but they're better than any of the boys I knew in school."

My mouth twitched, torn between amusement and regret. "We'll get you into that new school I found when all this is over. There'll be better guys there, or in college, or somewhere. You could probably skip the whole gangster part, since I've got that so well covered."

Marisol smothered a giggle. "I'll say. So, what are we doing now? How else are we going to hit back at the Gauntts?"

I sucked my lower lip under my teeth as I considered the question. "I guess we need to see how things are playing out with everything we've already done. Where's that remote?"

Marisol found it and switched on the TV, flipping to a news channel while I invited the guys back into our room. The table wasn't big enough for us all to sit around, so Ruin ended up tossing my and Marisol's selections to us on request and we snacked on our beds. The guys stood around the table, chowing down with their usual vigor and watching the newscast alongside us.

The first couple of stories didn't offer much enlightenment. It seemed that a truck transporting turkeys had broken down on a freeway, and now feathered menaces were gobble-gobbling and chasing cars all along the nearby exit ramp. According to the weather report, it was overcast with incoming rain, which was a little hard to buy into when the sun was beaming through the motel room window. But that was about as accurate as I found the forecast tended to be.

Then the newscast jumped to the "Top Story of the Hour." An image flew onto the screen of Marie Gauntt, flanked by Thomas and Olivia, speaking into a microphone while camera flashes went off around her.

"We have not and never will victimize any member of our community, let alone a child," she was saying. "These sick accusations must be the work of corporate opponents looking to undermine Thrivewell Enterprises for their own benefit."

"What!?" Marisol burst out. "That lying shit-cracker."

Apparently she'd picked up my tendency for creative insults. And I couldn't argue with her assessment of the situation.

"Of course they're going to put as positive a spin on it as they can," I said. "It doesn't matter what they say, only what other people believe."

But even as those words came out of my mouth, the feed switched to a couple of reporters in their studio. "What do you make of all this commotion, Ron?" the polished woman asked her colleague, sitting so stiffly straight in her chair she could have passed for a piece of furniture herself.

"They are incredibly disturbing allegations, Allison," the man said in one of those TV voices where every word is just a little over-emphasized. "It's hard to imagine that this kind of crime could have been going on for so long without being exposed before. From what I understand, there hasn't been any evidence or testimony offered by a named source. The so-called 'confessions' could be anyone, and they've left us with no way to verify their stories."

"I'm inclined to agree," the woman said. "The lengths these people have gone to in perpetuating their story seem more in line with the resources of a fellow corporate giant, not abuse victims seeking justice."

"Oh, for fuck's sake," Nox growled at the TV, the frustration in his tone echoing the matching emotion in me. "How the hell would you idiots know?" He jabbed the power button to switch it off.

Kai frowned. "Are they seriously saying that we went

*too* far in establishing our case? They'd believe us more if we'd been quieter about it? They'd never have heard about it if we'd been any quieter—the Gauntts would have raced in to squash our attempt faster than a cat on fire."

Marisol had drawn her legs up to her chest, hugging her knees. The chocolate bar she'd been eating lay on the bed next to her, only half finished.

"I can do it," she said abruptly.

My head jerked toward her. "Do what? Mare, you've done plenty."

She raised her chin, but her voice came out strained. "They want someone who isn't anonymous to verify their story. I can come forward. They can't say *I'm* working for some corporate enemy or whatever."

Oh, no. No, no, no. My heart sank even more than it had listening to the newscast. "I'm not letting you put yourself in the line of fire like that."

"It's my decision, isn't it?"

Kai raised his hand before we could debate further. "It's your decision, but you should make it knowing all the facts. And the facts are that they *will* claim you're being paid off by some opponent to make your claims. They'll say it's still not enough. You don't have any concrete evidence or witnesses, right? Your parents never saw what went on."

"As if those deadbeats would testify anyway," Jett muttered, and he had a point.

Marisol deflated so fast that my throat choked up as I watched her. "I guess not," she said quietly. "Maybe…

141

if we could convince some of the other people they messed with to speak up too…?"

"We can try," I said. "But I still don't want you being first. If you put yourself out there that obviously, who knows what the Gauntts will do to you now?"

She held my gaze, hers so haunted it nearly killed me. "Who knows what they're still doing to other kids? I don't want more people to go through that."

She had a point too. And she was sixteen—maybe not an adult, but old enough that she *should* be able to make her own decisions.

I sucked in a breath. "Look, we'll talk to the other marked people we found and see what strategy we can come up with that they'll get on board with." I had major doubts about whether any of them would want to step into the spotlight, though. The college kids hadn't minded sticking it to their parents from behind the scenes, but none of them wanted the entire world knowing about their painful history. They were barely comfortable with *me* knowing about it.

And the gang members we'd woken up… They'd be blowing their cover and risking wrath from both the Gauntts and their leadership. Plus I knew from personal experience that gangster men weren't super keen on openly sharing their vulnerabilities.

So I barreled onward, making up my plan as I spoke. "And I'll go back to the lake this morning. To the spot where the Gauntts do their rituals. I'll see if I can get any more information out of the spirits of the kids they left there. Maybe there's proof in the marsh."

Had they left *any* of the bodies of the older Gauntts behind? Or any other traces of their rituals? If they had, hopefully the lingering ghosts could point those out to me without too much additional pantomiming.

Marisol didn't look totally reassured, but she nodded and picked up the rest of her chocolate bar. "Okay. I want to come too, though."

"We should all go," Nox said firmly. "We stick together; we protect each other. That's why we're going to win this fight."

We finished the rest of our vending-machine breakfast with somewhat less enthusiasm than we'd started with, packed our remaining belongings in Fred 2.0's trunk, and explained to Nox why he no longer had a motorcycle. He growled so loud I was surprised the motel doors didn't shake off their hinges, but he got into the car with me, Marisol, and Ruin, taking the front seat for the first time since his bespelling.

It was definitely a relief having him sitting upright and fully conscious for once, even if his eyes were shooting murder daggers at everyone who crossed his path, like they were all complicit in the loss of his beloved ride.

"You can get a new one, right?" Marisol piped up from the back as I drove around the edge of Mayfield toward the lake.

Nox let out a harrumph. "It'll take a while to find another one that good. Fucking Skeleton Corps assholes have probably claimed her for their own." Then he shook himself and patted Fred's dashboard. "But we did a good job with this baby. I just don't like how long I had to be dependent on the rest of you lugging me around."

I shot him a bittersweet smile. "There was a lot of lugging, but we didn't mind it at all. I'm just glad you're back. We lost Professor Grimes's car, but we could swing back to Lovell Rise and pick up Ansel's old car so you have some kind of vehicle."

Nox grimaced. "Nah, I'm sure I can scrounge up a ride that's better than that today."

"If you get a new bike, I'm grabbing one too," Ruin said. "Even my insides barely hurt at all now. We need the whole brigade!"

"Let's see where we can fit that into our busy schedules," I said dryly.

I slowed as we came up on the end of the lane that took us closest to the Gauntts' marshland property. We hadn't passed any other vehicles in several minutes, and the stretch of scruffy grass where we'd stopped before was empty.

We parked there, Jett and Kai bringing their motorcycles to a halt on either side of the car, and peered apprehensively in the direction of the spit. No forms I could see moved along the nearby shoreline or between the trees that blocked our view of the spit itself.

"I'll stay here and stand guard," Jett said, pulling out his gun. "If I see anyone coming this way, I'll shout."

I wanted to suggest that Marisol stay with the car too, but one look at her told me that she wanted to be a full part of this expedition. Well, why shouldn't she? It wasn't as if the lake's spirits would hurt her, and if it'd make her feel more in control after the way the Gauntts had used her for so long, then she deserved to be included.

We tramped over the patchy fields toward the shore, giving the trees a wide berth so we could check out the spit from a distance before approaching it. The narrow strip of land jutting into the marsh was just as vacant as it'd been the last time we'd come out here.

A cool, damp wind licked over me, thick with the scent of algae. The thudding of our footsteps reverberated into my bones. I started to sing a soft, wordless melody under my breath alongside it, reaching for the inspiration to guide me in this quest. A sense of certainty settled over me.

When I'd broken through my own mark, I'd completely submerged myself in the marsh. Last time, I'd tried to commune with the spirits in the water from dry land. Maybe if I met them on their own turf, they'd be able to speak to me more clearly.

The guys had seen me go that far before, but my sister hadn't. I reached over to grasp her hand as we stopped at the foot of the spit. "This is probably going to look kind of strange. I'm just doing everything I can to get answers. Nothing I try will really hurt me. The spirits here want our help."

How much they could work through their communication issues to help us help them was a totally different story, of course.

Marisol nodded and squared her shoulders like she

was bracing herself. Nox gave my arm a quick squeeze. "Do what you need to do, Minnow," he said.

I walked out to the end of the spit and peered down at the water rippling around the stalks of the reeds and cattails. *Were* there bodies down there, sunk out of sight like my guys' had been by their murderers? The thought sent a shudder through me, but I peeled off my shoes and socks and dipped my toes into the water.

It was as cold as I'd expected. Gritting my teeth, I sat down on the edge of the spit and hopped into the water right where we'd seen Nolan Senior's former body go under.

I cringed as I slid into the water, half-expecting my feet to smack into a water-logged corpse. But they hit the silty bottom, feeling nothing but the slick mud and a couple of small stones. The lake came up to my armpits there.

Ignoring the chill seeping through my skin, I waded around the end of the spit. As I pushed through the marsh vegetation, I prodded with my feet every which way, half hoping for and half dreading the moment when I might encounter the bulge of a bone. A couple of times, I even fished hard lumps out to study them in the air, only to find they were ordinary stones.

It wasn't really surprising that the Gauntts would have covered their tracks at least that well. They owned this land, whether they publicized the fact or not. They'd hardly want there to be any chance of someone uncovering bodily remains on their property.

A few feet beyond the end of the spit, the water

lapped around my neck and tugged at my hair. I swished my hands through the lake in a rhythmic motion and closed my eyes. The hum in my chest reverberated through my limbs.

The spirits were still here. I needed them to come to me, to speak to me.

"I'm here," I said softly. "I want to know more of your stories. I want to know anything your killers did that would work as proof. Did they leave anything behind? Here, or in your old home, or anywhere else?"

The water shivered around me with a faint tug, like dozens of tiny fingers trying to catch hold of me. I balked instinctively for a second before following that tug and sinking all the way beneath the water.

As the cold liquid closed over my head, images rushed into my mind like the smack of a wave. It was like when the ghostly figures I'd summoned into watery form had splashed over me last time, only a longer and more intense deluge.

Impressions swam by of younger versions of the Nolan and Marie I knew as well as other adults I had to assume were the Gauntts' previous bodies—yanking the kids around, murmuring magical words to keep them still and compliant, alternating between cold aloofness, cutting anger, and brief moments of doting kindness. I got whiplash just watching it.

As far as I could tell, the Gauntts hadn't turned their perverted interests on their hosts-to-be. Maybe that had felt too close to incest, or maybe they'd been worried about somehow contaminating the bodies that would become theirs. I didn't have any faith at this point in them having the slightest moral compass. It was a small comfort anyway. Who'd want to choose between being molested and being murdered?

I didn't catch anything that looked like evidence we could turn against the Gauntts, though. Every action they took against their adoptive kids was either magical or designed to look like normal discipline. Nothing was done in public view where it might have been captured on camera, even accidentally. The spirits could hardly testify on their own behalf.

I opened my mouth, letting water stream in without fear. Moving my lips to form the question I wanted to ask. *Do you know where the bodies are?*

Visions swept over me of bloated corpses yanked out of the marsh and carted away with whispers through the dark of night. After that, the spirits didn't seem to have any clue what'd happened to the physical remains of the monsters who'd taken them over.

Damn it. Wasn't there anything I could use?

But another sensation was surging up through the fraught mix of fear and anger that resonated from the ghostly memories. I became aware of the entire marsh spread out around me, filled by the lake but a distinct part of that body of water. Water that'd been contaminated over and over by the Gauntts' dark rituals. They'd poured their influence into it, submerged bodies and then dredged them up, twisting sickening magic all through the currents.

Those impressions came with a rush of nausea. I'd

sensed that the marsh wasn't entirely happy the last time I'd come out here, but if the water rushing into me now contained any emotion of its own, it was revulsion.

It longed to bring life, to shelter the plants and creatures that called it home, but the Gauntts were polluting those intentions with their own psychotic purposes. A dark energy radiated through the liquid around me, but from the marsh's reaction, it felt more like binding chains than liberating power.

What would happen to the Gauntts if this place could manage to shake off those chains?

It didn't do me any good wondering about that when I could taste the hopelessness of its situation in the desperate roar of the water through my awareness. Then I was thrashing up to the surface, the nausea making my stomach lurch so I spewed all the water I'd swallowed back into the marsh.

I stumbled over to the bank and simply leaned against the end of the spit for a moment, my breath coming raggedly, my head spinning. A frog swam up to me with a concerned croak, and I tipped my head to it. Through our new supernatural connection, faint but steady, I sensed my men shifting on their feet, wanting to rush to help but not knowing how to. And I still didn't know how either.

The only thing I was sure of after my commune with the marsh's spirits was that I never wanted my sister to feel as terrified or desperate as they did. I'd protect her from the powers looming over us, no matter what I had to do.

# fifteen

*Lily*

When I finally dragged myself out of the water onto the spit's solid ground, the three guys and my sister hustled to meet me.

Ever practical in ways I appreciated more by the day, Kai had grabbed the emergency blanket from Fred's trunk. He wrapped it around my sopping clothes, and for a minute I just clutched it around me, waiting for my shivers to subside as my body regained its warmth.

"Did you see anything?" Marisol asked, her eyes nearly round. "What happened?"

I hoped she hadn't been too disturbed by watching me all but drown. I gave her a small smile. "Not a whole lot. Really just more of what I saw last time. The Gauntts treated their adopted kids like shit and manipulated them with their magic so they wouldn't make trouble. They take the corpses of the older bodies away from the marsh—none of the spirits seemed to know where to. It seems like they've been pouring more and more magic into the water itself so that it can help them work their rituals, and the marsh isn't happy about that."

Ruin rocked eagerly on his feet. "So how does that help us take down the Gauntts?"

"It doesn't," I admitted reluctantly. "At least not in any way I can see right now." I paused. "I guess it's possible that if I damaged Marie's heart the way I did with Nolan, they'd be forced to come out here and do their ritual again, and maybe we could arrange for them to be caught in the act... But I'm not sure how easy it'll be for me to get close enough to her. The whole family must have a ton of protection around them now, and they've got every excuse to."

"We can't give up," my sister protested.

Nox drew himself up to the full extent of his substantial height. "Of course we're not giving up. This was just one strategy that didn't pan out. There's plenty more we can try." He tucked his arm around me and ushered me back toward the car. "You gave it your best shot, Minnow. Not your fault those water-logged spirits couldn't cough up anything useful."

His words didn't really reassure me. I knew what strategy Marisol was thinking of trying, and it was the last thing I wanted her to have to do. I twisted my hair in my hand to wring out some of the lingering moisture, straining my brain for something else we could try right now before she started talking about making public statements again.

Jett lifted his hand to us in greeting as we approached our parking spot. Then his head jerked around at the same time as an engine's rumble reached my ears.

Two engines rumbling, it turned out. A couple of police cars roared into view along the laneway we'd driven down. I stopped in my tracks at the sight of them and then hurried the rest of the way to Fred 2.0, my pulse lurching.

Whatever they wanted, I didn't think it could be good.

"Get in the car," I called to Marisol. The Skullbreakers guys braced themselves around me, tensed for battle. We could have all leapt into or onto our vehicles and made a run for it, but the cops were coming up on us fast and blocking the lane. I wasn't sure we'd actually be better off in flight.

Kai nudged his glasses up his nose, his other hand dipping toward the gun wedged in his jeans. "We should hear what they have to say. If this is something to do with the Gauntts, they might give away something about their plans. But stay where you've got shelter."

We opened the car's doors and positioned ourselves with those as shields. The guys kept their guns out of view—for now. As the police cars skidded to a halt across from us, my heart thudded hard.

We'd faced off with gangsters and other criminals before, as well as bullies who'd been on the attack. Fighting with law enforcement felt like an entirely different level of trouble.

If we crossed that line, could we *ever* come back, no matter what happened with the Gauntts?

Several of my froggy friends had bounded over to join us. I didn't take more comfort from their presence as they croaked at the cops stepping out onto the matted grass.

The officers didn't have any concerns about showing *their* weapons. Four cops emerged, two from each car, with pistols pointed in our direction. "Stay where you are," one bellowed. His dark hair was slicked back so solidly you'd have thought he was a plastic action figure come to life. "You're under arrest."

When he didn't follow that up with anything, we all just stared. Kai cocked his head. "Under arrest for *what?*"

"Don't ask questions," one of the other cops barked. "Put your hands up where we can see them and march on over here, buckaroos."

Oh-kay then. I'd never been taken into police custody before, but I was pretty sure this wasn't standard procedure. I frowned at them. "If we haven't committed any crimes, I don't think you can arrest us."

I mean, we had committed various crimes—well, mostly the guys had—but if the cops didn't *know* that...

EVA CHASE

Two of them shifted on their feet, looking impatient and maybe a little puzzled, as if they weren't totally sure what they were doing here either. Weird.

"We don't need any of your back-talk," the first cop said. "Are you going to come peacefully or not?"

"We have a right to know why we're being arrested," Kai spoke up. "It's part of state law. Which I'd expect you to know about."

The cops exchanged a glance. "You know what you've done," another said in a threatening tone.

Ruin beamed at them. "We took a walk along the marsh. Nothing wrong with that."

"That's not— You have been implicated in a *very* serious crime." The cop scowled at us as if her doom-and-gloom expression would make up for the fact that it was becoming increasingly clear she had no idea what that "very serious crime" was.

None of them did. What was going on here?

My nerves prickled with apprehension. I sucked in a breath, trying to think of something I could say that might diffuse the situation, and the cops started striding forward.

"If you won't come peacefully, then we'll need to use appropriate force," the first one said robotically. Now he sounded like an action figure too.

Nox made a gesture to Jett, who nodded and surreptitiously tucked his gun away. I guessed they didn't want to give the cops any current excuses to enforce this arrest if we didn't have to.

But that didn't mean the Skullbreakers were going

to hand themselves over. As the cops got closer, the four guys stepped forward carefully to meet them, their hands partly raised.

"I'm sure we can clear up this misunderstanding," Nox said with a wry note in his voice.

One of the cops scoffed, and then the guys all moved at once.

Ruin and Kai lunged forward in unison, each swatting a different cop across the head like a momma cat cuffing a kitten. Kai's immediately swiveled and tackled the colleague next to him to the ground. Ruin's crumpled onto the grass too, raising his hands to his face as he turned into a blubbering mess.

Jett had snatched at the last cop's gun at the same time. The burly woman held on tight, but Jett wasn't looking to disarm her. Only to reshape the gun into a form that wasn't remotely threatening anymore.

The cop ended up holding a lump of metal in the vague shape of a leaping fish. She fumbled with it as if still trying to find the trigger. Then, with a savage snarl that seemed out of place with the professional uniform, she sprang at Jett.

Nox wasn't letting his guys fight this battle alone. He sprang in there as Jett raised his hands to defend himself and sent a wallop of crackling energy into the cop's midsection. The woman flew several feet back and fell on her ass. She sprang up again and launched herself at Nox.

Nox let her come and snatched at the woman's shirt at the last second, heaving the cop over his shoulders, spinning her around, and then sending her flying toward the lake. The sound of tearing fabric came with his heave. The woman whirled through the air like a maple key and thumped to the ground with the seam of her shirt sleeve gaping open.

And where it gaped open, a pinkish blotch about the size of a nickel showed against her bronze skin.

My pulse stuttered. "She's marked!" I said. "Maybe they all are."

Ruin leapt to check the sobbing guy, who was so distraught he didn't even bother trying to fend the gangster off. Ruin yanked at the guy's collar to reveal a matching blotch at the peak of his shoulder.

My stomach sank. Kai turned toward his dupe, who was still wrestling with his partner on the ground, and I caught his arm.

"I think we know what's going on well enough. Let's get out of here while we have the chance. I'd try to break the spell, but I don't know how much time we have. There could be more coming."

Nox clapped his hands. "You heard her. Move out!"

He dropped into the car, taking the driver's seat this time, and I jumped into the back with Marisol. As Ruin scrambled into the passenger seat, Jett and Kai mounted their motorcycles. In less than a minute, we were zooming across the bumpy field around the lane and back into the road as soon as we'd cleared the police cars.

"So... the Gauntts sent some cops to play with us?"

Ruin said as we zoomed toward Mayfield, trying and failing to keep his tone light-hearted.

"It looks like it." I let out my breath in a huff of a sigh. "They used their supernatural control to convince the cops that they had to take us in, since apparently they don't have any evidence they could use to get us actually arrested."

"They're just as stuck as we are in that area," Nox said with a low chuckle.

"Except they *can* call on anyone who still has their mark," I said. "If there are at least four county police officers they can manipulate… how many other people will they be able to send after us?"

"At least not all of the other people will have guns?" Marisol suggested in an attempt at optimism.

"There is that," I agreed. "Let's look on the bright side."

Ruin, naturally, was the expert at that approach. "Lily can break their marks, and then they'll be against the Gauntts!"

I grimaced. "Only if there isn't a bunch of them trying to attack us all at the same time. It does take a certain amount of concentration and time."

"You've got all of us working with you," Nox said. "Including me now, thank the Devil. We'll take whatever those pricks throw at us and send it right back at them."

It'd be nice to believe that it'd be that easy. But as we drove between Lovell Rise and the neighboring town, Mayfield's high rises looming in the distance, a deeper uneasiness gripped me. I couldn't help noticing that a couple of the cars cruising around on other country roads turned toward us after we'd come into their view.

By the time we were approaching the Mayfield city limits, we had three vehicles racing after us. Nox gunned the engine to stay ahead of them, his forehead furrowing.

"It'll be easier to lose them in the city," he said. "They look like regular people. I doubt they have a lot of experience with stunt driving."

He motioned to Kai and Jett through the windows, and they swerved off in different directions at the next intersection. The cars stayed on our tail. I guessed they were looking to maximize the number of targets they could tackle.

What did they think they were going to do if they "caught" us? *Were* they armed and planning to shoot on sight? Or were they just hoping to irritate the hell out of us?

They were definitely accomplishing that last part already.

As we passed into streets packed with buildings on either side, Nox pulled through a gas station's lot, tore down an alley, and doubled back on our previous course. We got a moment's relief of an empty rearview mirror before a car we drove by in the opposite lane pulled a sudden, screeching U-turn and barreled toward us.

Nox muttered a curse and whipped through another series of quick maneuvers that had us jerking in our seats. Every time we lost one follower, we seemed to pick up another before we'd driven more than a few blocks. The marked dupes appeared to be everywhere.

My pulse thumped on. I was starting to get dizzy with the adrenaline. "We're going to run out of gas eventually," I said. "Maybe we should leave the city."

"Then they'll have easy eyes on us for miles around," Nox said. "Fucking hell. If I could smack them around through the windows…"

"You'll only smash the glass if you try. Anyway, it isn't their fault, any more than it was Marisol's when she ran away."

He grumbled under his breath inarticulately, but he yanked and twisted the wheel until we'd shaken our current follower. Then he veered straight into an underground parking lot where we could stay out of view temporarily.

When we were sure no one had followed us in, he parked behind a column that hid us while still giving us lots of room to flee if we had to. Then he sank into the seat and reached for his phone. "I'll get Jett over here. He'll have to do a temporary makeover on your car. The Gauntts must be giving their marked people the impression of what it looks like so the idiots know what to go after. We've just got to make it look different."

As much as I loved Fred 2.0 as it was, I wasn't going to argue with his suggestion. We had to do what we had to do.

I squinted through the dim lot, my heart still racing. "That strategy will only protect us for as long as it takes before the Gauntts realize we've changed the vehicle... or until they find some other way for people to ID us."

Marisol rubbed her arms. "How are we supposed to figure out our next moves if we're being chased all over the place? We can't go back to the motel, can we?"

I shook my head. "I don't think that's safe. Too many people coming and going, too many who might have already seen us or the car there." Then I paused, an idea rising up that I examined reluctantly.

We'd already asked for a lot of help from people who hadn't been inclined to help us in the first place. But I wasn't sure we had a lot of choice. And keeping us in action against the Gauntts was for their benefit too.

"They're sending the marked people after us," I said. "So why don't we go to the people we've already unmarked?"

# sixteen

*Ruin*

When we pulled up outside the little cottage, Nox muttered something about it being a "shack." I thought it was kind of cute. The clapboard exterior was all soft if faded pastels, with a narrow front porch where the inhabitants could sit and gaze out over the lawn to the rocky beach. The strip of sand and pebbles stretched about five feet before reaching the edge of the lake. It had a peaceful atmosphere—maybe the right word was "quaint."

Peyton didn't seem to think too much of it, though, even with it being a place she'd spent time at as a kid. She'd told us it belonged to friends of her family who lived out of town and didn't use the cottage in the fall.

Her parents had a spare key, but there was no official connection between them and the property that the Gauntts could trace. She led us around the small building with a faint grimace that didn't budge.

"There are only two bedrooms," she said as she unlocked the front door. "But the couch in the living room is a pullout. And there should still be a couple of air mattresses stashed in the closet from when they'd have larger get-togethers here."

"That's plenty," Lily assured her. "We appreciate getting any kind of place to stay that's away from where the Gauntts' lackeys are looking for us."

Apparently Peyton had grown up near here in one of the towns a few over from Lovell Rise, farther along the edge of the large lake. We were almost directly opposite the marsh here—if I squinted, I could make out a greenish blur against the shoreline on the other side of the water.

That didn't mean the marked people the Gauntts had incited to hunt for us wouldn't come out this way, but hopefully even if they did, they'd have no idea that Lily's revamped car was the one they were supposed to be keeping an eye out for. It has a shiny new coat of gray paint thanks to Jett—"the color people are least likely to pay attention to," he'd said—and a slightly redesigned frame that had turned it more modern-looking than before.

Lily's lips pursed a little whenever she looked at it, as if it pained her seeing her car transformed into a different one, but Jett had assured her that he could change it back as soon as the Gauntts stopped being such dicks about everything.

He and Kai had shoved their motorcycles into the garden shed on the property, which had been just big enough to accommodate all of them except the back wheel. They'd closed the door as well as they could and draped a sheet of tarp over the bikes' rears so they wouldn't be identifiable.

Peyton hadn't said much during all that. She hadn't talked much in general since we'd come to her to make our appeal. With the door now open, she hesitated on the porch before offering the key to the cottage to Lily.

"I'll need it back afterward," she said. "And—if you could keep the cottage pretty clean… My parents' friends like to come out here with their family around Christmas, and I don't want them finding a mess."

"Of course." Lily offered her a smile that was only a bit tight around the edges. "You're doing us a huge favor. We don't want to make things any harder for you."

Peyton hugged herself even though the sunny day wasn't too chilly. "Well, we can't let those asshole Gauntts get away with how they've treated all of us. Come on, I'll show you around. Not that there's much to see."

Inside, she pointed out the doors to the two bedrooms, the bathroom, and the cramped kitchen that would have trouble holding more than one person at a time. Not that I figured we were going to be cooking any elaborate banquets while we were here, as unfortunate as that fact was.

I considered asking whether we could get delivery all the way out by the lake and decided it was better not to badger Peyton any more than we already had. Kai had managed to make a quick stop to grab a couple of bulging bags of premade grocery food, so we weren't going to starve, even if I was craving my spicy beef jerky. I'd finished my last package this morning.

Lily's sister didn't seem to have the same concerns about imposing on our obviously reluctant host. When we'd come to a stop in the middle of the living room, which held the pullout couch, a couple of armchairs, and a TV that looked old enough to have been in operation before our first deaths, Marisol prodded Peyton's arm.

"There are bigger ways you can help take down the Gauntts. If we all speak up together, show that we're not scared and we'll say what they did to us—"

Peyton jerked away from the other girl, her face blanching. "I'm not making any big speeches. To have everyone knowing what they did... what I went along with..."

"They were magically controlling us!" Marisol protested. "And we were kids. They were freaking intimidating even without the magic. No one's going to blame you for it."

"And if anyone does, they're a total asshat," Lily put in.

Peyton shook her head. "I just don't want that story

tied to me wherever I go for the rest of my life. Which will totally happen."

"It's not just us," Marisol said. "If we could get the other marked people from the college on board—if all of us stood up together—the spotlight wouldn't be on just a couple of us."

"I don't think they're going to go for it either. And what if they back out at the last minute?" Peyton shuddered. Her gaze darted to me, as if she hoped I'd rescue her somehow.

She still did that here and there—look at me as if searching for Ansel, hoping he'd suddenly appear. Not that he'd seemed to be very protective of her even when he'd had control of this body. I wasn't sure why she would want that jerk back so much.

"I wish I could stand with you," I told Marisol. "But I don't know what exactly happened to Ansel. I guess I could make it up based on what we've heard from the other guys who were marked…"

Kai brushed past me with a bump of his elbow. "Bad idea, Ruin. The Gauntts switched things up a fair bit, it seems like. If you say one thing they can prove isn't true and they catch you in a lie, then you'd undermine the whole case."

My momentary hopes deflated. "Yeah. That makes sense. I definitely don't want that to happen."

Lily squeezed my arm. "You help in all kinds of other ways."

"If our *other* marked 'friends' would be a little more helpful, maybe we'd be getting somewhere without

165

anyone needing to do a big public announcement," Nox said, glowering at his phone. He raised his head to glance at the rest of us. "Our man in the Skeleton Corps is having trouble bringing anyone else on board. The two other guys he found who have the marks have gotten skittish about letting us do anything about it since our last fight with the Corps. Worried they'll be punished for fraternizing with the enemy or something. It's like they *want* to be some rich prick's puppet." He snorted in disgust.

Jett waved toward me and Kai. "If we can at least bring them around, Kai and Ruin can force them to go along with Lily's cure."

Kai made a face at that suggestion too. "The first guy came to us willingly. I think we should uphold that pattern when it comes to anyone from the Skeleton Corps. We need these people to trust us, and they've got way more reason to be wary of us than the college kids did. We're better off if it's their idea. Otherwise they'll just see the Gauntts as *another* enemy while we're still one too."

Jett huffed, but he didn't appear to have any counter argument.

Nox glared at his phone again. "He's at least finally convinced them to meet with us so we can make a case. Not sure what we could say that he hasn't already, but we've got to take that shot." He ambled off into the corner, his fingers tapping away at the screen as he replied to the latest text.

Peyton watched him go, her posture somehow

getting even stiffer. I couldn't be the guy she wanted, and I wasn't interested in being anyone's guy except Lily's, but she was doing a lot for us. I wished I could make her feel better about it. Say something that would cheer her up even if I couldn't make the guy she'd dreamed about suddenly appear. He hadn't really existed even when Ansel had been alive.

Sometimes I worked best when I just went with the moment and figured out what was right along the way. I moved to her side and motioned toward the door. "Take a little walk with me?"

Peyton blinked at me, her eyes going wide. She hesitated, but this time it didn't look like wariness, only surprise. Then she nodded emphatically.

I shot a quick glance over my shoulder at Lily to make sure she wasn't bothered, but she just gave me a fond smile. She knew how important it was to me to see the people around me happy—or at least as close to content as I could make them. The fact that she understood was one of the reasons I loved her so much.

And she loved me too. The memory of her saying those words hovered in my chest like a giddy bubble, one that'd never pop as long as I lived.

Peyton ambled with me down to the water. Little twinges of pain still ran through my abdomen with my steps, but between the doctor's work and Jett's, the discomfort wasn't too bad now. I'd been able to taper off the painkillers enough that my thoughts no longer felt like they were swathed in cotton balls.

Peyton kicked at the pebbles with the toe of her

sneakers and peeked at me through her dark, wavy hair as it drifted across her face. "Did you want to talk to me about something?" she asked.

"Yeah," I said. "I know you're not really excited about all the ways we've intruded on your life."

Her cheeks flushed. "Well, I—I mean, it's been kind of crazy, and all the memories stirred up—and I still don't really understand what happened to Ansel." She gave me that hopeful look again.

I kept my tone gentle. "He's gone. But you're still here. And you're doing an amazing job fighting back against the Gauntts in the ways you can. I just thought you should know that."

Peyton's eyes narrowed abruptly. "Is this to try to get me to testify like Lily's sister keeps pushing for?"

I held up my hands. "No, not at all. That's got to be your decision. I just want you to feel okay, or even good, about everything you've already done."

"It's not so easy." Her gaze dropped to the rock-laced sand. "I barely know any of you. You've done some kind of shitty things too. Just not anywhere near as shitty as what the Gauntts are doing."

I found I couldn't argue with her point. But there were other things I could say. "That's fine. But, you know—you've probably noticed that I'm usually pretty upbeat about stuff. I like to find the positive in everything if I can. Yeah?"

A giggle slipped out of her. "It's kind of hard *not* to notice that, even not knowing you very well."

"Right. So, I first started being that way when I was

a little kid. My parents wanted me to figure out how to keep myself happy, so I pretended I was happy all the time, hoping that when they saw I'd managed it, they'd care about me more. But it didn't work that way. And the happiness I made myself feel was kind of hollow for a long time… I think I only really started meaning it after I found people who did welcome me and support me the way they should have."

Peyton arched her eyebrows. "Those other guys you're hanging out with?"

"Exactly!" I said. "I've always belonged with them, and when I knew I could have their backs and they'd have mine, everything got so much brighter. And I think it can be the same for you too. Your parents let you down. They didn't protect you from the Gauntts. Some of your friends let you down too. But I'm sure you can find the right people who'll let you be happy too. Let you know you're making the right decisions about your life. It's not us, and that's okay. Now that you've figured out more about where you're coming from, it'll be easier to find them."

Peyton studied me for a long moment with the warm sun beaming over both of us. Then she offered me a small smile that looked more genuine than anything I'd seen from her earlier today.

"Thank you," she said. "In a weird way, that is kind of nice to hear. And I appreciate that you bothered to say anything at all. I know… you have a lot of reasons to be mad at me for how I treated Lily before."

"That wasn't totally your fault either," I reminded

her. "You had the Gauntts egging you on. And everybody makes mistakes. You should probably apologize to her sometime if you haven't already, though."

She rubbed her hand across her mouth. "Yeah. Well. Like I said, thank you. I hope you guys come up with something even better to knock those pricks on their asses."

She went over to the car she'd driven here in, and I headed back to the cottage. Before I reached the porch, Nox stepped outside, rolling his shoulders.

"I'm going to see if I can talk some sense into those Skeleton Corps idiots," he said as Lily emerged behind him.

My success with Peyton had left me with more energy than usual zinging through my veins. Lily had told me before that my attitude was good for the group in ways I might not even be able to see, and maybe she'd been more right than she knew. Before I could second-guess the impulse, the words tumbled out.

"I'll come too. Maybe I can convince them the nonmagical way."

Nox gave me a slightly skeptical look, but he waved me along. "Let's go, then. We want to make this quick. They agreed to meet outside the city, but we're still going a little closer to Mayfield than I'd prefer. I don't want to stick around for long."

This time, since we weren't in the middle of a high-speed chase, he let Lily drive. It was her car, after all. He gave her directions until we ended up at a tourist shop standing alone along one of the country highways. The store clearly hadn't been open in quite a while. The grime on the windows looked almost as thick as the glass.

A few minutes later, another car pulled up. Three men got out—the one who'd come to us asking to have his mark broken and a couple of younger guys who I guessed were marked too. The first guy tipped his head to us, but the others just eyed us warily.

"Look," Nox said right off the bat, planting his hands on his hips, "you've got a bunch of rich bastards who've messed around with you, and they're stopping you from even knowing about it. What's the hold-up? You'd rather stay in the dark?"

One of the new guys narrowed his eyes at Nox. "Maybe we've seen too much of your craziness to think we should believe anything you say. *You* could be the ones who messed with us."

Parker groaned. "I've explained it to you guys. You saw what happened to Storek. Anything these guys have ever done wore off within half an hour. I've had these memories for days since they broke whatever was hiding them in my head."

"Who says we even need to know?"

I could answer that. Nox squared his shoulders, looking like he was about to try to berate them into submission, but I stepped forward first.

"I think we all want the same things," I said.

The second new guy scoffed. "How so?"

"None of us wants some assholes in a high rise

controlling us and what we do, right? Trying to keep us down. They *want* us to fight with each other so we're not fighting them and getting back that control."

The first newbie glared at me. "No one jerks me around."

"But they can," I said. "They're already doing it all over the city. Any second now, they might tug on the invisible leash they've got on you and start calling the shots, and as long as you've got that mark, you can't do anything about it. But we can break the leash. We can bark right back in their faces and shove the collars they tried to put around our necks down their throats instead. Why should those pricks get to call the shots? Isn't Mayfield *your* city?"

Nox stirred discontentedly at that suggestion, but the Skeleton Corps guys all perked up a little.

"It is," one said. "I don't know why the guys in charge keep listening…"

"They get paid off," Parker said with a sneer. "That's all *they* care about. They're keeping us down too."

"It doesn't have to be that way," I added. "We're already fighting back, and we can hit them even harder if we're all together in this."

The other newbie eyed me with continued wariness. "You hit *us* before. Why don't you try to hit us now and make us do what you want?"

"Because we're not like them," I said automatically. "We hit you to protect ourselves and find out who screwed us over. Now we know the biggest screwers of them all are the Gauntts, so that's where we're going to aim our fists from now on."

"With or without you," Nox said, with an approving tip of his head when he caught my eye. "We're not going to force you. This *should* be your battle too, but we can't make you believe that."

"I've never wanted to hurt anyone," Lily said quietly. "I just don't want them to get away with all the damage they've done that so many people don't even know about."

There was a moment of silence. But something one of us had said must have gotten through, because the first guy sighed and turned toward Lily, shrugging off his jacket. He raised his chin. "No one controls me. But if *you* do anything that feels like you're fucking with my mind—"

Lily raised her hands. "I'm only going to take off the spell that's already there."

The second guy folded his arms over his chest. "I want to see this before I do anything."

He would see. He'd see that we could be on the same side. And maybe my appeal had made that happen.

## seventeen

*Lily*

I tugged the hood of my jacket lower over my forehead to shade my face and glanced across the street at Kai, who was similarly clothed and lurking in the alley opposite mine. We hadn't really wanted to come into the city while there were untold numbers of the Gauntts' marked dupes on the look-out for us, but one of the new Skeleton Corps guys had given us an opportunity we had to pursue. So we'd just taken every possible precaution to avoid being identified.

The young Corps member who was lurking farther down the street had undergone a much more extreme makeover. He'd been able to point out the usual driver who picked up the Gauntt grandchildren from school

174

and brought them back to the house—the same man who'd picked up *him* a few times when the Gauntts had been "visiting" with him several years ago. Then Jett had used his magical powers of transformation to adjust the Skeleton Corps guy's features so they matched pretty closely.

We were counting on the Gauntts not scrutinizing the help in minute detail. And the Corps guy was counting on Jett being able to put his face back to normal after this little mission.

But before the mission could even get really started, we needed to create a distraction. Nox and Ruin were going to grab the actual driver before he could set off. Our guy was going to take the driver's place. We needed a bigger spectacle to divert people from the inevitable smaller commotion.

Kai signaled to me, and I raised the paintball gun he'd picked up somewhere or other with his usual resourcefulness. Not the Skullbreakers' typical weaponry, but one I felt a heck of a lot more at ease with. We weren't out to kill anyone today, only to do a little… rearranging and recording, and that was a relief.

Jett would have loved to play a part in this stage of the mission too, but we'd needed someone to stay with Marisol for her protection… and as Kai had pointed out with a snort when I'd commented to him about it, "Jett would have gotten too caught up in making it art instead of making them dance to our bidding."

Kai made the first shot, a blob of red paint splattering into the window of the limo company's building. I fired off a couple of rounds that smacked the dark compact limo just outside with splotches of bright yellow.

Ruin probably liked the makeover, but the company staff didn't seem too pleased. A couple of them hustled out just as Kai launched his next few shots.

Paint punched the man in the gut, the woman in the shoulder. I added a flare of magic to spray the paint even farther across them, gooping up their eyelashes and flecking their hair. It was makeovers all around today!

As they teetered and flailed, a couple more employees hustled out of the building to see what was going on. I fired between them, using my powers to improve my aim and making them jump apart as they dodged.

Just as planned, the driver we were targeting ended up a little farther down the street from the others. Kai and I alternated between shooting at the building, the other employees, and our target, aiming to compel him farther away. Soon that part of the street was looking like a kindergarten painting.

After the first few paintballs battered the sidewalk around his feet, our target hightailed it out of my view. I might have heard a muffled grunt.

The other employees were too busy squawking over their predicament and yelling at each other that someone should call the cops or a cleaning team or the boss—no one seemed to quite agree on who the proper authorities were. After several more explosions of color for good measure, we lowered our weapons.

A moment later, our replica driver strolled into view. He dashed past the others, motioning to them in a gesture designed to indicate that he had to hoof it to make it to his next job. His colleagues barely noticed him in their colorfully disturbed state.

Kai and I watched until another sleek black car with tinted windows purred out of the garage. When it'd disappeared down the street, we ducked down our respective alleys and met up a couple of blocks away where we'd parked Fred 2.0.

I dove into the driver's seat and started the engine. We wanted to be in place well ahead of time. As I pulled into the street, Kai flipped open his laptop. He still wasn't the most avid techie around, but his speed-reading skills and ability to quickly process information gave him a major leg up on his friends, who were just slowly creeping out of their twenty-years-delayed electronics knowledge.

"The camera is already on," he reported. "I'm getting the signal. Now we just need to record some usable footage."

That was the important part. And we needed to stay in range of the device for it to happen. I drew up a block away from Nolan and Marie Junior's school and turned off the gas. Kai studied his screen.

Was Nolan still going to school even though his body was now inhabited by a man who'd gone through more education than anyone in that building could have imagined? Or had the Gauntts come up with some excuse to disenroll him? I figured they'd probably set him up with some kind of home office or similar so he could keep contributing even in his child-like state. Remembering how pissed off he'd sounded that he was going to have to stay out of the public eye for years gave me a small twinge of satisfaction.

One tiny thing hadn't gone his way.

I squirmed uneasily in my seat, waiting for Kai's next update. It only took another few minutes. He sat up a little straighter, a smile crossing his lips. "Here we go. The kid's getting in—the granddaughter. Looks like she's alone. And our guy… he's attached the camera to her bag, just like we discussed. Perfect."

I got a glimpse of the camera's view on the screen, showing the girl perched in the limo's back seat, her legs swinging and her hands fidgeting with the plaid skirt of her uniform. She stared out the window with a dreamy expression and then leaned forward and asked for a specific radio station as the driver started the engine.

In that moment, she looked like a normal kid. We'd been hoping that'd be the case. The adult Gauntts obviously kept a tight rein on their adoptive children, but their supernatural control eased off over time just like Kai's and Ruin's did. After a full day at school, this was probably as close to being a typical kid as Marie Junior ever got.

Before Kai needed to prompt me, I pulled away from the curb and drove along a parallel route to the limo's, heading toward the Gauntts' mansion. Once, the feed jittered when I got stuck behind a teen doing a very slow parking job and the limo pulled too far ahead, but I hit the gas to close the distance as soon as I could.

The real success of this mission would depend on what happened once the limo got to the house.

I stopped at the side of the road just before the limo reached the mansion. As I yanked up the parking brake, Kai swiveled the laptop so we could both watch. I balled my hands on my lap and waited for the scene to unfold.

We might not get anything right away. We couldn't control what angle the camera ended up at when the bag was moved. But there should be a little something right off the bat.

The limo eased to a halt. The girl froze in her seat. Her head turned toward the window as she appeared to track someone coming over to collect her.

The door opened to reveal Thomas Gauntt. It'd been him and Olivia who'd carried out their perverted interests with our Skeleton Corps guy—our first confirmation that the two generations of Gauntts were equally predatory. I hoped he wouldn't feel too awful being that close to his molester right now.

Thomas didn't glance toward the driver. He grasped Marie Junior's shoulder with a clamp of his fingers that looked just shy of painful. "Come on then," he said in a flat voice that wasn't the slightest bit parental. "Quickly and quietly. And get your bag."

She unclasped her seatbelt and reached for the backpack. The camera's feed swam and rolled. She must have slung the bag over her shoulder, because we ended up with a view of the limo driving away from the front gate, which clanged shut afterward. The footage bobbed and swayed with the girl's footsteps all the way to the house. Her supposed father didn't say another word.

In the front hall, everything went still. All we could see was the door. Then Thomas said in the same firm voice, "Up to your room. We'll call you when it's dinner time."

Not a word of affection, not a single question about her day. But the girl followed his instructions mutely. We got the backward view of her tramping up the steps and into her bedroom—and then, miracle of all miracles, she set the bag down next to her desk with the camera facing her bed.

There wasn't much to see all the same. Marie Junior sank down on the edge of the bed, clearly visible on the feed, and just… sat there. And sat there. And sat some more, not moving other than periodic blinks and the slight rise and fall of her chest with her breath.

The longer I watched, the more my skin itched with discomfort. It wasn't any kind of in-your-face horror. The Gauntts weren't carving her into pieces or locking her in a cage. But there was something intensely awful about the sight all the same. A nine-year-old girl in a room full of books and toys doing absolutely *nothing* while she waited for her parents to tell her it was okay to take action again.

As if she only existed to carry out their will. Which wasn't far from the truth, was it?

After a while, Kai let out a low whistle. "You'd think

they could let her at least *read* or something. How bored must she get?"

"Maybe she doesn't even notice much," I said. "Everything might be a fog in her head because of their magic—like it was for Marisol when they used their magic to make her run away and stay with their people. Which doesn't make it better. They're already stealing away the little bit of life she should be getting before they totally murder her." I grimaced.

We waited until the dinner call came. That was the first time Marie Junior stirred on the bed. She got up and walked out like a puppet on strings.

While the Gauntts presumably ate their dinner, Kai and I dug into ours of grocery store sandwiches and chips. Our enemies had also murdered my access to decent food. It took about an hour before Marie Junior walked back into her bedroom, with her namesake right behind her.

Marie Senior stopped her granddaughter with a hand on her shoulder and squeezed her like Thomas had. "You'll stay here all night and not make a mess, won't you?"

"Yes, Grandma," Marie Junior answered in a vacant tone that sent a chill down my spine. Then she sat down on the edge of the bed again. And sat. And sat.

After another hour of the girl staring motionless at the wall, I motioned to Kai. "I don't think we're getting anything else tonight. Do you think this is enough to make the news?"

"You can definitely tell something's really not right

with how they're treating her," he said. "No healthy kid would act that catatonic. I think it'd work as proof that there's something wrong in paradise."

A deeper sense of relief washed over me as I turned the car in the opposite direction from the Gauntt mansion. I'd been braced for someone to notice us, to come at us somehow, but we'd escaped any consequences.

As I drove back toward the lake, Kai fiddled with the laptop until I heard the swoosh of a sent email. He folded his hands behind his head. "There we go. It's off to every major news outlet and a bunch of minor ones besides. Let's see how long it takes them to broadcast some clips."

He brought up several windows with various online newsfeeds to keep watch. I forced myself to keep my eyes on the road rather than the computer. Driving at legal speeds rather than Nox's preferred pace, it'd take us almost two hours to get to Peyton's cottage.

We were halfway there when Kai cleared his throat. He turned up the volume on the laptop. I didn't let myself look at the newscast he was streaming, but the reporter's voice pealed out loud and clear.

"We recently received footage from an anonymous source that appears to support the recent accusations that the Gauntt family is mistreating children. No one could see this video and not think that the youngest member of the family has had her spirit broken in some way."

Kai cackled. "We've got them now. I'd like to see

them explain how this is all a lie. Oh, one of the other channels picked up the story too! Wanting to be at least second to the punch."

A thrill raced through me. We'd taken a risk, and it'd paid off. It couldn't be too much longer before the Gauntts' façade started to crumble.

Then my phone chimed in my purse. Probably one of the other guys checking in on us, not realizing I'd be driving right now. I tipped my head toward it. "Answer it and put it on speaker phone?"

Kai fished out the phone and tapped the button on autopilot. I don't think either of us was prepared for the voice that crackled from the speaker.

"This isn't a game, darling," a woman said, and my heart lurched. I knew that coolly firm tone. It was Marie Senior. "You strike at us, we strike back—at everyone. Their demises are going to be on your conscience."

"What—" I started, but she hung up with a click. Kai stared at the phone. With a jerk of his hand, he smashed it against the door handle. Then he rolled down the window to chuck it into the overgrown field we were just driving past.

"Had to make sure they can't track it," he said, sounding more unnerved than I was used to. "I don't know how they got your number in the first place."

"Magic," I muttered, but my own nerves were still jumping. "What did she mean about striking back at everyone—about 'demises'?"

"I'll see if I can find any info." He tapped at the

keyboard, still in the hunt-and-peck stage of comfort. For the first several minutes, there was nothing but that sound and the thump of my pulse. Finally, he sucked in a sharp breath.

"*What?*" I demanded.

Kai wet his lips before they flattened into a grim line. His next exhale came out raggedly. "More kids. Not in any way we can prove is them. There are reports popping up of dozens of children across Mayfield and the surrounding towns suddenly being rushed to the hospital with some unknown illness. No, wait—" He tapped again. "Now they're saying it's a suspected poisoning. Oh, fuck."

"What?" I said again, but with less energy than before. My spirits had already plummeted before I braked so I could look at the screen.

"They're putting out a bulletin of the people they 'believe' might be responsible for the supposed poisoning," Kai said, swiveling the computer. "Thanks to an anonymous nudge from the Gauntts, no doubt."

Gazing back at me from the screen were five photographs—photos of me and the four lead Skullbreakers.

# eighteen

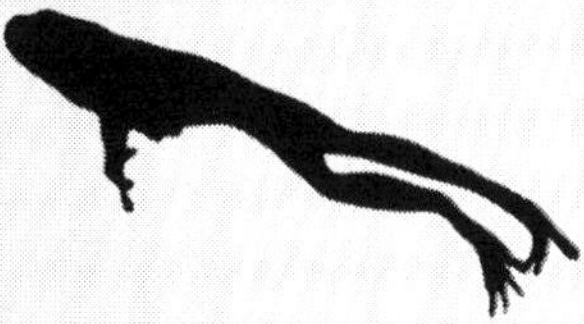

*Lily*

I stepped out of the hospital with a cloud of anguish hanging over me as dark as the deepening evening. The damp wind tugged at my hood, and I almost forgot to jerk it back down over my face. Cool drizzle started to speckle my cheeks as I hustled to the car where Kai and Ruin were waiting.

As soon as we'd heard the news about the Gauntts' latest act of war, I'd turned the car around and headed toward the nearest hospital. I had to assume that the Gauntts were causing the sickness in the kids—that these were kids they'd used for their supernatural and perverted purposes and left marks on that they were affecting them through. Marie was trying to punish us for our efforts by both hurting the most vulnerable

people she could and setting us up for a fall at the same time.

I could easily picture her sitting in her office drumming her fingers together and cackling like a maniacal dictator.

Kai had told the others what was going on, and Ruin had insisted on zooming over here on his motorcycle for moral support, despite my protests. But honestly, it'd been a bit of a relief to have his strong arms wrap around me when I'd gotten out of the car. I knew Kai cared about me, but he wasn't exactly one for huge gestures of affection.

But even though I'd snuck into the hospital with slightly higher spirits than before, those hopes had been dashed to the floor, stomped all over, and kicked into the corner within a few minutes. I'd done a quick makeup job on my face with a few basics I'd had in the glove compartment, pulled back my hair, and even smudged brown eyeshadow on my hairline so if anyone caught a glimpse, I wouldn't look like the blond girl in the news reports, but I still had to avoid notice. And even if I hadn't been a wanted maybe-criminal, I couldn't have walked up to the front desk and said, "I want to see any poisoned kids you've got in here!"

We weren't completely sure there *were* any kids at this specific hospital, even though it'd sounded like enough children had gotten sick that any hospital in the county should have at least one. Because of privacy concerns for minors, the newscasts hadn't given any details about their specific locations. I'd hoped I'd overhear a comment or catch a glimpse of some clue that'd point me in the right direction.

And maybe I had. I'd caught a murmur along the lines of, "so young… no idea what's causing it…" and followed the nurse who'd said it down a hall. But the room she'd gone into had been guarded by a stern-looking police officer. I didn't think he'd let some random hoodie girl go wandering in—definitely not without a close enough look to give me away.

If the kids were getting sick through their marks, then I could cure them by breaking those marks. But I didn't know how to bring my magic to bear without touching them, or at least being close enough to see who I was working on. The Gauntts were exerting their influence from afar, and my range was so limited.

So when I trudged back to Fred 2.0, my hopes were as slumped as my shoulders. The drizzle felt like an appropriate accompaniment to my feelings.

Unfazed by the rain, Ruin sprang out before I reached the car. He gave me another hug and then checked my expression. "What happened?"

"I couldn't find any kids who're affected, if there are any in there," I said. "I came across one possibility, but there was a cop staked out by the room. Which I guess makes sense if they think the kids were purposefully poisoned instead of just getting sick."

Ruin gave me a reassuring smile. "Kai and I can take care of that. We'll walk right in and convince him you need to get inside."

"Ruin could probably get one of the doctors in a

state where they'd point you to anyone else with the same condition who's in the place," Kai put in, leaning his elbow out the window he'd rolled down.

I shook my head. "There are too many people. You can't brainwash everyone in there simultaneously. And if you start pushing doctors and cops around in a crowded hospital, then they'll definitely believe the story about us being some kind of child-murderers."

"We could try to work our powers on all of them," Ruin offered with his dogged optimism.

Kai sighed. "No, Lily's right. Do you want to try another hospital?"

I glanced back at the gloomy gray building. "This is one of the smaller ones. The big ones in the city will probably have *more* security, not less." My hands balled at my side. "I need a better plan. Or better magic. Or… something."

As I growled that last word, a sliver of an idea occurred to me. It was a longshot, but that was more than the no-shot-at-all I had right now.

I went around to the driver's seat. "We're going out to the marsh again."

That declaration made even Ruin frown. "Those cops found us out there last time."

"We'll take a different route and walk the rest of the way—and keep a close eye out," I said. "If there's anyone nearby, we'll get out of there immediately. But… the Gauntts put a bunch of their magic into the marsh so they could build up their powers there and use it more effectively for their rituals. Maybe we can use that magic against them. And the spirits of those kids should be more upset about what those douche-canoes are doing now than anything before. If they can lend a hand, make some kind of a cure, help me extend my power with their energies… I need to ask."

The guys didn't debate my strategy. Kai kept watching the newscasts on his laptop as I drove toward the lake, but he didn't report any details that'd help us get to the kids to help them. The Gauntts hadn't inserted themselves directly into the conversation about the hospitalized kids either.

No one was talking about our video of Marie Junior anymore. Strict parenting was barely a blip on anyone's radar when children might literally be dying.

Would it occur to anyone to blame the Gauntts? They'd been accused of hurting kids multiple times in the past few days. But none of that hurt had been the type to send anyone to the hospital. There'd be no evidence of foul play when the sickness had been conjured by supernatural means none of the doctors would even believe in.

God, how many of the hospital staff might be marked too?

I shook off that thought as the stretch of water, currently slate-gray under the darkening clouds, came into view up ahead. I was abruptly self-conscious of the beams of the car's headlights streaking through the thickening night. But there weren't any streetlamps along these rough country lanes to guide my way otherwise. Ending up in a ditch wouldn't do us any good.

After a brief internal debate, I drove straight on toward the lake instead of veering down one of the side lanes that would have taken me closer to the spit. We were still a mile distant from that part of the marsh, and anyone keeping watch would *only* be able to see the lights. They had no reason to assume those lights belonged to a suspicious vehicle unless I headed toward the Gauntts' property.

I parked at a lookout spot at the end of the road just a short walk from the water's edge. During the summer, families would have come out here to have picnics and let their kids chase after frogs amid the reeds. The autumn days had gotten cool enough that I doubted there were many of those excursions happening now. Definitely not on a drizzly night.

Hugging myself, I stepped away from the car and peered through the dusk toward the spit. The last haze of the sun's light was fading along the horizon. Unless some vehicle over there flashed *its* lights, I had no way of telling how closely the spit might be monitored.

Both of the guys had followed me. "It's not worth the risk of going closer, is it?" I said to Kai, figuring he'd give me the unvarnished truth.

He frowned. "I don't like our odds. It'd be too easy for them to lie in wait and ambush us if there are minions over there keeping watch. But if you think it's worth it—"

"No." I paused, grappling with my sense of

hopelessness. "The magic the Gauntts put into the marsh must stretch all through the marsh to some extent, not just around the spit. They haven't stopped the water currents from flowing around. The energies they've sent into it have got to be what I absorbed after I nearly drowned. Maybe they're what helped your spirits stick around for so long instead of fading away."

It was an unnerving thought that the very people we were desperate to destroy might have given us the powers we were depending on to do so—but also fitting in a way. I squared my shoulders. "I can call to the water. I should be able to reach out to the power in it from right here, and maybe the lingering spirits of their victims too."

"Anything you need from us, just say the word!" Ruin declared.

I walked down to the edge of the marsh, where a chorus of froggy croaks greeted me. It wasn't any hassle sitting on the damp ground when the drizzle had made me pretty damp already. I shucked off my shoes and socks, rolled up my pantlegs, and dipped my feet in the water up to my calves.

The now-familiar hum inside me expanded as if resonating with the lapping of the lake. I stretched my awareness out through the currents and eddies, a swampy flavor congealing in the back of my throat.

Could I feel a faint tremor from the direction of the spit? An answering energy that recognized me?

"I need your help," I called out to it. "You know all about the Gauntts' magic; you hold so much of it.

They're using it to hurt people—kids—even worse than before. If you could lend me some of what they've given you so that I can really take them on, if you could give me the strength to break all the spells they're casting… Please."

I couldn't sense any kind of response. The cold water kept tickling over my feet. The cattails rustled around me. I might have tasted the faintest hint of resistance and fear.

"I'm not like them," I said. "I won't be like them. I won't use the power in you for awful things. I—"

I halted, memories surging up that made what I'd just said a lie. My throat closed up completely.

Kai's voice reached me from just behind. "What's the matter, Lily?"

I rubbed my hand over my face. "It's not totally true, is it? I've used the powers I already got from the marsh to *kill* people. I essentially killed Nolan and made the Gauntts come out here so they could murder their grandson. Why should the marsh or the spirits in it believe me?"

Ruin let out a dismissive sound. "You're nothing like them! You're the most wonderful person I've ever met."

My voice came out dry. "I think you might be a little biased."

"He's right, though," Kai said. "You're nothing like the Gauntts. Why did you strike out with your powers when you have? *Why* have you hurt people?"

I paused. "To stop them from hurting you, or Marisol, or me. But still—"

"No buts," he said. "As much as I enjoy yours. The Gauntts are totally selfish with their magic. They're hurting people who've never done anything to them so that they can have more life, more power, more everything than any human being is supposed to. They don't even care about the kids they're raising. But you— you're giving everything you have to protect people you've never even met. That's love and compassion the Gauntts would never comprehend."

"Yeah," Ruin put in. "They've got no idea how to be like you."

Kai nodded. "You stand for hope, for everyone getting to live a *real* life, not a few taking more than their fair share while the others suffer."

I swallowed hard, absorbing their words. Yes. I'd hurt and even killed people, but it was true that it'd never been because I'd wanted to. And never to get some special benefit for myself. I wished I never had to again. More than anything, I wanted the Gauntts stopped, unable to harm anyone ever again. Less pain, less suffering.

Love. Compassion. Hope. That *was* what I stood for. I had to hold on to that conviction. Right now, it resonated through my nerves with a glow that condensed at the base of my throat.

I opened my mouth, and a melody spilled out, as if maybe I could sing the marsh into trusting me, working with me. "Let them all rest and heal, let all the evil be sealed. We can do this together, we can stop them forever, if you'll only believe in me."

My voice fell away, but no response came. I couldn't tell if the marsh was even listening now. Sighing, I got up.

"Hey," Kai said, with unexpected gentleness in his tone. He hesitated for a split-second before slipping his arm around me. "We keep finding more ways to get at them. We aren't backing down." He stopped and shook his head at himself. "That's true, but that's not what I should be saying right now. Ruin's right. You're something special. No matter what the marsh or the spirits in it think. No matter what the Gauntts try to blame on you. You're something fucking precious, and I don't want you to ever forget that I think so too."

I peered at him through the darkness, his face all in shadows, his eyes barely visible behind the faint gleam of moonlight off his glasses. What I could see of his expression was solemn and intense.

Kai didn't normally talk like that. I wasn't sure how to take it. Or the way he carefully stroked his hand down the side of my face.

Maybe he thought I was breaking down like I'd started to when my searches for Marisol had failed, and he thought he had to force himself to act sweet to hold me together.

"I'll be okay," I felt the need to say. "I just—it's frustrating. I wish stopping the Gauntts wasn't so hard, but of course it is. You don't have to worry about me giving up."

Kai let out a hoarse chuckle. "I know that. That's not why— You know, I've always been the way I am, even when I was little. Wanting to learn everything I could, figuring things out quickly, seeing how to read people... It freaked my parents out, so they just kind of stopped dealing with me other than the necessities, and most of the other people I ran into didn't like how sharp I was either. I can't say I really had friends before the Skullbreakers."

An ache formed in my heart at the thought of the bright, brilliant, lonely boy he'd been. "I'm sorry."

"Don't be. That's not the point. They didn't matter anyway, not really. But you do. You're everything I could want, and I—I don't want to be sharp with you. Other than when it helps you. But the rest of the time... I'm trying to find the softer parts of me, even if they're smaller than what the rest of the guys can offer, so you can have that side of me too."

Sudden tears pricked at the backs of my eyes. Before I could figure out how to respond to his emotional confession, Kai tugged my face toward his. He caught my lips in a tender but passionate kiss that warmed me from my toes to the top of my head, chasing away the chill of the damp night.

Without breaking the kiss, he walked me over to a lone oak tree that stood several feet from the shoreline. The sweep of the branches, autumn leaves still clinging to them, gave us more shelter from the thin rain. Kai pulled me flush against him, one hand around my waist, the other lingering against my hair.

"You tried telling the marsh who you are and what you stand for," he murmured. "Maybe it'd be better if we showed it how much love you've got surrounding you." He glanced over his shoulder toward Ruin, who'd followed us over at a respectful distance. "Both of us, if Mr. Enthusiastic wants to join in as much as I suspect he does."

Ruin hummed and stepped around us to rest his hands on my waist from behind. "I'm always happy to give our woman a demonstration of just how much I adore her."

A giddy shiver ran through me. I wouldn't normally have gone for something like this, outside in a theoretically public place, but it was so dark I could barely see the car twenty feet away. We hadn't noticed any sign of anyone nearby.

Maybe Kai was right that making love would prove something. All the Gauntts seemed to do out here was inflict death. And even if he wasn't right, I wanted to show *him* how much his declaration meant to me.

"No arguments here," I said, and leaned in to kiss him again.

As my mouth melded with Kai's, he caressed my hip. Ruin pressed against me, pinning me between them. He swept my hair to the side and lowered his head to nibble the side of my neck.

More heat bloomed through my body everywhere the two of them touched. It might as well have been blazing summer around us with the way I was feeling now.

Kai stayed tender in his attentions, slipping his hand under my shirt and cupping my breast through my bra. He circled his thumb over the peak in increasingly tight circles until the quivers of pleasure had me whimpering against his mouth.

Ruin tucked his hand between Kai and me to massage my mound through my pants. I swayed with the motions of his fingers, a moan stuttering out of me. My ass brushed the bulge of his erection.

I rubbed back against him and teased my hand down to Kai's groin at the same time. The other guy was just as hard behind the fly of his jeans. I couldn't resist tugging down the zipper right then and gliding my fingers over the silky skin of his shaft. His groan made my heart leap.

I loved them too—so much. Maybe our relationship was crazy in all kinds of ways, but it was thanks to them that I'd found who I could really be, gained the confidence to stand up to Mom and Wade and now the Gauntts, become a force to be reckoned with while I stood between our enemies and my sister…

That was what real love was meant to be, wasn't it? Something that helped you grow into a better version of yourself.

Say what you want about my four ghostly gangsters —they'd supported me in spades.

Ruin tugged down my jeans and eased his hand right inside my panties. He made an approving sound, his breath spilling hot over my neck. "So wet for us. I love feeling how much you enjoy this. Nox is right— you're a *very* good girl."

Kai laughed as he squeezed my ass. "And a naughty

one. Both at the same time. Aren't we lucky to have her?"

"Oh, yes. The luckiest." Ruin pecked kisses along my shoulder and dipped his fingers right inside me.

I couldn't contain my cry. As I rocked with Ruin's pulsing fingers, I fumbled to yank Kai's pants down far enough to fully free him. "I think I'm the lucky one. And I'd be even luckier with you inside me."

Kai let out a stuttered breath thick with longing, but the next second he was turning me between them. "My friend didn't get that honor last time. You should have all of us every which way." He lifted his chin toward Ruin. "Lean against the tree so you don't strain yourself."

Ruin followed his instructions with an avid grin. As he propped himself against the oak so it could take most of his weight, I unzipped his jeans too. His cock sprang into my hand, and he let out a groan of his own as he shoved his pants and boxers down farther. Then he slid his hand around me to pat my ass.

"Every which way," he said with undisguised fervor. "Are you going to take both of us, Angelfish?"

Kai had stayed with us, stroking his fingers up and down my sides. Now, they briefly stilled. My heart stuttered with a jolt of giddy nerves. "I— Do we have everything we need?"

Kai pressed a kiss to my shoulder and the nape of my neck, slipping his hand between me and Ruin at the same time to tease across my sex. "I think we can make sure it's nothing but enjoyable for you with what we have." He tugged my pants farther down and trailed the slickness from my sex to my back entrance.

As Kai started to massage me there, Ruin rocked against me, provoking my clit with his straining cock. Kai paused just long enough to retrieve a foil packet and hand it to the other guy. Ruin chuckled as he ripped it open. "It is good having friends who are always prepared for the important things."

A giggle tumbled out of me. I helped roll the thin material over his length, giving him an extra pump of my fingers so he groaned again.

"I want you to feel every bit as good as I can possibly make you," I said, my voice gone low and husky.

I felt Kai's smirk against the corner of my jaw before he nipped my earlobe. "And we both want the same for you. Isn't it perfect how that works out?"

He hefted me up so I could sink onto Ruin's shaft. Ruin grasped my ass, spreading my cheeks wider as if to offer Kai even easier access. We stayed there, me simply enjoying the sensation of being filled and held, as Kai worked more of my natural lubrication over my other opening. Then he nudged his own cock against it.

As he eased into me bit by careful bit, a thin whine escaped me, but it was nothing but ecstatic. I wasn't sure I'd ever stop being amazed by the delight of two of my guys taking me at once. The heady sensations rippled through my whole body, setting me alight even when we were barely moving.

And then we did start moving. Ruin stayed braced

against the tree trunk and Kai leaned into us, and together they lifted me up and down, impaling me deeper on their cocks with each iteration. The rush of pleasure became a flood, all-consuming.

This was love too, wasn't it? Giving yourself over to the people you trusted most in the world. Honoring the joy you could create between your bodies because of that trust.

A soft, wordless song spilled over my lips and carried through the air. I shivered and quaked with the increasing pace, my breath quickening, but the melody only rising.

Kai thrust even faster and came with a groan and a tighter hug around my torso. "Fucking love you," he mumbled.

The sound of his release tipped me over the edge in turn. I clamped around Ruin, my head bowing as the final wave rolled over me and wrung me out to drift in the afterglow. Ruin kissed me hard on the mouth, his hips jerking as he followed me.

When we came to a stop, still clasped in our joint embrace, I couldn't tell if anything had changed in the marsh air. If any powers thrumming through the water had taken notice of our display or cared. But there was a new steadiness inside me.

I cared about so many people. I cared about getting to the truth and helping those harmed by it heal. And nothing the Gauntts did could stop me from pursuing that goal all the way to the end.

# nineteen

*Jett*

I'd saved the main Thrivewell building for last, for good reason. The other satellite companies in the county had security around them, but nothing on the same level as the Gauntts' home base. As I kept watch for the first several minutes from a shadowy alcove down the street, I started to feel more like a vigilante superhero than a rogue artist.

Well, maybe I was a little of both tonight. I'd certainly been taking to the air more than the average person did.

Two security officers were patrolling the outside of the building. At one point, the first stopped to talk to another guard just inside the lobby. I had no idea how many other officers might be staked out inside, but they weren't my concern.

I needed a chance to do my work on the outer walls without getting caught. And this wasn't a process I could rush if my magic was going to work right, especially when I was getting tired from the half a dozen spectacles I'd already designed tonight.

When I'd gotten a good sense of the security guards' rhythms, one of them pacing back and forth in front of the building while the other completed regular circuits of the full thing, I hustled farther down the street where I'd be out of view, crossed the road, and approached again by slinking through the dark patches between the glow of the streetlamps. I didn't walk right up to the Thrivewell building, of course. Instead, I darted around the side of the neighboring office building.

That one didn't have anywhere near the same kind of security. The squat concrete structure which only stood ten stories compared to Thrivewell's twenty housed a bunch of different companies on different floors, including an accounting firm and a recording studio, based on the sign out front. None of them were apparently inclined to put a big budget toward securing the building overnight, but then, unlike the Gauntts, they had no reason to anticipate an attack.

I gripped the handle and used a surge of my ghostly energy to shift the shape of the lock so it no longer held the door in place. As I eased the door open, the sound of footsteps made me freeze. I ducked down behind a large potted shrub in the side hall and watched as the sole security guard in this building ambled by, looking more interested in whatever he had playing on his phone than in his surroundings.

With a little luck, no one would ever realize the crime I was about to commit had taken advantage of his lax attitude. I had nothing against the guy. It had to be awfully boring walking around in dark halls for hours on end while shit-all happened.

Thankfully, I found a stairwell just a short distance down the hall. I hurried up the steps, less worried about noise now that I knew I'd left the security dude behind. The only time I paused was at the fourth floor, where the recording studio's vibrant red-and-yellow logo was emblazoned on a plaque next to the landing's door. I studied it for a second, committing the name to memory as I thought of the career aspirations Lily had talked about.

Wouldn't it be a punch in the Gauntts' teeth if she saw through that dream just one building over from where they'd tried to crush her?

I couldn't do anything more about that mission right now, though. I strode up the rest of the flights, cursing the lingering effects of my nerd host's lack of fitness as my breaths turned ragged, and pushed past the door on the top floor.

Now all I needed was a window on the side of the building facing Thrivewell. Or at least a wall. I could make do with whatever, but it was helpful to be able to see what the hell I was doing.

To my satisfaction, I found a room toward the back

of the building on the correct side with a spread of waist-height windows stretching the entire length of the space. I didn't need to reach Thrivewell in *exactly* the spot where my magic would take effect, only to make some kind of contact, and there'd be less light back there to expose my efforts.

Taking slow and even breaths to build up my focus, I marched over to the farthest end of the row of windows. There, I set my hands against the glass. Then I willed it and the concrete beneath it to stretch out like a diving board toward Thrivewell's glossy wall.

After my recent efforts, a prickle of exhaustion passed through my arms at the attempt. But the materials bent to my will, folding down and yawning across the ten or so feet between the buildings. To preserve energy, I only made the ramp a couple of feet wide. If I took an actual dive, it'd be my own clumsy fault.

The process was entirely silent, other than the wind that seeped through the now-open window pane and ruffled the papers on a few of the nearby desks. The patrolling guard walked by ten stories beneath me with a faint rasp of his shoes against the pavement. I peered down at him, waiting until the vague impression of his form in the darkness disappeared around the bend, and then crept out onto my enchanted ramp. Beat this, fairy godmothers.

To ensure my balance, I scooted along on my ass with my legs splayed and my knees gripping the edges of the ramp. It wasn't the most visually appealing display of coordination I'd ever put into the world, but I told myself that didn't matter when no one was supposed to see me anyway.

When I reached the far end, where I could brace my feet against Thrivewell's sleek siding, the plank was wobbling a little with my weight. I debated pulling more concrete along it to thicken it but decided it felt sturdy enough. I didn't have time or energy to waste. This was the keystone in my first real public show, the masterwork around which all the others were centered.

Leaning forward carefully, I rested my hands against the smooth surface just like I had with the window. But I didn't reshape the building in front of me. Instead, I closed my eyes and pictured the impressions I wanted to mark into the face of the structure.

Colors and forms and the lines of letters swept out from my imagination. I paused here and there to pay special attention to one detail or another, making sure every effect I created shared the same reflective quality. It wouldn't do if the curtains rose too soon and the Gauntts had a chance to cover up my show before the rest of the city got to see it.

Sweat trickled down my back and over my forehead. I didn't dare raise my hand to swipe it away. I just kept pushing the images in my mind into the surface in front of me, on and on, no matter how the mass of concrete and glass I was perched on bobbed with the rising of the wind.

A jab of fatigue shot through my mind. I shoved against it with one last burst of power, and then I sagged backward, dropping my hands to my sides to steady myself.

It was done. At least, as far as I could tell, I'd finished what I'd set out to do. I wouldn't know for sure how well it'd turned out for another few hours.

I scooted back to the other building looking just as dorky as I had on the way out, though considerably more relieved with each butt-length closer I got to solid ground. As soon as I'd scrambled through the opening, I turned to finish the last part of my task. With a yank of my supernatural voodoo, I pulled the glass and concrete back into place.

Okay, so maybe that window was now more of a parallelogram than a proper rectangle. And maybe the wall was slightly lumpier than it'd been before. Wiped-out artists did wiped-out work. If anything, I was shaking these office drones' lives up in some tiny way. They should thank me for the fresh perspective.

I snuck down through the stairwell and out the same door I'd entered through. When I reached Lily's car, several blocks away, she was still asleep in the backseat where I'd left her. A gun was tucked in her folded arms like a teddy bear.

She'd insisted that none of us should go into the city on our motorcycles, since the Gauntts' lackeys were probably keeping an especially close eye on our favorite type of vehicle. And after she, Kai, and Ruin had gotten back to the cottage to tell their story about the attack on the marked children and I'd declared that I had a mission of my own to see through, she'd insisted that I shouldn't go alone. That was okay with me. It was fitting that she'd be one of the first people, if not the very first, to witness the greatest work I'd made yet.

She only stirred briefly when I started the engine. I drove around to an underground parking lot where we could stay out of sight and tipped the driver's seat back as far as it would go. I needed to catch up on my sleep too. Before I closed my eyes, I set the alarm on my phone for just before dawn.

I woke up before the alarm at the rustle of Lily sitting up. "I'm sorry," she whispered when I glanced at her. "You can go back to sleep. I just needed to stretch a little."

I checked the time and shook my head. "No, I was going to need to be up soon anyway. We need to get into place to watch the sunrise. Then you can see what I made."

She clambered into the front passenger seat and watched me with open curiosity as I drove us back toward the center of the city. We walked the last few blocks, keeping our hoods up and heads low.

I'd picked out the perfect vantage point: a sixth-floor café in a shopping complex almost directly across from the Thrivewell building. It wasn't technically open yet, but I made quick work of the lock on the doors and led Lily over to the floor-to-ceiling windows at the front of the space.

It was still dark out, a faint glow just starting to touch the edges of the sky. Lily peered through the glass at the Thrivewell building. "What am I looking for?"

"Just wait," I said. "I made it so that it'll only show up when the sunlight hits it. We've got maybe another five minutes."

I tapped out a quick message to Kai telling him to alert whatever news contacts he'd picked up that there was something to see at the Thrivewell head office. I would let word about the other buildings I'd "painted" spread more organically. This one—this one needed to be blasted all over TVs and computer screens for the entire county to see.

The edges of the supernaturally painted shapes started to shimmer with the expanding light. Lily stepped closer to the glass, and I moved with her, tucking my arm around her waist. It still felt like some kind of miracle that I could simply be with her in every way I could possibly want, so easily. That I could offer something that would mean so much to her, even if it was hardly a romantic gift in the traditional sense.

Because the artwork I'd imprinted on the front of the Thrivewell building wasn't pretty by any stretch of the imagination. As the first news van rumbled into view on the street below us, the colors and lines came into clearer focus.

A quartet of monsters with the adult Gauntts' faces loomed over a crowd of children with sickly green skin. Thomas and Olivia dribbled toxic purple liquid over them. The beast that looked like Marie was wrenching one child's arm. He was wearing only an undershirt, and a blotch like the ones that marked so many other victims shone on his upper arm.

Words rippled around the image, framing it. *The Gauntts brought the poison. Check your children. See the marks they left.*

More vehicles were stopping outside the building. A yell carried faintly through the glass, too muted for me to make out the words. Lily pressed her hand over her mouth.

"It's horrible," she said. "And it's perfect. You pointed the finger right back at them and gave the parents and doctors the evidence to look for."

"They won't be able to prove that the marks came from the Gauntts or had anything to do with the kids getting sick," I admitted. "But all those parents *know* that they gave the Gauntts access to their kids at some point. I figured they could use a reminder."

"Yes," she said softly, and gave me a smile that was sad and grateful all at once. I wrapped my arms tighter around her and took one last look at my masterpiece. We needed to get going before the café workers came to prepare for the official opening.

The picture I'd painted wasn't the kind of subtle art that was usually my preference. It was so literal I'd normally have cringed. But right now, with what we were up against, it'd hit the exact note I was going for. It really was the most perfect piece I'd ever made.

And if I could create one piece of artwork that said exactly what I needed it to in every hue and stroke, who was to say I couldn't do that again in my usual style, sometime down the road. After all, I couldn't have asked for a better muse.

# twenty

*Lily*

When I woke up after a much-needed nap, the guys and Marisol were gathered around the little TV in the cottage's living room. Mid-day sunlight was streaming through the front windows. It'd have felt like a cozy little scene if not for the name "Gauntt" carrying from the speakers.

As I reached the couch, Nox grasped my hips and tugged me down onto his lap so I could join the three of them on the sofa. Ruin leaned forward in the armchair next to us and offered me a blueberry muffin. My stomach grumbled with the reminder that I hadn't eaten anything at all so far today. Despite the tightness in my gut, I took the muffin and dug in as I watched the news story play out.

"Repair crews have worked quickly to cover up the vandalism done to the Thrivewell buildings last night," the man on the TV was saying. "But images of the strange graffiti—if you can even call something so elaborate that—are circulating throughout social media. The Gauntt family has released a statement accusing their competitors and saying this is more corporate sabotage. And during all this, I'd have to say the children still fighting for their lives in hospitals throughout the county are the true victims here."

My throat constricted. I forced down the last bite of muffin. "No kidding," I muttered as the newscast moved to another story. "Is *anyone* actually investigating the Gauntts or considering that they could be lying?"

Kai rubbed his forehead. "The reporter mentioned that there've been some public petitions circulating, people calling for more transparency, whatever the fuck they think that means."

"The most important thing is the parents seeing that message, right?" Ruin said in his usual optimistic way. "Thinking that they made a mistake."

"If it actually bothers them to see their kids sick after what they already put them through," Marisol said with a grimness I didn't like. I reached over to squeeze her hand.

Nox took my other hand in his, stroking his thumb over my knuckles. "There's a lot of buzz around the images. We've got them talking even more than before.

We're getting there. Now we just need to decide how to hit them next."

The words had only just left his mouth when a mechanical groaning sound emanated from outside. We all sprang up. Heart thudding, I raced to the window to peer across the terrain.

My car's hood had lifted open. I didn't see anyone around it. It looked like it'd just popped up of its own accord. Frowning, I eased out the front door.

As I walked over to take a closer look, all four of the guys flanked me with Marisol trailing close behind. But there was no one around at all. Just us and Fred 2.0… whose hood was now swaying up and down like it was doing an imitation of a shark's chomping mouth.

Static crackled from the car radio and formed into a voice. The hood kept swaying along with the words, giving the ridiculous impression that it was Fred talking to us.

"Lily Strom. This is a message for Lily Strom. Bring her here or repeat this message to her."

"What the fuck?" Jett said. He stepped closer to the car and leapt backward when the hood snapped momentarily shut like it'd hoped to devour a body part or two.

The next words weren't anything I'd have expected my loyal vehicle to ever say to me: "Lily Strom, this is your last chance to negotiate the return to health for all those children. If you care about seeing them live, you'll meet with a representative of the Gauntt family in the field east of the Strom family home. He will come alone. So must you. If you arrive with aggression, your chance and the children will be forfeit."

The hood crashed down once more with a resounding clang. Ruin sputtered a laugh. He ambled over and tapped at the metal frame as if trying to wake Fred up again.

Marisol folded her arms over her chest. "That's some crazy magic."

"They found your phone and then your car," Nox said with a growl. "Those fuckers had better learn to back off." He smacked his fist into his palm and glanced at his friends. "We should tear right over there to that field and show them—"

I held up my hand, even though my heart was still pounding painfully fast. "No. They said I should come alone."

Nox stared at me. "You can't go along with what those assholes want. They'll be looking to destroy *you*."

"Maybe," I said, "but it'd be hard for them to arrange an ambush in that spot. There's nothing around but grass." I could see the field in my mind's eye—it'd been my view from the front porch for most of my childhood. "It sounds like they might *kill* all those kids right away if I don't at least try to talk to them. I'm not going to go along with any crap they ask, but hearing what they say might tell us where they're vulnerable, right?"

Kai grimaced. "She does have a point." He gave me a firm look. "If you see *any* sign that there's more than their one representative in the area, you'll want to take off immediately. And keep a grip on his blood so you can take him down before he can try anything on you, if he decides to."

Nox let out another growl and shifted his weight on his feet. "I don't like this. They don't get to call the shots."

"They are, though," I said. "To some extent, we can't stop them until we figure out how to save those kids."

"I know." Scowling, he nodded to the car. "But you're not going anywhere in that. Now that they're turning your ride into their very own ventriloquist dummy, I think we've got to put it on ice until the Gauntts are out of the picture. Kai, do you think you can scrounge up another car quick?"

Kai clapped his hands together. "I'm sure I can take care of both problems at once."

I waved Fred 2.0 a fond farewell, hoping it wouldn't be for too long, and Kai zoomed off. He returned just half an hour later in a modest sedan that I couldn't imagine anyone glancing twice at, which I guessed was the point.

"No one will miss this for the time we'll be keeping it," he said as he got out. "Jett, you want to give the license plate a little makeover just in case?"

While Jett went around to the back to make a few adjustments, Kai tossed me the key. I got in, and Nox dropped into the passenger seat next to me.

"What are you doing?" I demanded.

The Skullbreakers boss gave me a look so fierce it'd

have seared the flesh off my bones if it hadn't been mixed with protective devotion. "I'm not letting you really go out there on your own. You'll want to park far back from their guy anyway. I can keep out of sight. But this way, if you yell for help, there'll be someone to deliver it."

I couldn't bring myself to argue with him. I didn't want to face the Gauntts' representative and whatever else they might have in store for me alone. But I gave him a fierce look right back. "You need to make sure you're not seen and stay put unless it's *really* obvious that I'm in trouble that I can't take care of on my own. You know I can deal with a lot."

He huffed. "I do, Siren. I can keep my hands to myself. When I'm specifically asked to." A sly gleam lit in his dark eyes that set me on fire in all kinds of other ways.

"Fine," I said. "We'd better get going. They must have left some extra time in case I wasn't here to get the message right away, but I don't know how long they'll wait before they decide I'm not coming at all."

Jett walked around and pressed his hands to the windows one after another. "Adding a little tint so no one can see in," he told us. "Easier than having the boss squash down on the floor."

Nox grinned at him. "My ass thanks you."

I swatted him. "Once we get out by the field, you should stay low anyway, just to be safe."

In preparation, he pushed the passenger seat back as far as it would go while I drove. Then he stretched out his legs, which still reached almost all the way across the space.

"Is this how big you were in your original life?" I asked. "Or are you still filling out Mr. Grimes?"

Nox chuckled. "Worried I'll get too massive for you to handle? I think you'll do just fine, Siren."

I rolled my eyes, my lips twitching into a smile. "I'm only wondering."

He glanced down at himself. "I think this is about back to normal. It's hard to remember exactly after twenty-one years in limbo. It feels pretty right, anyway." He looked back at me. "Speaking of which—you know it's not right that the Gauntts are putting those kids' lives on your shoulders, right? *They're* the ones doing the killing. They're the ones who messed with them and marked them in the first place. They're just trying to get you to back down because of how hard you've been working to protect those kids from them."

I did know all of that, but hearing him say it so plainly released one or two of the many knots in my stomach. "I can't help thinking about how if I backed down, they might let the kids recover."

Nox shrugged. "And then they'd fuck up a whole bunch more kids because no one got in their way. You've seen how we work, Minnow. There's a lot of collateral damage in our chosen career. I know you're not used to that, but the way I see it, it's really just a reflection of how the whole world goes, just a little more in your face. There are always choices. Someone always loses. You just try to make sure it's mostly the people who deserve it, and that you make the choices that save as many of the people who matter as you can. But you have to realize you can never save everyone."

I swallowed hard. "Yeah." Then I didn't know what else to say. He was right. And the Gauntts *were* the ones forcing me to worry about saving anyone at all.

But all the same, if I saw an opening that'd let me save every one of those kids without losing even more, I'd take it.

Nox reached over and squeezed my knee. "That doesn't mean there's anything wrong with you wanting to protect everyone. That huge heart of yours is part of the reason I love you."

Those words still provoked a flutter through my chest. "Just part?" I teased.

He winked at me. "I do have a healthy appreciation for the rest of your body as well. And this brain that seems to be nearly as good at scheming as our know-it-all." He tapped the side of my head lightly.

The conversation hadn't changed anything in a concrete way, but the worst of my nerves had settled by the time we came into view of the field the Gauntts had directed us to. I spotted a figure standing in the middle of the grassy expanse, half a mile from the nearest building, which was my old house, standing on its lonesome in the distance. There was no one else around and nowhere for them to be hiding unless they'd shrunk to about six inches tall. Even if the Gauntts had staked out backup at the house, they wouldn't be able to reach me very quickly.

Nox sank low in his seat without prompting. I pulled onto the shoulder of the road at the edge of the field and parked. It was going to be a bit of a hike just for me to reach the messenger.

"If I need you, I'll shout really loud," I told Nox before I opened the door.

He saluted me. "And I'll run really fast."

I tramped across the field toward the waiting figure, a middle-aged man I'd never seen before. The familiar scent of the nearby marsh washed over me with the breeze. The Gauntts might have claimed part of the shoreline as their own, but this was my home turf. I wasn't going to let them intimidate me.

Remembering Kai's suggestion, I directed the hum of energy inside me at the Gauntts' man, getting a feel for the pulse of blood through his body. I could shove it all toward his heart in an instant if I needed to. I kept a close eye on his hands, watching for any attempt to reach for a weapon. He was holding a tablet, but that didn't mean he couldn't have a gun concealed.

I came to a stop about ten feet away from him. "I'm here. What did they want to say to me?"

The man didn't speak, simply tapped the tablet and held it up. The screen showed a video chat feed. Marie Gauntt peered at me from wherever she was conducting this virtual meeting. The new Nolan, the kid containing his old soul, came over to stand next to her chair.

"Miss Strom," she said in her usual cool voice. "I take it you're willing to consider a ceasefire."

I raised my chin. "I just want to hear what you have to say."

Marie gave a slight lift of her shoulders. "It's quite simple. You've seen how so many people are suffering because of your actions. You can end that all right now and have everything you ever wanted at the same time."

"And what exactly do you want from me for that to happen?"

Nolan piped up, his dry tone sounding odd in his newly youthful voice. "Give up your allies—this gang that's been causing havoc around the city. Come and work with us. We can set you up with whatever career you'd like, and you can keep it for as long as you want —just as we do. And all the animosity between us can end."

Every bone in my body balked at the suggestion of becoming like them in any way. I wanted to hear every detail they'd offer, though, in case we could use anything in the fight against them.

"What would you do to the Skullbreakers?" I asked.

"They seem to center their activities around you," Marie said. "I expect if you step aside, they'll be much easier to contain."

To kill, she meant. My jaw clenched. "And you're saying you'd make all those kids better again? They'd completely recover?"

"They were only ever ill because of your actions," Marie said. She was being very careful not to admit any of the Gauntts' involvement, I noticed. Probably worried I might be recording this conversation to use against her.

They could be doing the same with me. I crossed my arms. "I didn't do anything to the kids, and you know it. *You* made them sick to get back at me."

Nolan let out a huff. "See it however you like. Do you want to spare them or not? You know how far we can go and how much power we wield beyond anything you and your ruffians are capable of. You're never going to win. Why are you holding onto this grudge while so many children suffer by your hand?"

A prickle ran down my back. Did he really think that ending the supposed poisoning would end the suffering? What about all the other crap they'd put the kids through?

"Are you going to stop the rest of the stuff you're doing to kids like them?" I demanded. "You've been messing them up for longer than I've even been alive."

Marie tipped her head to one side, giving me a look so patronizing I wanted to punch her in the face. "I don't know what you're talking about. Any associations we've had with the people in those towns have solely been for drawing the necessary resources to keep our legacy going and satisfying what urges need addressing. The most vital energies come from youth, but we've never taken too much. We've never done any *harm*. We don't take things that far."

So that was why they targeted kids—because the energy the Gauntts could draw from their young bodies was the best for maintaining their magic? I guessed that made a sort of sense given that a lot of the family's magic went into keeping their spirits eternally alive from host to host.

Still, I had to snort in disbelief. Did she honestly buy her own story? I didn't know whether the energy they seemed to harvest from the kids hurt them any in the long run, but did she think somehow there were levels of molesting that were acceptable, just because they had some perversions to "address"?

Any amount was too far for the people they'd messed with. I'd witnessed the emotional harm done in my sister and in every other person I'd freed from the marks. If the Gauntts' repeated passage from adult bodies to juvenile ones had warped their proclivities toward "youth" in every area, then that was just one more sickening way their domination over this community had polluted it.

"Either you're lying or you're nowhere near as smart as you seem to think you are," I said. "I've seen the effects of your 'legacy' all over town. *I* felt it when you stole seven years of my life to cover up your dirty secret. And now you think I want to be a party to that sick behavior?"

Marie's face stiffened into a mask of disapproval. "We've made you a generous offer. You should think twice before throwing it back in our faces. Having observed you in action, we'd prefer to work with you to keep this all simpler. Having another ally who understands where we're coming from could benefit all of us. But if you insist, we'll have to enforce our authority the hard way."

The threat chilled me, but I couldn't see any way to get around it. I wasn't going to give the Gauntts control over my life, and I wasn't going to buy into their psychotic philosophy.

Nolan had said I was never going to win, but they wouldn't be making this offer in the first place if they weren't afraid that I could, would they? They were worried about how much *they* might lose if the battle continued. That meant even they believed that we had a chance of stopping them completely.

"Then make it hard," I said firmly. "Just know that you'll take the fall for every kid who dies under your spell. You have no idea how many cards we have left to play."

Both Nolan's and Marie's gazes hardened even more. "We'll see about that," Marie said tartly. "You've chosen your fate."

The video feed blinked off. The man tucked the tablet into his jacket and strode away without a word.

# twenty-one

*Lily*

My skin creeping with apprehension, I hurried back to the car. Nox didn't straighten up in his seat until I'd pulled the door closed. He took in my expression.

"They didn't dangle any bait you wanted to take?" he said.

I shook my head. "I mean, I didn't really think they would. But I didn't find out anything all that useful either. They were really cagey in what they actually admitted to, which isn't surprising. I did my best to persuade them that it'd be a bad idea if they make those kids even sicker, but I don't know if I was convincing enough."

Nox gave me one of his slow, broad smiles. "You can

be plenty convincing." He paused, still studying me. "Is something else wrong?"

I swiped my hand across my mouth. "I don't know. They were talking about coming down on us 'the hard way,' as if they've been going easy on us before. I don't know what they meant by that. But they might have been bluffing just like I kind of was."

"Probably," Nox muttered. "Sounds like those fuckers' MO."

I started the car and swerved around to head back toward the cottage, scanning the landscape around us as I went. I couldn't see any sign that we were being watched, and the Gauntts' messenger hadn't come anywhere near Fred. That didn't mean they couldn't have some scheme to find out where we were hiding out now. I bit my lip.

But Kai, being the brainiac he was, had considered that concern before I needed to voice it. Nox had just texted the other guys, and at the ping of the responding message, he motioned to me. "Our know-it-all gave me the address for a parking garage we should stop at in Lovell Rise. He's arranging for us to swap cars there. When we come out, anyone keeping an eye on us won't know we're in the new one."

I exhaled in relief. "Perfect."

The garage Kai had directed us to was at the bottom of a large shopping plaza—at least, large by Lovell Rise standards. Cars were coming and going pretty regularly on this Saturday afternoon. One of our few remaining new Skullbreakers recruits waved to us and handed us the key to our new car. We drove out and zoomed off toward the cottage with the weight of that immediate threat lifted.

The cottage had just come into sight up ahead when my new burner phone rang. Nox fished it out of my purse for me and held it up on speaker phone. I didn't recognize the number.

"Hello?" I said.

An urgent voice spilled from the speaker. "Hey—it's Lily, right? I—I'm not sure what to do. It seems like they're coming for me. I don't think I can stay here any longer."

It took me a moment to place the guy with an image of him hunched at the base of a tree near the Lovell Rise College parking lot. "Fergus? What happened?" I'd broken the Gauntts' mark on him weeks ago, and he'd helped us with our plan to strike out at Thrivewell through their victims' parents. He hadn't sounded this distraught the last time I'd spoken to him, but then, we hadn't talked at length. The last contact I'd had was when I'd texted all our unmarked allies my new number in case anything important came up.

"I'm not sure," he said in the same rushed tone. "I can just tell—it's not safe here. They figured out I was trying to screw them over, and now they're trying to destroy me. I had to leave campus... I don't know how long it'll take them to find me..."

I had the sense of him pacing, his breath already ragged from an extended flight. My chest constricted. "You mean the Gauntts. They've come after you?"

"Yeah. Yeah. I didn't want to bother you, but—"

"No, it's okay," I said quickly. It was my fault he was becoming a target all over again—I'd drawn him into this fight. "Look, we've got a place where you can hide out safely. Can you borrow a car they wouldn't be able to trace to you? Or get a cab with cash?"

Relief rang through his voice. "I should be able to manage. Thank you."

"It's no problem at all. This is where you'll want to go."

I rattled off directions to the cottage as I parked next to it. Fergus offered many more effusive thank yous and hung up. I hurried over to the building, my stomach knotting all over again.

How long would it take before the Gauntts went after the other victims who'd helped hit back at them? Were any of them safe? Now I was doubly glad we'd taken so many precautions to make sure our enemies couldn't find our current hideout. It could be a safe haven for all of them if we needed it to be. We'd make do.

"Hey," I said as I came into the living room where the other guys were sitting around the table. Marisol appeared in the doorway of the second bedroom. "We're going to have company. The Gauntts have gone after Fergus, so I told him to come here. We can give him one of the spare air mattresses. I should probably check in with the other college kids who've been working with us."

Jett frowned, getting up from the table. "What are those pricks doing to the guy?"

"I don't know," I said. "He didn't get into the details. But he was obviously really upset. I think—"

Before I could finish that thought, my phone rang again. I snatched it up, thinking maybe Fergus needed more urgent assistance, but this time it was Peyton on the other end.

"Lily," she said without preamble. "Did you hear from Fergus today?"

I paused where I'd gone to the closet to pull out the air mattress. "I did. Has he talked to you too? Have you heard from anyone else at the college? It sounds like the Gauntts are starting to crack down."

Peyton exhaled audibly. "Yeah, I think they are, but maybe not in the way he might have made it sound. He called me up an hour ago and was asking some kind of weird questions about you guys—if I knew where you were or what your plans were. Trying to make it sound like he just wanted to pitch in, but something about it... The more I think it over, the more I'm convinced he wasn't asking for himself."

A chill washed over me. "What do you mean?"

"I mean I think maybe the Gauntts have already gotten to him. And convinced him to throw the rest of us under the bus to save his skin or get some kind of benefit. I don't know him that well, but I wouldn't say he's super strong in the spine department."

"Shit." I had to agree with her assessment. I stared blankly at the closet door as her suggestion sank in. "I told him about the cottage—how to get here. I thought he was in trouble."

Peyton echoed my curse. "You'd better get out of there then. Find someplace else to hide out at least until we can be sure. I could be wrong. But—"

The growl of an engine cut through her voice. "Wait," I said, and hustled to the window.

Not one but three cars were approaching along the lane that led to the cottage. And it was way too soon for Fergus to have gotten here from Lovell Rise. My stomach sank. "I think we're already out of luck. *Someone*'s coming, and it's not Fergus. I've got to go."

"What's going on?" Ruin asked, breezing over to the window as I hung up.

I motioned to the cars. "Peyton thinks Fergus caved to threats from the Gauntts and double-crossed us. It looks like she was right."

"He's a fucking nitwit," Nox growled, and started waving to the room around us. "We don't have time to make a run for it. It's better if we have walls around us for a standoff. Grab your guns and anything else you can use as a weapon. We've beaten them down before; we'll do it again."

In the time it took for the cars to reach the cottage, we'd pillaged the building for all other possible weapons. I held a butcher knife in one hand. Marisol had grabbed a heavy bronze bust from the dresser in her bedroom that she could use as a bludgeon, clutching her little gun as well. The guys each had their pistols in one hand and the other free for inflicting their powers, but they'd gathered a heap of knives, frying pans, glass bottles, and even the ceramic logs from the decorative fireplace near the door in case they needed to switch weapons.

We watched from the windows as men burst out of the cars. Unlike our last stand-off, they didn't make any attempt at caution. I guessed it must have been pretty obvious that we'd see them coming. They opened fire from the moment they were clear of their cars.

The front windows shattered in on us. We'd all ducked down at the boom of gunfire. I yanked my arms over my head to shield my face and tugged at Marisol to do the same.

As the shards rained down on us, more bullets whizzed by over our heads. They weren't giving us the chance to bob up and get a single shot in ourselves.

My awareness raced over to the nearby lake, the hum from within my chest reverberating through the water's currents. With a heave of concentration, I brought an epic wave soaring up over the lawn and crashing down on where I thought our attackers were still standing.

The water pounded against the grass—and several bodies thumped onto their backsides with the liquid pummeling. The gunfire briefly cut off. The Skullbreakers sprang up and pulled their own triggers, sending a hail of bullets to follow the deluge of lake water.

Unfortunately, most of our attackers had stayed close to the cars, and even with those who didn't have shelter, it was hard to land an effective shot from a distance on someone sprawled on the ground. The men behind the cars started shooting over the trunks and around the windshields, and for several seconds there were so many bullets flying back and forth it was a wonder the air itself didn't crack up.

Of course, when you're firing a million bullets a minute, you tend to run out pretty quick. It was only a matter of time before the clicks of empty chambers carried from all around me, both on our side and our attackers', after multiple re-loadings. The guys tossed their guns aside and snatched up whatever they could set their hands on from the heap.

Our attackers had other plans for us. One of them hurled something that looked like a pop can through the smashed window, and it thudded to the ground in the middle of the living room, streaming smoke. In an instant, we were coughing, my eyes burning at the noxious gas billowing from the canister.

We had no choice but to flee. As we burst out onto the lawn in front of the cottage, I summoned another wave from the lake with a roar of rushing water. The Gauntts' people—it looked like a mix of Skeleton Corps guys and a few more official bodyguards, based on the suits three of them were sporting—scattered in an attempt to dodge. All the same, I managed to smack several of them onto their asses again. A couple I even swept with the flow of the water all the way back into the lake, where they splashed around like half-beached whales.

Ruin swung a cast iron pan at one guy's head, braining him with a cracking sound like his skull was an egg. That was one way to make an omelet.

"Skewer your colleagues!" Kai ordered another with a whack of his fist, and shoved a meat thermometer into the guy's hand. The Skeleton Corps dude spun around and plunged the makeshift weapon into the chest of the man next to him. The thermometer made a whining sound as if to indicate its target needed more cooking.

Another car roared toward us, and I tensed, catching my balance on the sopping and therefore slippery ground. But I recognized this car—it was Peyton's. From the way she tore down the lane, she'd raced straight here as fast as the vehicle could go after I'd hung up.

Some of our attackers spun around to respond to the new threat. And she proved to be a threat indeed. Peyton parked on the other side of our enemy's cars with her window already rolled down and immediately started hurling objects at the nearest men. A full water bottle clocked one guy across the temple. Her ice scraper battered another square in the face.

A third guy lunged at her door, and she whipped out a little cannister of pepper spray. At its hiss, he started to do an impromptu jig of pain, clawing at his eyes.

One man grabbed something out of his trunk and leapt toward us, a fresh gun in his hands. Marisol yelped in warning and jerked her gun hand up, and my pulse lurched.

Maybe she could have gotten off the shot. Maybe it'd have made more sense to let her go for it. But I knew what it was like to carry lives ended on your conscience, even of people you had no reason to mourn. I didn't want that for my little sister.

I was supposed to be protecting her.

I flung my powers at our attacker first, pummeling his heart with his own blood like fists converging on every chamber through the arteries and veins. The guy stiffened and keeled backward, hitting the ground before Marisol had quite gotten her finger around the trigger.

I glanced at her to check her reaction, and in my distraction, one of the other men snatched the gun from his colleague's hand. As my head jerked back toward him, he fired.

Kai's body wrenched to one side. The blare of pain echoed faintly but unmistakably through our supernatural connection. He crumpled, his hand pressing against his chest.

A cry burst from my throat. The rest of my guys gaped at Kai for a split-second, horror flashing across their faces. Then their expressions flashed to pure, scorching rage that radiated into me alongside my own inner turmoil.

True chaos erupted across the lawn. Nox barreled forward, sending out punches of supernatural energy in every direction he could reach. Ruin gave a vibrant battle cry of his own and whirled around our attackers with his frying pan thudding into flesh and bone on one side and his fist sending the men into fits of terror or dismay everywhere he could reach. Jett raced to Kai, pressing his hand to his friend's shirt just below the wound, his face tensing with concentration.

It should have been enough. We'd already almost won. But in the bedlam around me, I didn't see the dickwad charging straight at Marisol until it was almost too late.

He had a knife in his hand. Possibly he'd planned on taking her hostage rather than killing her, not that I'd have been super pleased with that outcome either. As he grasped her wrist and wrenched her arm behind her back, I flung my powers at him.

His heart burst. His body seized as a metallic flavor filled the back of my throat. The knife fell from his hand, glancing off my sister's shoulder with a nick of blood—but his fingers momentarily clenched around her wrist as he fell. There was a snap of breaking bone, and she sobbed, groping at her arm that now hung limply at her side.

A surge of my own fury loomed inside me. I dashed to her and spun around, ready to smash anyone who was still standing to smithereens.

There was no one. Just us and a whole lot of corpses —and Kai slumped against the side of the cottage, looking like he might soon add to that number.

# twenty-two

*Kai*

I'd never felt pain like this. Or maybe I had, in the fleeting seconds when the bullets had hit me just before I'd died the first time. That memory had gotten hazy over the years in limbo. I wasn't sure how much I'd absorbed the sensation before I'd kicked the bucket anyway.

This agony I was fully aware of. It blazed through all my other senses, making it hard to even focus my eyes or process the shouts and bangs around me. Every thump of my pulse sent the pain spiking harder through my chest.

At least the fact that my heart was still pumping meant the bullet hadn't hit me there. I hurt because I was still alive. See, I could look on the bright side just like Ruin did.

Through the throbbing, I registered someone's hand on me. A gruff voice giving curt instructions. That was definitely Jett, even if I couldn't focus enough to distinguish the words. Something was shifting, stretching, melding against my ribs... The pain dulled just slightly. I blinked and managed to fix my attention on his face.

"I don't know how long that'll hold," he was saying, his normally sullen voice laced with unusual urgency. "I don't know how much got damaged in there. We should bring the guy who patched Ruin up."

I attempted to agree and only managed to let out a vague "mmm" sound. When I inhaled, my lungs burned but held the air. Had they been leaking before? I couldn't remember how much I'd been breathing during the worst of the agony. It was the sort of thing I usually took for granted.

Couldn't take anything for granted anymore. Fucking corporate pricks with their attack dog gangs and crazy voodoo.

I coughed with a bit of a sputter and managed to croak, "My phone. Dr. Morton. Tell him... we'll pay double last time."

Jett had no idea how much I'd paid him the first time, so he took that in stride. Our funds weren't in the best state since we'd been spending more time waging war than conducting business after we'd made our grand return, but we could manage it.

The sounds all around me had fallen away. I squinted past Jett and noted that the only people still standing were the ones I wanted to see—well, and the college girl who had the crush on Ruin's host, but as far as I could tell, she was on our side at the moment.

They'd all turned to stare at me. Jett rattled off what I'd said about the doctor—well, he was a vet. That was a kind of doctor. He knew how all the parts were supposed to be attached, which was what mattered. Nox stepped toward me and then hesitated.

"I don't know if we should move him." He peered at me. "Do *you* think we can move you?"

I should know that, shouldn't I? I was the know-it-all. I opened my mouth and closed it again, tasting the dryness that'd crept through it. The image of Ruin in the back seat of Lily's car, blood spurting from a wound we'd thought we'd closed, flashed through my mind.

But it wasn't good for us to stay here, either. The Gauntts knew our location now.

Of course, it looked like all their remaining goons were now lying dead on the lawn. Could we hope we'd finally run them dry?

"I'm not sure," I said finally.

Nox's mouth twisted. He might not ever have heard me say those words before. Possibly they disturbed him. They kind of disturbed me.

"I'll bring him here," he said abruptly. "Let him decide. The Gauntts have never sent two onslaughts right after each other—and if anyone else *does* show up, the rest of you know how to deal with them."

Jett handed him my phone with the contact. Nox jammed it to his ear as he hustled to the car, and the artist moved to Marisol. For the first time, I noticed that her arm was hanging limply, her wrist twisted to the side in a way that didn't look right at all. Lily was hugging her gently as her sister blinked back tears.

I wasn't the only one those pricks had injured. The urge shot through me to push to my feet and apply whatever medical knowledge I'd accumulated across my life so far to the problem, but just a tiny shift of my body sent the pain inside me from aching to stabbing again. I gritted my teeth and resigned myself to staying where I was, leaning against the side of the building.

Peyton raked her fingers into her hair and stared at the scene around us. "Oh my God. Fucking hell. We can't leave this place like this! How in the world could I ever explain— If they find out I let a shoot-out go down on their property—"

She sounded like she was starting to hyperventilate. Ruin shot a concerned look at Marisol but seemed to think his skills could be put to better use with the other girl. He gave her a light pat on her arm which calmed her down in an instant.

"We'll clean things up," he promised with a smile. "I'll help you."

"We'll need a truck," I rasped. "Get all the bodies together and then… hose the rest of the grass down. Call Lamont. He'll get something together."

I wasn't sure my instructions had been coherent, but Nox paused where he'd been about to get into the car.

"You shouldn't be hauling corpses in your condition," he told Ruin. "Or we'll need the doc for you too. We're lucky you didn't already bust your guts out all over again in that fight." He let out a growl of frustration before stalking over to our man of sunshine and shoving my phone with the vet's address into his hand. "*You* go get the doc. Then you can mostly be sitting, and you can make sure he understands the importance of getting here quickly."

Ruin nodded with a swift bob of his head and jumped into the car. As he tore off, Nox pulled out his own phone, presumably to call Lamont. He grumbled a few orders into the phone and then got to work dragging bodies off to the side of the property near Peyton's car. The college girl shuddered but moved to help him, her lips curling with disdain.

Jett was murmuring to Marisol in a low voice as he worked over her arm with obvious care. Her jaw was still clenched with pain, but her expression looked more hopeful now. We'd have the good doctor take a look at her too after he got here.

Maybe only her. I couldn't tell whether I'd actually make it that long. The pain kept zapping through me at odd intervals alongside my breaths and any twitch of my body. There were plenty of vital organs that might have been scraped, nicked, or outright punctured.

If I went now, at least I'd protected everyone who mattered in the meantime. I'd showered Lily with all the adoration I was capable of. I'd leave her knowing just how much she'd meant to me. That was the best I could ask for.

And hey, maybe I'd get to return all over again. I'd be a little more thoughtful in picking my next host, that was for sure. No pushy family members or asshole friends.

I swallowed and coughed. I hadn't realized she'd gone inside, but Lily emerged from the cottage a moment later and carried a glass of water over to me. She held the glass to my lips for me.

The cool liquid slid down my throat like some kind of paradise. I knew the bullet had hit significantly higher than my stomach, so at least I didn't have to worry about whether quenching my thirst was a fatal move.

Lily let me drink my fill. Then she set the glass down and touched my cheek. For a few seconds, she just gazed at me. Her face was etched with tension.

"I'm sorry," she said abruptly.

I managed to raise an eyebrow. My voice came steadier now. "Pardon? I'm pretty sure *you* weren't the one who shot me. Difficult to accomplish when you're not even holding a gun."

Lily gave me a baleful look and glanced over her shoulder at her sister. When she met my eyes again, hers were even stormier.

"I got distracted," she said. "If I'd been paying enough attention to everything, I'd have seen that guy in time. I was trying to keep Marisol safe. Maybe I went a little overboard. I just don't want... I don't want her to have to deal with even more crap than she's already had heaped on her. But I don't want to see you get hurt because I freaked out either."

The anguish in her voice made my heart ache in a very different way. I leaned my face into her touch. "You didn't bring the danger into our lives—or your sister's life—any more than you called it into your own." I halted to catch my strained breath before going on, stating what to me was utterly obvious. "This is all on the Gauntts. And you can't protect her from everything, you know. There'll be times when you can't be there. It's better if she learns how to defend herself, isn't it?"

Lily grimaced. "Just because I was okay with Nox teaching her *how* to shoot doesn't mean I want her to have to put those lessons to use."

"You might not get the choice," I had to point out with as much gentleness as I could offer. "That won't be your fault either. I don't think she's going to blame you."

"No." Lily let out a laugh that sounded almost startled. "She might even blame me for interfering. But she's only sixteen."

I couldn't quite shrug. "We were already building up the Skullbreakers when *we* were sixteen. What do they say—age is nothing but a number."

Lily narrowed her eyes at me again, but she didn't argue. She sank down on the grass next to me and swiped her hand over her face. "We're going to have to go on the run again—as soon as we can safely move you. I don't know what to do next. How are we going to beat them? The longer this fight goes on, the worse it gets."

"We're running out of options," I agreed. "And they've upped the stakes. But we still… we have a chance. We can defeat them. We hit them back one last time with everything we have, do whatever it takes…"

I just couldn't see how. My thoughts wouldn't arrange themselves into a coherent strategy. Too much pain was prickling through them, nudging them in odd directions instead of their usual orderly flow.

The Gauntts' minions hadn't just taken me physically out of the picture. They'd messed with my ability to contribute my brains to our operations as well.

A rare flicker of panic shot through me, but I clamped down on it and turned all my focus on the woman next to me. The sweet yet fierce woman who'd stayed strong through so much.

"You'll figure it out," I told her. "You're smart, and you've got something even more important than that."

She cocked her head. "Which is what?"

"You understand. You know what the Gauntts' victims have been through, what it's like to have your life controlled by outside forces. You know how to find the strength to rise up and fight against someone who's so much bigger than you." I coughed but managed to regain my voice. "We have an army of people out there. We just need to figure out the most effective way and time for them to strike… we have to make them totally committed… You can do that."

Her head drooped. "I don't know. You're the one

who can always see how to nudge people in the right directions, how to use all the information you have as leverage."

"This isn't about leverage," I told her. "It's about... connection. You've got this. I don't know if I'm going to be alive to see it, but I'm absolutely certain you'll pull it off."

I couldn't tell if those words were enough, but Lily tipped her head in acknowledgment. She squeezed my hand, searching my face as if I might still have the answers to our predicament there even if I couldn't find them myself. "Thank you," she said.

When she got up to check on her sister, I watched her walk away, hoping against hope that I'd given her all the push she needed to do what I couldn't.

# twenty-three

*Lily*

"How does it feel?" I asked Marisol, studying her arm.

She held it gingerly in the makeshift cast Jett had conjured for her using dirt he'd scooped off the ground. "I think it's okay. Jett said it felt like only one of the bigger bones was fractured, so he sealed that up. It doesn't hurt badly anymore, just kind of aches, so I think he must have been right. If we need to, we can crack the cast open so the doctor can take a look."

I wasn't sure the doctor we were relying on had enough experience with human bone structure to identify any more subtle problems, but I knew how adept Jett had become at using his powers. If she wasn't in major pain, we could wait until I could safely bring her to a proper hospital.

She was taking this whole situation in stride so easily. Somehow that made me feel almost as bad as when I'd heard the bone crack. She shouldn't have needed to live a life where facing off against gangsters and having her arm fractured was a normal occurrence.

But like Kai had said, it hadn't been my choice. The Gauntts were forcing us into this situation, and blaming myself wasn't going to fix anything.

The other things he'd said were still running through my mind. I understood what it was like to have my life torn apart by the Gauntts better than any of the Skullbreakers did. I knew how it felt to lose time and memories you should have had, even if it wasn't quite the same as what the other victims had experienced. I'd gone through the same frustration of having someone else calling the shots, taking over control.

We needed to rally our allies and end this war as soon as possible, before the Gauntts destroyed even more. Before they decided I couldn't make good on my threat and murdered all those kids as their psychotic version of punishment for my disobedience. And maybe there *wasn't* anyone better to figure out how to stop them than me.

I'd let the guys take the lead so often in this conflict, figuring it was their world more than mine. I hadn't minded serving mainly as backup. But the conflict with the Gauntts actually belonged to me more than them. It was my life and my sister's that family of asswipes had purposefully ruined. I didn't think they'd even known about the murders of the Skullbreakers—that'd just been the Skeleton Corps handling their own sorts of business.

And it might not be a matter of figuring out the right plan, only of finally stepping up and saying what we needed to say to carry out the most obvious one.

Nox was still busy hauling bodies into the growing corpse mountain he was building with Peyton, and Kai had closed his eyes while he rested. Ruin had taken his phone anyway. I went over to Jett, who was temporarily unoccupied as he recovered from the energy he'd expended with his attempts at healing.

"You've got Parker's phone number, don't you?" I asked.

He studied me as he pulled out his phone. "I do. Why?"

"I don't think we can let this go on any longer. And if we're going to tackle the Gauntts, we need to take away their soldiers first. I'll just have to see if I can talk our guys on the inside into taking that final step."

Jett nodded and brought up the number to show me. He didn't argue or suggest that he or one of the others should handle it instead. I still had an anxious twinge in my gut, but his lack of concern settled my nerves a little.

I tapped in the number on my own phone and raised it to my ear. I wasn't sure I'd get an answer, since

Parker might be in dangerous company, but he picked up on the second ring. "Hello?"

"Hey," I said. "It's Lily. From—you know."

Before I could go on, he groaned. "I'm so sorry—I only just heard about the guys that got sent after you. It was people I'm not very connected with. Is everyone okay?"

I wasn't surprised that he wouldn't know everything immediately. He worked under one of the Skeleton Corps's head guys, but they segmented their operations without a ton of communication between the different squads to make it harder for anyone to damage them. It was kind of a relief hearing Parker sound so concerned about us.

But then, he'd already been rebelling against his bosses when he'd first come to the Skullbreakers. Knowing what his bosses were supporting had only strengthened his resolve.

Would it be enough for him to strike against them in a much more overt way?

I glanced toward Kai, debating how to answer Parker's question, and just then our new car pulled up with Ruin behind the wheel. He ushered out the man who'd stitched him up before. Another waft of relief swept through me.

"They hit us pretty hard, but we all made it through," I said, praying silently that my statement remained true. "The Gauntts have made even more threats, though. I don't think we have much time left unless we want to see kids dying all across the city—and it's getting almost impossible for us to stay out of their reach. We need to pull out all the stops to take them down first."

Parker's voice turned more cautious. "What did you have in mind?"

I sucked in a breath. "You and your friends are our secret weapon. The Gauntts have mostly been able to threaten us and keep us on the run with all the Skeleton Corps guys they keep sending after us. I think we have to topple the Corps leadership completely, end the gang's ties to the Gauntts, and then we can go right at them. Maybe we can even convince some of the other members lower down the ladder to join in the revolt."

There was a moment of silence and a rustle of fabric as Parker shifted his position. "I don't know... You haven't had to work with these guys. If we make one wrong move..."

I gathered my own resolve. "Then what? They'll hit you back? What could really be worse than having them make you do the dirty work of the family that messed you up for all these years? Don't you want to start living your *own* life finally?"

"Of course I do," he said. "I just... It's not that simple."

"I know it isn't." I closed my eyes, gathering my thoughts. "Look—the Gauntts had me shut away in a psych ward for seven years. I lost a third of my childhood—completely gone. They took away your sense of security and your ability to make decisions for your own life. They've done it to hundreds of other people. And that means we're not alone. We're in this together. There are a hell of a lot more of us than them. We don't have to let them terrorize us into being victims all over again. We can take back the control they stole from us."

I hadn't been sure exactly what I'd say until the words spilled out, but they felt perfectly right. They resonated through my chest and over my tongue, and something about them must have hit Parker in just the right way too.

He sighed. "I don't want those kids getting even more hurt. I don't want to keep being bossed around by people who'd support those sickos. If you're in this with us—"

"We are," I said, and a lightbulb lit in my head. "And *you* get to take control right now. You call the shots. Figure out with the other guys when the best time to strike would be, tell us when and where, and we'll race right over to back you up. We know you want to win this war just as much as we do. We'll put our lives in your hands."

A note of awe came into Parker's voice. "Okay. All right. I think we can pull together something pretty quick. With everything that's going on, I can probably plant the idea with the bosses that they need to have a meeting today. I'll be in touch soon."

He hung up, and I hurried over to see what the doctor—animal or otherwise—had to say about Kai's current state of being.

The man was crouched down across from Kai,

who'd opened his eyes and was nodding in response to something the doctor had said. His eyes looked bleary, but he was at least conscious enough to carry on some kind of conversation. My heart thudded faster as the doctor peeled back Kai's shirt to examine the wound Jett had sealed.

He tutted to himself and shook his head. "I don't know what strange voodoo you all can work. Never seen anything like this." He pulled out a stethoscope, which he pressed to Kai's chest and then his back, instructing him to breathe deeply. Then he tutted some more, as if he thought he could heal wounds with his disapproval.

"There doesn't appear to be anything urgently wrong, but he needs his fluids replenished and plenty of rest. And it'd be good to keep him monitored somewhere with proper equipment in case he takes a turn for the worse. If I could give him an X-ray, that'd cover even more bases."

"Well, we need to get out of this place anyway," Nox said, and lifted his head. A small delivery truck was just rumbling toward us along the lane. "And there's our clean-up crew. Perfect."

It seemed like a little bit of an overstatement to call the one recruit who was driving the truck a "crew," but he did dive right in with Nox, Jett, and Peyton carting the bodies from their heap on the grass into a new heap in the back of the truck. The doctor looked the other way and started tutting more quietly. If he regularly took gangsters as clients, I supposed he'd seen plenty of bodies he couldn't stitch back together in his time.

I grabbed the cottage's hose and washed the blood down to the lake, sending silent apologies through my humming energies for adding to the violence it'd been roped into. I didn't know what we were going to do about the smashed windows on the cottage, but that problem seemed much farther off than the others staring us down.

As the last corpse thumped into the truck, my phone's ringtone chimed. It was Parker. I whipped the phone to my ear. "Hey. Any news?"

"Yeah," he said, a little breathless but with undisguised eagerness. "We've set things in motion. There's a meeting happening, and we'll all be there—if we move on the inside and you guys charge in from the outside at the same time, I think we can topple them. There aren't many people left for guards. Just be at the Castle Top Bakery at five o'clock. Wait until the icing hits the window."

"We can do that," I said, wondering what to make of his last strange instruction, but he dropped the call before I could clarify.

Nox was watching me from where he was standing by the truck. "What's going on?" he asked.

"We're going to take down the rest of the Skeleton Corps bosses," I announced, "and then we're going to go straight at the Gauntts."

In a hasty back and forth, I explained what I'd told Parker and the instructions he'd given us. Nox rocked back on his heels as he took it in.

Ruin was bobbing on his feet with typical enthusiasm. "We're going to go crush them, right?"

"We can't leave them hanging," I said. "I told them we were coming."

Nox rubbed his jaw. "Are you sure we can trust them, Minnow?"

That was the big question, wasn't it? But I already knew the answer. I wouldn't have reached out to Parker if I hadn't.

I nodded. "He came to us from the start. He put his life in our hands, going against his bosses back then, trusting *us* that we'd do the right thing and give him his memories back. That we wouldn't backstab him. He and the other guys he brought to us know how awful the Gauntts are. We've got to stand with them now. It's our best chance of breaking the Gauntts' hold and weakening them enough to stop them for good."

"All right then," Nox said, so easily my heart swelled with love. He really meant it when he called me one of the Skullbreakers—he trusted *my* word that much.

He motioned to the recruit. "The doctor and Kai will ride with you. Drop them off where he tells you, ditch the truck where we discussed, and meet up with us at this bakery." He turned to Peyton. "I'm guessing our college friends won't be up for much of a fight, if we can even trust *them* now."

She hugged herself. "I came to help because I set you up here, but I'm not rushing into another gang battle, thank you. I don't know where the others are at, but I wouldn't be surprised if the Gauntts have put pressure on more than just Fergus."

"We appreciate that you came out here at all," I felt the need to say.

She caught my eye and tipped her head in what felt like the first really respectful acknowledgment she'd given me since all the insanity had started. Maybe it was even friendly.

"That's fine," Nox said, and pointed to Marisol. "Can you bring the kid with you just for—"

"Hold on." My sister stepped forward, interrupting him. "I'm not just a kid, and I don't want to be left behind. *I* can fight."

My stomach lurched. "Mare—"

She shook her head and met my gaze. "I've still got my good arm. I can still shoot a gun. It's my fight too— maybe more than any of yours."

Every particle in my body clanged with the desire to refuse her, to force her to stay away. But I didn't know if I even could. And should I?

The Skullbreakers had wanted to protect me every way they could, but I'd insisted on fighting alongside them for the exact same reasons Marisol had said. Because I could, and it was my battle too.

I'd tried to protect her from so much. I'd stood in her way when she'd wanted to go public with her story of abuse, I'd intervened when she might have shot that guy—and she'd gotten hurt anyway.

I couldn't defend her from every possible threat, and I did have to let her grow up sometime. She'd already had to grow up faster than any sixteen-year-old should in the worse sorts of ways. Didn't she deserve to reclaim more control over her life too?

I wavered and swallowed hard. "Okay. You can come with us. But you're injured and you don't have powers, so you stay at the back where we can give you a little extra protection, all right?"

She grinned at me like I'd approved an epic sweet sixteen bash. "Deal."

"Then we're set," Nox declared. "Everyone move out! Let's take these fuckers so far down they'll find themselves having dinner with the Devil himself."

# twenty-four

*Lily*

I was going to guess that at least one member of the Skeleton Corps leadership had a sweet tooth, given their habit of holding meetings in places like ice cream parlors and bakeries. Castle Top looked like a pretty tasty venue, with a castle-shaped chocolate cake on its sign and fanciful pastries etched on the front window. Definitely not a gangster vibe.

A CLOSED sign hung on the door, and the window itself was dim. It had a pinkish tint that made it doubly reflective, showing more of the street outside than what was going on within. I just hoped we'd be able to identify Parker's signal when he gave it.

We were poised in our car just a couple of buildings down the street on the opposite side, all of our gazes trained on the broad pane of glass. Tension coiled through my chest, vibrating with the hum of my supernatural energy. My thoughts kept tripping back to images from our standoff at the cottage—Kai crumpling, Marisol's arm cracking.

Was Kai definitely secure wherever the doctor had taken him to give him more thorough treatment? I guessed he was safer than he'd have been here, anyway.

My sister shifted in her seat in the back where she was poised between Ruin and Jett. She had the gun Nox had given her in her hand, ready to go, like they did. Glancing at her in the rearview mirror, I felt my stomach twist.

This time, I wouldn't leap in when she was about to defend herself. I didn't know what worse outcomes I might fail to prevent if I tried to save her even from the discomforts she was willing to face. But that didn't mean I liked being in this position.

Nox stared through the windshield with an air like the calm before the storm, silently ominous. "They'd better not screw us over like the whole Skeleton Corps did last time."

"We know *why* the bosses double-crossed us," I reminded him. "They found out we were after the Gauntts, and they didn't want to lose their corporate backing. They even double-crossed one of the other bosses. These guys haven't got any reason to."

"Other than not wanting to risk dying," Jett put in.

"Pretty sure they're risking that just by being part of a gang in the first place," Marisol said with typical teenage snarkiness. I did appreciate hearing her show her spirit—and anyway, she had a point.

"We mow them all down, right?" Ruin said, rubbing his hands together. "All the bosses. Can't trust any of them after last time."

I nodded. "They're the ones who made the deal with the Gauntts—the ones who take their orders. With the bosses gone, maybe the Skeleton Corps will fall apart, or maybe Parker and his friends will step up and change their direction... Maybe the Gauntts will be able to find new leadership to work with them again, but not fast. It's going to be chaos for at least a little while."

A savage smile crossed Nox's face. "And while that's happening, we cut them off at the knees—and then slice and dice them into as many pieces as we feel like."

Jett grunted. "Let's not get ahead of ourselves. We haven't even gone at the Skeleton Corps yet."

A crash sounded from inside the bakery, loud enough that it filtered through the windows. We all stiffened in our seats. My hand shot to the door handle.

Then, with a creamy squelch, a blob of icing as big as a fist smacked into the window just beneath the etching of a churro, making it look like the balls on a pastry dick.

"That's our cue," I shouted, shoving open the door.

We hurtled across the street as more thumps and bangs emanated from inside the bakery. Nox slammed right into the locked door. An electric crackle vibrated through the frame as he smashed the lock open with a combination of physical and magical strength, both of which he had no shortage of.

We charged inside, skidding on the goopy mixture of icing and mashed dough that coated the floor. Our three allies were guarding the back of the building as promised, preventing the three remaining Skeleton Corps leaders and their handful of lackeys from leaving. A couple of those lackeys and one of the bosses already lay face down on the floor. From the looks of them, with bits of cake and pastry splattered all over them, you'd have thought they'd died by over-gorging on desserts if it weren't for the pools of blood spreading into the sugary mess.

The other Skeleton Corps members had thrown themselves behind the large display case that stretched the length of the room. Most of the cakes, tarts, and other sweet delicacies behind the glass had been the other casualties of the battle so far. The display window had been shattered and several confections blasted apart as if someone with a grudge against gluten had stormed through.

The final two bosses and their lackeys had been scuttling toward the front door in the hopes of escaping, crouched down below the level of the display. Glass shards and shiny sprinkles dappled their hair as if it were post-modern cupcake frosting.

Our arrival cut off their escape route, and they didn't take very kindly to the affront. I'd barely had a chance to suck in a breath of the sugary air before they were raising their guns in the hopes of blasting us away.

The energy inside me instinctively reached for the most liquid objects in the room. Pies full of jellied filling that'd escaped the initial massacre flipped off their stands and smacked into faces, throwing off the men's aim—and leaving their faces drenched in a gelatinous mess. As they swiped at their faces to clear their eyes, we closed in on them.

With a surge of energy, Nox punched the cash register next to the display case and sent it flinging into the nearest dude's head. Ruin purposefully slid on his feet across the slick floor toward our allies, spraying bullets as he went. A few more pastries bit the dust. The Skeleton Corps dudes sank even lower in their dwindling shelter.

"Truce!" one of the bosses yelled. "Ceasefire! We don't have to do things like this."

"Oh, yeah?" Nox snarled. "How do you suggest we do them, then?"

"We came to an agreement once. We could join forces again."

The Skullbreakers leader snorted. "The only thing you joined forces in was trying to send us to an early grave all over again. We know who's holding your leashes. We don't make deals with lapdogs."

"There's no point in sticking with them if they don't have our backs," the other boss said. "Aren't you better off with us on your side than having us dead?"

"Why should we trust *you* to have *our* backs?" I demanded, stepping forward. I could sense the racing of the man's pulse through his veins from here. He was legitimately terrified, but that didn't guarantee anything more than the most temporary loyalty.

I fixed my glare in his direction. "You've only ever served the Gauntts. You didn't even look after your own people! You turned on one of your own when he realized the people you've obeyed are sickos. You didn't give a shit what they might have done to any of the men working under you. Why do you think those men are turning on you now?"

I swept my hand toward our three inside guys, who nodded.

"You sold us out too many fucking times and in too many ways for us to believe a single word out of your mouths now," Parker snapped.

I focused on the lackeys hunched around their bosses. "The people in charge are the ones who made the really shitty decisions. The rest of you can make better choices. We're happy to have any of you step away from them and join us now. It's just the two who were at the top who're going to have to pay for how they helped the Gauntts terrorize this city."

There were five lackeys still surrounding the bosses. They glanced at each other and at their employers with queasy expressions.

"Don't you fucking dare," one of the bosses growled, but if anything, his attempt at a threat had the opposite effect to what he'd intended. Faces hardened. All five of the men started to scramble away.

"You goddamn traitors!" the other boss shouted, and opened fire at the men leaping over the glass-scattered countertop. The lackeys dove out of range, and our guys let loose a hail of bullets that had the bosses diving into the compartments right under the counter.

They had nowhere left to run, but they were the ones who'd backed themselves into this corner. Imagine how differently it might have gone if they'd listened to their colleague about how toxic the Gauntts were and supported us in our campaign against them weeks ago.

We might have taken the family down so much sooner. Those kids might never have gotten sick. Nolan Junior might not have lost his life to contain his adoptive grandfather. We'd dealt out a lot of violence, but the worst of it was on their consciences, not ours.

My men and our allies marched closer to deliver the final judgment—and one of the lackeys who'd abandoned ship staged a reverse mutiny. Maybe he thought there was still a chance of his bosses coming out on top and that if he orchestrated it, he might nab one of the vacant spots alongside them. Maybe he was simply incredibly offended by the blatant destruction of cake. For whatever reason, he launched himself at Nox, whipping out his gun.

Before I could yank my supernatural energies toward him, Marisol yelped, the sound merging with a thunderous bang. A bullet blasted into the side of the guy's skull, toppling him before he could get in his own shot.

My sister sucked in a breath, staring at the slumped man and then at the gun braced between her two trembling hands. Her eyes darted to me. Her face was pale but firm.

"He was one of the guys who helped the Gauntts keep me away from you," she said in a rough voice. "I remember him from the bits of memories. He laughed at me, thought it was hilarious that he could spit on me or push me around and I couldn't fight back…" Her gaze settled on the dead man again. "He deserved it."

A lump rose in my throat, but I smiled in spite of it. "I'm sure he did."

Nox swiveled to take in the other lackeys who'd joined us. "Anyone else want to take a pointless stand for assholes who didn't give a fuck about you? No? Good."

As the lackeys backed away, a couple of them even tossing aside their weapons to make a more emphatic show of good faith, Nox motioned to the other Skullbreakers and our allies. They circled the ends of the counter, positioning themselves just out of view so the bosses couldn't shoot at them. Then Nox barreled toward the counter on the shop side, swinging both fists at the same time.

The energy he propelled with his strikes smashed right through the wood and sent the men in hiding tumbling out of their shelter across the floor. At the same moment, the rest of our men sprang into action. Bullets tore up the floor and into the two stunned figures from both sides. In a matter of seconds, the last of the Skeleton Corps bosses were as holey as a box of donuts.

Ruin raised his gun and let out a whoop of victory. A startled laugh of what sounded like relief spilled from Parker's lips. We looked around at each other, a sense of finality sinking over us—and then the walls of the bakery shuddered.

We spun around. "What the fuck?" Jett demanded.

My first thought was that we'd been struck by a very coincidental earthquake. But as the building around us continued to creak and rattle, I made out a familiar posh sedan that'd pulled up across the street. The windows were tinted, the figures inside hidden, but I was gripped by total certainty of who they were.

The words creaked from my abruptly constricted throat. "The Gauntts have come for us."

# twenty-five

*Lily*

Ruin bounded over to get a closer look out the bakery window. "This is a good thing, right? We wanted to blast them apart too, and now we can."

I wished I could share his sense of optimism, but in this particular case, the groaning of the building's foundation and the cracks I spotted spreading through the ceiling were putting a damper on my sense of victory.

"We've exhausted some of our powers, and they're probably fresh," I said. "And if we're not careful, they're going to use *their* powers to bring the whole building down on our heads."

I tried to reach my awareness across the street and

through the car, but with the distraction of the quaking building and no visual to latch on to, I couldn't focus in on a single pulse. The cracks overhead were widening. I didn't have time to get my act together.

"Let's get out of here before we're buried!" I hollered, and tugged Marisol toward the back door.

The men all ran with us: the Skullbreakers, our original Skeleton Corps allies, and the four lackeys who'd thrown their lot in with us when they'd realized their bosses were about to go down. We'd been on opposing sides in the past, but now we were united in one common goal: survival. There was a kind of harmony to the thudding of our racing feet and the rasps of our urgent breaths as one guy yanked open the door for the rest of us, another waved us along while he braced against a trembling wall, and a third yanked us faster out into the alley behind.

It wasn't just survival, was it? It was freedom. Freedom from the asshats and shitheels who'd tried to keep *us* down, who'd used us for their own ends, who'd demanded our obedience without offering any loyalty in return.

And I'd helped bring about this harmony. I'd woken up the marked guys—I'd said enough to get through to them and the other lackeys, to give them the conviction to step away from their bosses.

As we hustled down the alley, hearing the first screeching thuds of the bakery's framework collapsing, an idea bloomed in my head like a blossom unfurling.

We had to stop the Gauntts, but we couldn't do it

alone any more than we could have tackled the Skeleton Corps leadership with just the six of us. And I knew exactly the allies we needed now. If I could empower gang members who'd once wanted to shoot us down, then I had to be able to do the same for the people I wanted to turn to next.

I stopped at the end of the alley, watching the street beyond in case the Gauntts pulled around to launch another attack.

"We've got them scared and desperate," I said between ragged breaths. "They risked coming out here to take us on themselves. I don't like our chances if we go head-to-head with them right here, but I think we can lead them into a different kind of trap."

Ruin grinned and gave the air a couple of eager punches. "All right. We'll show them who's boss."

I hoped I could follow through. I grabbed my phone and dialed Peyton's number.

"What now?" she said when she answered, but her mildly irritated tone was offset by the concerned question she couldn't help following with. "Are you all okay?"

My lips twitched with wry amusement, but I got straight to the point. "For now. I need you to pass on a message—tell all the marked people from college whose memories I cracked. At least one of them should report back to the Gauntts."

Peyton audibly perked up. "What's the message?"

"Tell them we figured out a way to destroy the Gauntts' source of power. We're going down to the marsh to do it now, so no one who's been hurt will have to worry for much longer."

She inhaled sharply. "Are you serious? Then why—"

"It's complicated," I said. "But it'll work if the Gauntts come chasing after us. Can you pass the message on?"

"Yes. Just the first part and not the chasing bit." A brief, raw laugh spilled out of her. "I hope you give them all the hell they deserve."

Nox drew his impressive frame up even taller and motioned to the people around us, assuming he knew my plan. "All right, we're taking this to the marsh. Head out, grab the nearest vehicle you can, and converge for an ambush near the entrance to the lane off—"

"Hold on," I interrupted. We didn't have much time to get this right now that word might be passed on to the Gauntts at any moment. Sirens were wailing in the distance, speaking of more complications we needed to avoid. "I don't want everyone there, and we're not going to ambush the Gauntts. I've got another idea, but I don't think anyone should come except those of us who have… extra ways of protecting ourselves."

"And me," Marisol insisted. I squeezed her hand, knowing there was no point in arguing.

Nox frowned, authoritative menace radiating off him. I knew how badly he wanted to crush the Gauntts on my behalf, and the best way he knew how was to blast them hard with everything we had. "We can do this," he insisted. "But we need all the manpower we can get."

I held his gaze with a pointed look. "We have other allies down at the marsh."

He made a scoffing sound. "They haven't managed to do anything other than drench you."

"I don't think I encouraged them the right way. They either weren't able or willing to help me, so this time *I'm* going to offer my help to them. I'm sure it's our best chance of destroying the Gauntts. Please, trust me."

Nox stared back at me, and something in his expression softened just a little. He did trust me, or we wouldn't be here to begin with.

"All right," he said. "I haven't got any feet to stand on arguing against crazy tactics. You just tell us everything you need." He waved at the Skeleton Corps guys, unable to resist aiming a little more of his commanding attitude toward the people he could order around. "Get going. Lay low, keep quiet, and we'll call on you if we need you. Just steer clear of the Gauntts and the other pricks you worked with."

Parker nodded and ushered the other guys away with an unexpected air of authority of his own. Maybe the Skeleton Corps would still have a future—a better one—once the dust had cleared.

The rest of us slipped out of the alley in the other direction. Nox ran for the car and brought it swerving around to collect the rest of us. Then we raced off toward the marsh with the Skullbreakers boss's usual disregard for all speed limits.

"Are you going to tell me exactly what the hell you're going to do out there?" he asked me.

I swallowed against the sudden dryness in my throat. "I think it's more of a 'I'll know what to do once I'm actually doing it' kind of a situation."

He let out a discomforted sound but left it at that.

Not long after we'd zoomed past the city limits and were roaring along the country highways between the smaller towns, Marisol twisted around in the back seat. Her voice came out wobbly, and not just because of the vibrations emanating from the straining engine. "I think they're behind us."

I swiveled to check. In the distance, I made out a darkly shiny car that did look suspiciously like the Gauntts' sedan. My pulse thumped faster. But—

"That's good," I said. "We want them to come. We need them out here if we're going to take them out."

As long as this gambit worked the way I thought it should. As long as we got to the marsh far enough ahead of them for me to make the necessary preparations.

This *was* the right way, wasn't it? What if I was going too far off the deep end?

I closed my eyes and gathered my faith in myself. Letting out my inner crazy was what had allowed me to do so much—to fend off my bullies, to break open my memories, to save Marisol. This strategy felt *right*.

If the battle against the Gauntts was mine more than the Skullbreakers, and Marisol's more than mine, then it belonged to the spirits and the marsh where they'd been abandoned more than anyone. Sometimes you just needed someone to show you the way.

The Skullbreakers hadn't pulled me from the marsh all those years ago, after all. They'd simply urged me to find the strength to save myself. That was when I'd gotten these powers, and now I could pass on the same favor.

Nox maneuvered the borrowed car with far less care than he'd shown for Fred. He drove it right past the end of the final lane, as far as he could get the wheels to keep turning over the uneven field beyond. That left us with just a short dash down to the spit.

"Stay close to the water," I yelled to the others as I darted down the narrow strip of land to its tip, where the Gauntts cast their magic. "Shield Marisol as much as you can. I'll try to be ready before they get here."

But the dark car was closing the distance by the second, growing larger against the horizon. I didn't hesitate. As the guys spread themselves out in a human wall near the foot of the spit, keeping my sister behind them, I plunged right into the water.

The cold water closed around me up to my shoulders, soaking my clothes in an instant. I reached out through the rippling currents for the energies I'd felt before and the spirits still lingering alongside them.

"Please," I said, or thought, or maybe both. With all my concentration fixed on the hum inside me and the contrasting resonance in the water, it was hard to pay attention to anything else. "Bring out all the power they've poured into you. I want *you* to use it, and I'll be right here backing you up with everything I have in me. We can do something better with it. We can break the hold they have over you, to save lives instead of taking them. *Please.* This is what I want to do for you."

I brought up an image in my mind of how I pictured this showdown playing out if the lake would cooperate, how I'd lend my powers to the anger and horror I'd sensed here before. Shivers of energy tickled over my skin through the water, as if the spirits were prodding me with giddy fingers. At least, I hoped that was giddiness and not fear. I needed them to be on my side too.

"They stole your lives," I urged them. "Both when you were living those lives and after. You can make sure they never do that to anyone else again. This is your war, and now's your chance to really fight it."

Deeper quivers reverberated through my flesh. I gathered the hum inside me and urged it out toward those spirits, toward the water that had held them for decades. An answering thrum flowed back into me, intensifying the energies inside me.

Was the marsh answering? Would it come through as much as we needed it to?

I was about to find out. The growl of a nearby engine penetrated my water-logged daze. I tuned into the shore enough to see the dark sedan bumping to a halt near where we'd parked our car on the grass. The doors flew open, and a sizzling wave of energy whipped through the air.

Nox struck out with both his fists, and Jett and

Ruin fired their guns, unable to do more across the distance. They only got out a couple of shots before the Gauntts' powers slammed them and Marisol back on the bank.

My heart flipped over. We had no time left at all. The next second might mean a fatal blow.

"*Now!*" I screamed, inside and out, and raised my arms.

The marsh water rose with me as if I were summoning it upward like a conductor for some grand aquatic orchestra. It surged higher and higher into one, two, three, four—then more forms than I could make out around me. They loomed over me and the spit like liquid giants, towering fifteen, maybe twenty feet off the ground. Gleaming arms lifted from their watery sides; massive translucent heads turned toward the Gauntts' car.

With the marsh's power combined with my own, I'd given the spirits of the murdered grandchildren the only kind of life I could offer them. Massive, vengeful life.

More energy wrenched in and out of me as I swept my arms toward the shore. The gigantic figures rushed forward, sloshing water around them as they went. They charged right up onto the shore, splattering the grass but holding their humongous forms.

Someone in the Gauntts' car tried to strike out at them. Magic warbled through the air; the watery legs wobbled. But their forms held, powered as much by the fury I could sense shrieking through their makeshift bodies as by my own magic now.

I couldn't tell how much of that rage belonged to the marsh or the spirits when both of them hand been equally used by the villains they were bearing down on. Either way, they intended to have their revenge.

"Stop!" a voice I thought was Marie's cried out, while those around her chanted in the strange language I'd heard during their ritual. "You're *ours*. You do as we say. We—"

The person behind the wheel must have realized they weren't taking back control right now. The engine gunned abruptly, the doors slammed shut in anticipation of a hasty escape—but the marshy giants were already on them.

The spirits plowed their immense fists into the windows, smashing the glass. The water that gushed into the body of the car flipped the Gauntts out through the holes of the front and back windshields and tossed them onto the open ground. It was just the four of them: Marie Senior, Thomas, Olivia, and Nolan in his new younger body, squirming and sputtering on the soggy terrain like fish that'd leapt out of their tank.

The spirits poured more water down on them, and more, and more, saturating them from the inside out. The Gauntts cried out words of power, erected a transparent shield over them, but the forms that now contained so much of their magic cracked straight through those with a few thunderous punches. They poured their water down the Gauntts' throats and up their noses until their frantic panting turned to gurgles and their chests swelled.

And on and on and on, until all four bodies finally lay still. It was done. All of them were dead, and no one was left to carry their spirits over into a new victim. Their reign of horror was finished.

A headache was spreading through the back of my head, every nerve felt like it was on fire, but I was gripped by a dazed sense of release.

The Gauntts had infected the marsh with their sick intentions, and those intentions had come back to claim them. All I'd done was provide a conduit to make that vengeance possible.

And now I was utterly exhausted.

I teetered and toppled backward into the marsh, the water closing over me as if it meant to reclaim *me* after my narrow escape fourteen years ago.

# twenty-six

*Nox*

Before I'd even managed to shove myself back to my feet, I was drenched. I grabbed Ruin's hand to help him up and then all we could do was gape at the lumbering masses of water as they pummeled the Gauntts into total submission. They beat those bastards with their watery fists until they were bloated and broken, and then they crashed down on them in what felt like a final "Fuck you," vomiting their watery selves over their murderers.

As the flood of water swept back toward the marsh, I spun around—just in time to see Lily sink beneath the surface, looking close to lifeless herself.

"No!" I hollered, defiance roaring through me. I'd let Lily take charge against all my instincts because she'd connected with the spirits here in ways the rest of us hadn't, but I wasn't letting the marsh take her away from me, no matter what it'd done for us. No fucking way.

"Look," Marisol gasped, pointing in the other direction. My head whipped around, and I realized that not all of the marsh monsters had flowed back to where they'd come from.

One of the colossal heaps of water was still poised over the farthest body. The body that'd once been Nolan Junior before the Senior had taken over residence inside a couple of weeks ago. A jolt of understanding shot through me.

It *had* only been a couple of weeks. The body had been kept living all that time—and it couldn't have changed much. There was a chance, wasn't there?

Every bone in my body ached to race to Lily's rescue, but I knew what she'd want me to do more.

That didn't mean I was abandoning her, of course.

"Jett," I said, jabbing my hand toward the spit. "Get Lily. Make sure she's okay." Then I hurtled toward the boy's corpse.

Images raced through my head alongside my pounding feet across the squishy ground. Fragments of my childhood rose out of nowhere into my mind.

I was wincing away from the swing of my father's fist. I was huddled in the closet to avoid another of his and Mom's drunken screeching arguments. Shivering under my thin blanket in three layers of clothes because they'd forgotten to pay the heating bill.

It'd been a shitty childhood until Gram had pulled me out of it. How had I repaid her, really?

But I could do this. I could pay it forward instead. I could do my very fucking best to give *this* kid another chance at an actual life.

The boy looked just as swollen and vacant as the others. His skin was already turning blue from the chill of the water. But unlike the adults, he wasn't quite as battered—his limbs lay at regular angles instead of unnatural ones, and I couldn't see any sign of broken ribs in his bloated chest.

I dropped down next to him. Rolling him onto his side, I thumped him between his shoulder blades, and the water gushed from his mouth and nose. Then I pushed him onto his back again.

The human-shaped heap of water was still crouched next to us. I glared up at it. "You've got to do some of the work here. Leave the marsh behind and jump on into him. Slam your heart—get it started again. I'll do my best, but if you're not in there, your jackass of a grandfather might try to yank it back."

The liquid mass shuddered. Then the water started to slough off it like it was shedding its skin, shrinking by the second.

I sucked in a breath and placed the heels of my hands on the boy's chest, dredging up every memory I could from the CPR course I'd taken years and years ago in case I ever needed it to save Gram.

I hadn't been there when she might have needed me, but I was here now. I was saving someone. And I liked to think if she was watching, she'd have given me one of her toothy grins with a double thumbs-up.

How many compressions was it? Ten? Twenty? Thirty? I just keep going—*pump, pump, pump, why won't you start, you fucker?*—as an ache spread through my arms. Maybe the spirits had drowned him too much. Maybe his soul didn't have the energy left to dive back in after all. Maybe—

I jammed my hands down one more time, and a bolt of energy zapped past them into the boy's chest. I slapped at my fingers, my skin searing, and then stared at the body in front of me.

The chest rose and fell. I pressed my palm to it again, and the erratic thump of a heart echoed against my hand, growing steadier by the moment.

Had the kid made it, or had I inadvertently brought that asshole Nolan back to life all over again? I hovered over the body, my fists ready to give him a pummeling of my own as need be.

The boy's eyes blinked. He peered up at me. Then he flipped over and coughed and gagged as a whole bunch more water heaved out of him. Apparently I hadn't done the most thorough job.

As he lay there, panting, he managed to find his voice. "Thank you," he said raggedly, sounding only like a kid, not like a corporate megalomaniac pretending to be one. "I—he—thank you." Then he started to cry.

I might be okay with doing a little heroic life-saving, but I had no clue at all what to do with a sobbing child. To my relief, Ruin and Marisol had followed me sometime during my grand effort. They sank down on either side of the restored boy, who I was going to guess would like to pick a name other than Nolan Junior now that he had the choice. Ruin tapped his shoulder, and the kid automatically relaxed.

"It's going to be okay," Marisol said in a soothing voice, patting his damp hair with her good hand. "You're going to be all right now."

I spun around with a stutter of my pulse, my gaze darting to the end of the spit as I thought of the other soul I wasn't sure we'd saved.

But there was Jett helping Lily walk with swaying steps along the spit, both of them soaked through, his arm around her back and hers slung across his shoulders. She caught my eyes with a shaky smile that grew when she noticed the boy beyond me. Tugging at Jett, she urged her feet faster across the muddy ground.

I hurried over to meet her and caught her in a hug that could have rivaled any of Ruin's, not caring that my drying clothes were getting soppy all over again.

"You did it," she said, breathless with disbelief. "You —you brought him back? Nolan Junior, not the old Nolan?"

"I think he did the hardest part," I allowed generously, and hugged her even tighter. "And *you* did it. You let them unleash holy terror on those menaces. They're gone. It's all done—it's over."

She pulled back with a sudden look of concern. "Do you think all their magic is gone with them?"

I didn't need to be Kai to figure out what she was

talking about, and neither did her sister. Marisol had already pulled out her phone and started tapping away at it.

"It's so soon," she said. "I'm not sure how long it'd take before—oh! Here, one of the kids who was in the hospital, her brother is posting about how she's just snapped out of her coma. She seems totally fine now." She glanced up at us, her eyes shining. "If one of them recovered when the Gauntts died, then they all must have, right?"

Ruin cocked his head. "I wonder if all the marks will fade too. Will all those people remember what the Gauntts did to them?"

Lily's smile turned crooked. "That won't be all happy for everyone. But at least they'll know. And if there's enough of them willing to speak up after we've already put the story out there, maybe they can make sure the Gauntts get the right legacy *after* their death."

"They fucking well better," I declared. "But right now, we deserve to celebrate ourselves. We'd better make sure Kai's insides held together too. And…" I looked back at the boy, who was sitting up, staring at his hands while he turned them frontward and backward like he couldn't quite believe they were his again. "What are we going to do with him? With all of them?" My gaze traveled to the water-logged bodies.

Lily went silent with thought, exuding the calm confidence that was starting to come more naturally to her. I loved seeing it so much that I had to restrain myself from kissing her—which I'd definitely do later, but distracting her in the middle of a brainstorm seemed counter-productive.

"We leave them here," she said after a minute. "*We* didn't touch them. It was their own magic that killed them. There'll be an investigation, and probably the police will be confused about how they died, but it shouldn't come back on us. And him…"

She eased out of my arms and walked over to the boy. When she reached him, she crouched down next to him. He raised his head, his eyes still gleaming with pooled tears.

"Where would you like to go?" she asked. "We could take you to the house that was your home. I think… Now that the people who hurt you are gone, it's technically yours. There'll be lawyers who can figure out all the details. But if you don't want to go there again, that'd be okay too. It must have a lot of awful memories for you."

The boy cleared his throat, but his voice still came out rough. "I— Marie will still be there, right?"

It took me a second to realize he meant Marie Junior, his sister. Lily rested her hand on his shoulder. "As far as I know. She might be in a tricky situation—it doesn't look like they officially adopted her."

The boy raised his chin. "I'll make sure she's okay. I can look after her now. That's the way it *should* have been."

Lily beamed at him, and right then I really hoped that our ghostly swimmers still had some juice, because damn, would she make an amazing mom one day.

"All right," she said. "We'll make sure you get home. Come with us for now." She caught my eyes. "Do you think our false limo driver would be up for making a repeat performance in his role?"

I grinned back at her. "I bet he would. You drive, and I'll tell him where to meet us."

And then everything and everyone would be where it should be, possibly for the first time in my entire life. Or should I say, lives.

# twenty-seven

*One year later*

*Lily*

"And that's a wrap," the producer said over the intercom, giving me a thumbs up and a broad grin through the sound booth's window. "That last take was fantastic, Lily. I think we've nailed this track."

I pulled off my headphones, a laugh that was both relief and exhilaration tumbling out of me. "Just three more to go, then."

As I headed out of the recording studio for the day, I had to resist the urge to pinch myself and make sure I wasn't dreaming. After months of writing songs, making contacts with musicians, and putting together a demo tape, I'd somehow managed to land a record deal. I'd been in and out of the studio working on my debut album for weeks now, but it still didn't feel quite real. How could this be my life?

Whenever I mentioned any thoughts along those lines to my guys, they scoffed and said things like, "How could it not be?" After we'd settled into a new, much more peaceful status quo with the Gauntts gone, they'd all encouraged me to pursue what really was a dream, even if I'd made it come true. Jett was the one who'd pointed me to this studio, just next door to the Thrivewell building, saying he had a good feeling about it.

We all liked to think the Gauntts were rolling over in their long-delayed graves, hearing the joy in my voice that they hadn't been able to extinguish.

Kai was waiting in the reception area, tapping away on his phone. I walked over and nudged him. "You're becoming a regular internet addict after all."

He snorted. "It's still full of garbage. But if you know the right way to look for things, there *is* plenty of information there too—stuff you can't get anywhere else." His eyes gleamed at me from behind his glasses. "Uncle Stu sent me a link to a blog on investment strategies. I think I can double the amount of money we're making without anyone having to get their asses kicked, just like you prefer."

"You're going to put the gang out of a job," I teased as we took the elevator down to street level.

A couple of months after the Gauntts' fall, another of Kai's host's relatives had reached out to him, and Kai had discovered a kindred spirit. Apparently Zach's mom's brother wasn't from the same all-American jock mold as the football player's immediate family, and he'd been off pursuing his intellectual pursuits all on his lonesome. Kai had been ready to send him packing before they'd started talking and immediately hit it off by showing off how much they both knew about pretty much everything. Now they kept in touch with regular emails and texts.

It was amazing seeing how delighted their conversations made Kai. He was still the same know-it-all he'd always been, but he'd loosened up even more from the efficient and practical guy he'd been when I first met him. From what he'd said, no one in his own birth family had ever understood his quick mind or love of learning. It might have come decades late, but I was glad he'd found that kind of connection now.

I often drove to the studio on my own in Fred 2.0. The car was purring along good as new despite the Gauntts' temporary possession. But when the guys were available, I still got a thrill out of riding with them on the back of one of their motorcycles. Kai led me over to where he'd parked his, and I hopped on easily, wrapping my arms around his waist.

"Nox headed over to the graveyard a little while back to check up on things," he said. "Should we swing by and remind him he's got another engagement tonight?"

I leaned into his solid frame. "Sure. I'd like to see the final result anyway."

We roared through the streets toward the cemetery where Nox's grandmother was buried. It wasn't hard to spot her section of the graveyard now. Nox had put a bunch of his recent earnings into designing and building a monument to replace her previously spartan gravestone. Sunlight gleamed off the pale gray marble slab that stood a couple of feet taller than the massive man gazing up at it.

I hurried up the hill to join Nox, slipping my arm around his when I reached him. He tugged me closer and nodded to the slab, which held a life-sized etching of a broad-shouldered woman with a steely gaze but a warm smile, her arms crossed over her bosom and her chin held high. She looked like she was about to demand to know what exactly we'd been up to—and to praise us for a job well done, as long as we'd committed to it fully regardless of exactly how legal it was.

"It's lovely," I said.

"She wasn't any angel, and she'd have laughed if anyone suggested she was," Nox said. "I figured she'd like this a lot better than some cheesy statue with wings. The stoneworker Jett found did a great job from the photographs I managed to scrounge up. It's almost like she's right there."

Jett had offered to imprint an image on the marble with his supernatural powers, but Nox had refused, saying his Gram would have seen that as cheating. *I'm going to pay for it to be done the usual way,* he'd insisted. And he looked nothing but satisfied with the outcome.

"It's not the home I wanted to give her while she was alive, but at least she's got a real presence in the afterlife," he said as we headed back down the hill.

"Granite would have been more durable," Kai couldn't help piping up.

Nox shot him a narrow look. "As you mentioned before. But she deserves something that's pretty too. If that one gets messed up, I'll just buy her a new one." He guided me toward his own bike. "You ride with me the rest of the way."

Despite the way he said it, I knew it was a request, not a command. But I didn't mind following through anyway, and Kai certainly wasn't offended. I squeezed onto the seat behind the larger man and let him carry us home.

As much as I'd loved our first apartment in Mayfield, it'd gotten awfully tainted by unpleasant memories during our few weeks there. And it hadn't really been big enough for all of us. After the Skullbreakers had gotten some time to revitalize their, er, business interests, we'd paid a generous fee to break the lease early and found a couple of three-bedroom condos in the same neighborhood up for sale that we'd been able to renovate into a larger two-story home.

The upper floor was technically mine and Marisol's, although the guys hung out up there with us plenty. It included a terrace where we'd been able to set up a little artificial pond for the various amphibious friends who still liked to stop by now and then. The lower floor was where the Skullbreakers hosted their new recruits and business partners as need be. Only for non-criminal activities, of course, but Kai wasn't the only one who'd branched out from that area.

When we came into the lower level, a waft of spice hit me in the face, making my eyes water.

"Sorry!" Ruin called cheerfully from the kitchen over the whir of the fans that were displacing the worst of the airborne burn. "Just finishing up a new batch. My ghost pepper blend!"

"It'll burn your tongue off," my sister informed us, appearing in the doorway with safety goggles, an amused expression, and several orange smears on her apron.

Ruin had discovered that he enjoyed creating hot sauce as much as he did eating it—possibly even more, since that way he could customize it exactly to his tastes. After he'd shared a little of his personal blend with a man the Skullbreakers had been negotiating with who worked in food processing... among other things... our spice addict had found himself with a production deal.

Ruin cooked the stuff here in the apartment, various workers came to collect it, and the manufacturing company bottled it, labeled it, and distributed it to select high-end grocery stores. The manufacturing guy had been bugging him about handing over his recipes for mass production, but Ruin wasn't interested in that.

Especially since his favorite part was experimenting with new flavors, not making money.

Marisol had taken to helping him out in the kitchen if he was at work there when she got home from school. Her smile as she peeled off her apron gave me a much deeper rush of relief than anything I'd felt earlier.

"Your history test went okay?" I asked.

"Yeah," she said brightly. I was starting to think Ruin's high spirits were rubbing off on her. "I aced all the questions except one I wasn't totally sure about, but I checked the textbook afterward, and I'm pretty sure I covered that completely too."

I studied her face, taking in the faint blush that'd come into her cheeks which I didn't think had anything to do with her studies. "Did something else good happen?" I asked with a gentle poke of her shoulder.

Her smile turned both shy and sly. "That guy I think is pretty cool, Jason—he asked me to go see a movie this weekend."

"Hmm," I said, as if I were debating whether to approve the date, but I couldn't stop a grin from springing to my own face. "That's awesome. Just make sure he stays cool."

"Or we'll cool his heels in all kinds of ways he won't like," Nox piped up from behind me.

Marisol rolled her eyes, but her expression of teenage rebellion only made me happier. We'd arranged for her to talk to a counselor about all the crap she'd been through with both the Gauntts and Mom and Wade, but I was pretty sure her own innate resilience deserved a lot of the credit for how well she'd bounced back. She was stronger than she maybe even realized.

I hoped that was true for all the formerly marked victims. The Gauntts' magic had clearly departed along with their long-overdue souls as I'd expected, cracking open sealed memories all across the county. A couple dozen people had come forward to speak up about their treatment at the family's hands shortly afterward, and we had no idea how many more were dealing with the lingering trauma more privately. I suspected local therapists had experienced quite the boom in business.

There hadn't been much we could do about it directly, but I'd insisted that we donate a healthy portion of the Skullbreakers' early business profits to Mayfield's pro bono mental health initiatives.

"Okay!" I said. "Everyone grab something to eat, preferably something that will leave your tongue intact. We've got to be out of here in half an hour. We don't want Jett thinking we've forgotten."

Kai chuckled. "The way he was talking this morning, I'm not sure if he'd rather everyone in town showed up or no one at all."

Nox cuffed the other guy in the shoulder. "You know how he is. No heckling him at the show."

Kai arched his eyebrows at his boss. "I would never."

Ruin emerged from the kitchen with another whiff of spice and pulled me into one of his exuberant embraces before planting a kiss on my lips. "We fried up some burgers while we were at it. I don't think *too* much pepper got onto them."

"They're safe," Marisol confirmed.

We chowed down on the burgers, and I changed from my studio-comfortable tee and yoga pants into a silky knee-length dress that had all three of the guys eyeing me appreciatively when I came back downstairs. I swatted Nox's hand away when he reached to squeeze my ass and wagged a finger at him. "Practice your self-control."

He smirked at me. "Oh, I'll be practicing it all night, but it'll be worth the wait."

I glowered at him, but thankfully Marisol was upstairs getting herself ready, so she didn't need to hear the suggestive remark. When she reappeared, we all headed out together, the guys coming in the car with us for once since they didn't want to mess up the more dapper clothing they'd put on for the occasion.

Jett was having his first ever public show for his art at a small but hip gallery in downtown Mayfield. Like Ruin's new business endeavor, it'd kind of happened by accident. He'd been tossing some of his old canvases in the dumpster behind our building, and the wind had caught on a sheet of paper and tossed it over to the sidewalk, where the gallery owner had just happened to be walking by. When Jett had gone running to retrieve the piece, the gallery guy had struck up a conversation, and three months later, here we were.

Sometimes I wondered if there weren't some other spirits watching out for us that we didn't even know about. Maybe Nox's Gram had stuck around after all. Maybe the ghosts we'd helped get their vengeance against the Gauntts sometimes took a trip up from the marsh to lend us a hand.

Or maybe fate simply figured that my guys had been through enough bad times during their first lives that it was time to heap on some good luck to balance the scales.

I was happy to see we weren't the first to arrive, even though we'd shown up right at the show's start time. A few browsers were already circulating through the white-walled space, peering at the paintings and mixed-media compositions. I saw one woman knit her brow as she eyed a streak of reddish brown that I was pretty sure Jett had pulled from his veins rather than any paint tube. There might have been some hot sauce mixed into a few of the pieces too.

He did like to make use of whatever materials were available to him—and to literally bleed on the canvas.

Jett hustled over us with uncharacteristic energy, his posture stiff but nervous excitement vibrating off him through the supernatural connection that still tied me and all the guys together. "There might be a reviewer from an art magazine coming," he said. "And someone already asked about buying one of the paintings. Someone actually wants to hang my work in their house." He looked dumbfounded.

I elbowed him. "Hey, *we* hang your art all over our house."

He made a face at me. "You have to."

"I want to. And it's great that this critic is coming, but it doesn't matter what some magazine dude thinks anyway, right?" I glanced around at the array of pieces, each of them provoking little jolts of emotion in me as if I could re-experience what Jett had been feeling when he'd applied himself to them. "How do you think it turned out?"

He rubbed his mouth, his gaze darting around the room. "I mean, there are always things that aren't quite what I was going for, no matter how I try... but I think this came together pretty well. It's got the vibe I wanted. That's what matters the most."

Several more people meandered in, including a few familiar figures. "Hey!" I said to Peyton, giving her an awkward little wave. She waved back with a lopsided smile.

We'd been on friendlier terms since we'd faced off against a murderous gang together, but we definitely weren't besties. I was never sure exactly how warm to be with her. But we'd at least established some kind of consistent dynamic of tolerant respect, which was more comfortable than the animosity between us before.

I did see her more often than I'd expected to, because somehow she'd ended up clicking with Parker, who I greeted next. He and a couple of the Skeleton Corps guys who'd continued their alliance with the Skullbreakers had turned up to see Jett's other kind of work.

Peyton stuck close to Parker as they moved through the room, tucking her hand into his. I didn't totally get their relationship, but then, stranger things had definitely happened. Who would have thought *I'd* end up dating not one but four gangsters—and resurrected ones, no less?

"Whoa," I heard one of the Skeleton Corps guys say under his breath as he stared up at a painting that stretched wider than he could have spread his arms, streaked with violent reds and violets like a fiery thunderstorm. Jett's lips quirked into a grin of pride.

The next patrons I recognized arrived an hour into the show. I turned around after grabbing a glass of wine just as Nolan and Marie Junior walked through the door, a man who must have been one of their guardians behind them.

Two kids, who were now ten and eleven years old, should have looked out of place in an indie art gallery, but the Gauntts' adopted grandchildren had picked up a few useful skills from their departed family members. They held themselves with the poise of CEOs—which they would be, once they hit eighteen. The Skullbreakers and I had worked as hard as we could behind the scenes to make sure the kids the Gauntts had meant to exploit came out of the situation as well as possible. We hadn't seen them in person in ages, though.

Nox sauntered over as they eased into the room. "Are you sure you should have come around for this?" he said in a wry tone. "It seems like associating with people like us could be bad for your reputation."

Nolan Junior, who like his sister had opted to keep

his name for now in the hopes of writing a new legacy to go with the overused moniker, gave the gang boss a smooth little smile with a twinkle in his eyes. "We're expanding our cultural horizons," he informed us with his childish bravado. "It's very important to be well-rounded. Our teachers tell us that *all* the time."

A burly guy in an expensive suit brushed past us, clearly not recognizing the Gauntt children from the past news stories. "Kids in a gallery," he muttered in a disdainful voice, and proceeded to down two glasses of wine back to back before shooting the server an equally disdainful glance. "This is garbage. You really should provide better for an event like this."

"Prick at two o'clock," Nox murmured under his breath, sizing the guy up from the corner of his eye. He exchanged a look with Kai, who started tapping on his phone. Ruin rubbed his hands together.

Seeing how the Gauntts had exploited so *many* people had left the Skullbreakers with a slightly revised perspective on how they wanted to carry out their own domination of the city. These days, they mostly stuck to jobs that involved ripping off or intimidating whatever jerks they happened to run into. "Asshole tax," Nox liked to call it.

There seemed to be plenty of ideal targets around here, thankfully none of them as powerful as the Gauntts had been. We'd been keeping a close eye out for any signs that those psychos' souls had stuck around and managed to make a grab at new bodies, but so far, so good.

I liked to think that their victims in the marsh had not just destroyed their bodies but swept their spirits all the way out of our world into the next, from which there was no returning.

"No 'taxing' until *after* the show," I ordered Nox now.

"Don't worry," he said, grasping my waist from behind and giving me a quick peck behind my ear. "We're not going to ruin Jett's big moment."

The show lasted until midnight. At ten-thirty, I sent Marisol home in an Uber with instructions to get some sleep before school tomorrow. By the time the gallery was closing up, Jett had sold nine pieces—two of them to the young Gauntts—and looked so pleased I half wondered if Ruin had swatted some joy into him.

Kai, who'd had the least to drink, volunteered to drive Fred. I ended up in the back seat with Nox and Jett.

Nox walked his fingers up from my knee, displacing the skirt of my dress. "I don't think the night's over for us yet. We've got a mark to chase down. But I could use a little inspiration first."

I cocked my head. "Oh, yeah? Are you turning into an artist now?"

He guffawed. "Just a simple man who needs your lovely moans and whimpers to keep me going, Siren." He glanced across at Jett. "Although I'm sure the actual artist here would love to celebrate his muse too."

Jett traced his fingers up my other thigh. "I'll

definitely never say no to a chance to expand my creative vision."

"I think we *all* need to celebrate," Ruin declared. "Find a good place to park, Kai!"

A giggle spilled out of me, turning into a gasp as Nox's thumb grazed my already dampening panties. I gave myself over to their collective embrace.

A little more than a year ago, I hadn't been able to focus on anything except surviving—and on making sure my sister did too. The journey toward really living had come with a lot of hitches along the way. But we'd found our place in this mad world, and it seemed like we'd even made it a little better with our own special brand of insanity.

I couldn't wait to see where that craziness would take us next.

# about the author

Eva Chase lives in Canada with her family. She loves stories both swoony and supernatural, and strong women and the men who appreciate them. Along with the Gang of Ghouls series, she is the author of the Bound to the Fae series, the Flirting with Monsters series, the Cursed Studies trilogy, the Royals of Villain Academy series, the Moriarty's Men series, the Looking Glass Curse trilogy, the Their Dark Valkyrie series, the Witch's Consorts series, the Dragon Shifter's Mates series, the Demons of Fame Romance series, the Legends Reborn trilogy, and the Alpha Project Psychic Romance series.

*Connect with Eva online:*
www.evachase.com
eva@evachase.com

Made in the USA
Las Vegas, NV
27 July 2023

75299913R00166